TO RIDE THE WIND

THE FOUR KINGDOMS AND BEYOND

THE FOUR KINGDOMS

The Princess Companion: A Retelling of The Princess and the Pea (Book One)

The Princess Fugitive: A Reimagining of Little Red Riding Hood (Book Two)

The Coronation Ball: A Four Kingdoms Cinderella Novelette

Happily Every Afters: A Reimagining of Snow White and Rose Red (Novella)

The Princess Pact: A Twist on Rumpelstiltskin (Book Three)

A Midwinter's Wedding: A Retelling of The Frog Prince (Novella)

The Princess Game: A Reimagining of Sleeping Beauty (Book Four)

The Princess Search: A Retelling of The Ugly Duckling (Book Five)

BEYOND THE FOUR KINGDOMS

A Dance of Silver and Shadow: A Retelling of The Twelve Dancing Princesses (Book One)

A Tale of Beauty and Beast: A Retelling of Beauty and the Beast (Book Two)

A Crown of Snow and Ice: A Retelling of The Snow Queen (Book Three)

A Dream of Ebony and White: A Retelling of Snow White (Book Four)

A Captive of Wing and Feather: A Retelling of Swan Lake (Book Five)

A Princess of Wind and Wave: A Retelling of The Little Mermaid (Book Six)

TO RIDE THE WIND

A RETELLING OF EAST OF THE SUN AND WEST OF THE MOON

FOUR KINGDOMS DUOLOGY BOOK 1

MELANIE CELLIER

LUMINANT PUBLICATIONS

Luminant Publications
PO Box 305
Greenacres, South Australia 5086

melanie@melaniecellier.com
http://www.melaniecellier.com

Cover Design by Karri Klawiter
Editing by Mary Novak
Proofreading by James Packer

For my goddaughter, Teresa,
with the hope that you will grow to love
both adventures and happy endings

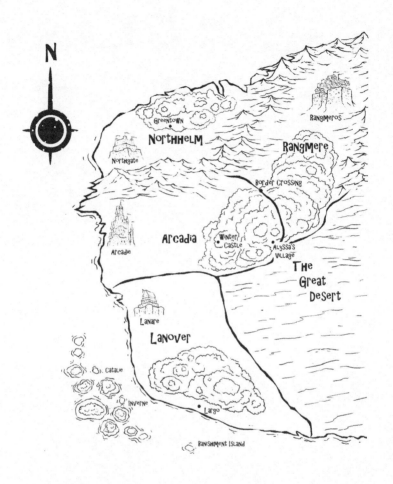

CHARLOTTE

A flash of white caught Charlotte's eye, unnaturally clean and bright among the greens and browns of the forest. She turned to face it, but it was already gone.

"Elizabeth!" A surge of unease in Charlotte's stomach made her tongue trip over her sister's long name. "Odelia?"

She still remembered the childhood years when they had been Bettie, Dellie, and Charli. But it had been many years now since her older sisters had turned into prim young ladies who insisted all three use their full names.

She called again, more loudly, but heard nothing in return. The silence around her was deep—too deep for a forest in mid-afternoon. She opened her mouth to call again but was silenced by a piercing scream.

Launching into motion, she sprinted toward the sound only to run headlong into her middle sister. The two girls bounced away from each other, Odelia falling while Charlotte just managed to keep her feet.

Her sister glared up at her from the forest floor.

"What is it?" Charlotte asked, too frightened to worry about Odelia's irritation. "Why did you scream?"

Odelia stood and brushed off her dress. "That wasn't me." Her voice carried a note of superiority. "Elizabeth was the one who screamed."

But Odelia couldn't entirely hide the anxiety in her face as she glanced back the way she'd come.

Charlotte sucked in a breath. "Is she all right?"

She started in the direction of the scream, but she hadn't made it more than three steps before her eldest sister appeared, stalking through the trees with stiff dignity.

Charlotte raced to her side, grasping her arm. "Are you hurt?" She tried to examine her sister, but Elizabeth shook her off.

"I'm fine," she said shortly, glaring at Odelia. "I can't believe you abandoned me! I suppose you were hoping I would be eaten first, giving you a chance to escape."

Odelia turned pink but stuck up her chin defiantly. "Your legs work as well as mine. It's not my fault you froze."

"Eaten?" Charlotte asked, impatient with their bickering.

Both turned on her with a synchronized movement, glaring at the youngest. Charlotte winced. Elizabeth and Odelia might bicker at times, but they were barely a year apart and had always formed a united front when it came to her.

She sighed, but for once she was concerned enough not to back down. "Is there a dangerous creature about? I thought I saw something among the trees..." She trailed off, unable to think what predator might have been responsible for that flash of white.

"It was an enormous bear," Elizabeth replied in a small voice, apparently subdued by the memory. "A white bear."

"White?" Charlotte gasped. "I thought they only lived in the far mountains! What was one doing down here in our valley?"

"As for that, who knows." Odelia looked at Charlotte with narrowed eyes. "But where were you?" She spoke as if she suspected her sister of setting the bear on them.

"I saw a flash of white earlier." Charlotte pointed toward a place between the trees. "I couldn't think what it might be."

All three young women turned to stare at the place she indicated, their earlier fear overwhelming their disharmony. Elizabeth and Odelia might have been pretending to be unaffected, but they were clearly still afraid.

Something moved between the trees, mostly out of view, but none of them could miss the glimpse of pure white. Odelia screamed, and all three sprinted away from the bear toward their house.

Elizabeth and Odelia soon outstripped Charlotte. Given her petite frame, she had never been a great runner. As she fell behind, she knew she should be afraid, but she couldn't help a surge of curiosity.

She glanced over her shoulder, scanning the trees for any glimpse of a snow-white bear. Did such a thing really exist? And, if so, what was it doing in her forest? In the five years her family had lived in the region, she had never heard tell of a brown bear in the area, let alone a white one. Could Elizabeth or Odelia have mistaken what they'd seen?

Her steps slowed even further, and she half turned. She knew she shouldn't look behind her while moving—she was going to walk into a tree if she kept it up—but she couldn't bring herself to blindly flee for home. It was rare for anything new or interesting to occur in this remote valley.

But her momentary courage fled the moment an enormous, white-furred shape lumbered out from between two trees. Her steps faltered and she stumbled to a halt, her mouth falling open. The creature was even larger than she'd imagined, and its fur seemed impossibly white for a wild creature. Charlotte herself never wore white, since the material didn't stay that way for long.

The bear lifted one foot to step forward, and her eyes caught on its long black claws. Her heart took off into frantic flight, and

3

her muscles tensed, ready for her body to join it. But just as she sprang into movement, her eyes found the bear's.

Her breath caught. Objectively, they looked just like those of any bear, but there was something in the creature's expression that she couldn't dismiss.

She wanted to pause, even to reach toward the bear, but her body was already running. Within steps, trees blocked a clear view of the animal's face. She slowed, but the memory of the claws returned, and she shook herself. She must have imagined the look in the bear's eyes. There was no way an animal could display such sympathy, despair, and longing with a single glance.

She didn't look back again as she fled, and within minutes she had reached her family's wooden home. It was smaller than ideal for five people, and the paint was long since peeling, but at least the walls and door were sturdy. No wild animal had attacked the structure in the past, and there was no reason to think a bear would do so now.

She pulled on the door, meaning to fling it open and tumble inside, but it resisted her tug. Someone had latched it, although they didn't usually secure it during the day.

"Elizabeth!" she cried. "Odelia! Open the door!"

A shuffling sounded inside, and a crack appeared. Her oldest sister's eye peered through, as if checking to see that Charlotte wasn't a bear speaking with the voice of a girl.

Charlotte huffed and pushed the door the rest of the way open, shoving her sister back. Lately her relationship with her sisters had regressed, and she had been restraining herself around them, but she was too irritated to hold it inside.

"You locked me out there? Are you serious? You were just going to leave me to be eaten?"

"I'm very thankful no one has been eaten." Her mother spoke with a faint trace of amusement. "But was there really such a need for concern? White bears in the forest sounds like one of your childhood tales, Charlotte, but I don't know what to make of it when all three of you claim you saw the creature!"

Charlotte winced. Her childhood claim that an invisible girl lived in a tower in the woods had been proven true in the end, but apparently she was never going to live down her reputation for being fanciful.

She directed an extra glare at her sisters, although neither of them was looking in her direction. It was partially thanks to her sisters that she had acquired the reputation in the first place. They had known the truth of the girl in the tower but had still taken delight in undermining Charlotte's claims. Her relationship with both Elizabeth and Odelia had seemed much improved in recent years, however, thanks to their leaving their old town behind and moving to such a remote area. But lately, it seemed as if nothing had changed after all.

"Perhaps you all imagined a bear," her mother said in a more comforting tone. "Sometimes the shadows among the trees can be positively fearsome."

The older two protested this suggestion, but their manner lacked the certainty Charlotte felt. Now that they were in the comfort and security of home, they were clearly both feeling ashamed of their reaction among the trees.

Charlotte shook her head stubbornly, however. "I saw it clearly. It was definitely a bear—and an enormous one too. I knew bears were large but not that large. And its color..." She shook her head. "It was such a pure white it would have hurt to look at its fur if the sun had been higher."

Neither of her sisters responded to her words, and her mother soon set them to chores around the house, separating Charlotte and her sisters in the process. It was an intentional act, Charlotte knew. Her mother was trying to give them space in the hopes it would soften the other two toward Charlotte. She had been doing similar things ever since the recent resumption of her sisters' old hostility—a change triggered by the celebration for their cousin's wedding.

But though Charlotte knew her mother meant well, she was tired of feeling alone and just wanted someone to take her side for once. It had been different in their old home. As young children, the sisters had been close enough, and by the time Elizabeth and Odelia pulled away from Charlotte, she had friends she could turn to in their place. When she was younger, she had solved the problem of her sister's growing animosity by escaping the house and them as much as possible, spending her time with her friends instead.

But it was different this time. When their father had first announced the family was moving to join his sister and her family in the far eastern valleys, Charlotte hadn't been too worried. Elizabeth and Odelia had complained that their destination was too remote, but the family had always lived in one of the remotest towns in Northhelm, so Charlotte had dismissed their complaints. The timing had even seemed perfect since her closest friend had just left the village.

But it turned out that the unscalable peaks forming the eastern border of Rangmere were even more remote than the forests of Northhelm. And while a number of secluded valleys were hidden in the lower part of the range, very few humans made those valleys their home. Charlotte had assumed they would at least have their cousins for company, but even they lived several hours' ride away. It had been a shock at first, and she had feared living in such an isolated way with only Elizabeth and Odelia for company.

But the isolation had worked to her advantage. It had been the presence of others that had first caused the issues in the sisters' relationship. First, the girl in the tower had chosen Charli as her closest friend, despite Elizabeth and Odelia being closer to Daisy in age. And afterward, the youths who caught her sisters' eyes had looked past them to their younger sister and the growing promise of her great beauty.

Elizabeth and Odelia, so close in age, had always been closer to each other than to Charlotte, and it had been easy for them to form an alliance against her. But in the valley, it was only the three of them, and her sisters had softened toward Charlotte, growing less distant and severe until she had even started to think of them as friends again, as they had been as children.

All of that seemed over, though. Their cousin had recently married, and everyone from three valleys had gathered for the occasion. There had been several new young men, recent arrivals to one valley or another, and it had also been the first gathering since Charlotte had turned eighteen. Since social customs decreed her birthday made her eligible for potential courtship, it had been a disastrous combination. Not one unattached young man had looked in the direction of either of her sisters, and in such an isolated living situation, that was too great a blow for them to bear.

Charlotte hadn't felt a connection with any of the young men, but it hadn't mattered. Before they even arrived home, all the progress of five years had been lost. Their memories of her supposed past crimes had reemerged, and Charlotte was back to being a source of resentment, an *other* her sisters could unite against. As the younger sister, she was supposed to wait her turn, not constantly steal the attention her sisters desired.

The door thudded open, and their father strode into the house, his cheerful smile banishing Charlotte's gloomy memories. If Charlotte had the qualities of a dreamer, she had inherited them from her father. It was no surprise he had followed the rumor of prosperity to a distant land—the true surprise was that he had remained settled in Northhelm for so long.

Looking back, Charlotte should have known it was the beginning of the end when a royal tour visited their old town. Not that her father bore any resentment toward King Richard or his heir, but a place visited by royalty was far too established to satisfy the explorer inside him—the one who wanted to carve order from the wilderness and uncover riches for his family in the process.

Her sisters still resented their father for ignoring their protests in favor of his own urge to go. But Charlotte couldn't maintain resentful feelings in the face of his obvious pleasure in their new home. He could never hide his joy after a day spent taming their land without another soul in sight, and she could rarely help smiling in response to his happiness.

His eyes fell on Charlotte first, standing closest to him. He immediately swept her into a hug, his bulky jacket emphasizing their size difference.

"Charli-bear!" He squeezed her as her broom dropped to the floor, and she buried her face in the soft leather of his jacket, barely holding back tears. Her father had his faults, but he was always warm and affectionate, and lately she had needed those qualities more than anything.

"You can't call her that anymore," her mother said in a tone of indulgent amusement. "The girls have seen a real bear in the forest."

"A bear?" Her father released her and stepped back, turning to look at Elizabeth and Odelia with a chuckle. "Here in the valley? It must have been a shadow you saw, although I'm sorry to hear you had such a fright."

He glanced at Charlotte, clearly as surprised as her mother that it was her sisters and not Charlotte spouting tales of a bear on the loose. And it was true that in the past she had shared her discoveries without first stopping to consider how credible they might seem to others.

A small, resentful part of her wanted to stay silent—or even to speak up in agreement that it had only been a shadow. She knew from bitter experience that her sisters wouldn't hesitate to undermine her in such a fashion. But the idea of being dishonest made her stomach squirm.

"Actually, it couldn't have been a shadow," she told her father. "It wasn't dark but white. I've never seen a creature with such pristine white fur."

She expected her father to protest, possibly even to laugh at her, but he did neither. Instead, a strange look passed over his face—an expression almost like fear. Charlotte frowned, but before she could question him, his smile returned.

"Well, well! I suppose anything is possible. These mountains must hold secrets unknown to any man. It is enough that he wasn't able to get his claws into any of you."

He gathered up his older daughters into the same hug he had given Charlotte, but they both protested and squirmed out of his grip.

"Tomorrow I'll check the closest sections of forest before you go out," he promised them. "If there is any sign of the creature, I'll drive it off."

He glanced at the enormous bow and arrow hung beside the door, and Charlotte felt an unexpected tug in her chest. The emotion she had imagined in the bear's face couldn't have been real, but she couldn't shake its lingering effects. It hurt with a melancholy ache to think of the majestic beast riddled with arrows, red blood marring his white fur.

"He wasn't aggressive," she said quickly. "I don't think he meant to hurt us."

Elizabeth and Odelia both shrieked protests at this suggestion, but her father looked at her with raised eyebrows.

"You don't wish me to drive it off?" He hesitated and then smiled. "I suppose you must feel a sense of kinship, Charli-bear."

Elizabeth sniffed loudly. She and Odelia had long ago insisted their father give up his childish nicknames for them, and Charlotte knew they looked down on her for allowing him to still use hers. But while she had submitted to the use of her full name in all other circumstances, she couldn't bring herself to reject her father's use of her old pet name. Every time she heard it, she felt warm, like being wrapped in a blanket made of affection and memories of happy times.

"I'll do my best to scare it away without harming it," her father said in a softer voice. "Indeed, I would prefer not to harm it. It is no small matter to fight a creature of that size, and who knows what the consequences would be."

He said the last part quietly, almost to himself, and he didn't seem to notice the odd look Charlotte gave him. Her mother's call for them to help prepare the evening meal interrupted the moment, and she lost the chance to question him further. But when she finally lay on her pillow, her ears full of her sister's even breathing, the image of the bear returned to her mind.

He had almost looked as if he would speak, and as she drifted off to sleep, she realized she would very much like to hear what he was going to say.

CHARLOTTE

*S*he slept fitfully, her rest disturbed by strange dreams of snowy tundras and snarling bears. Consequently, she slept in, and by the time she woke, her sisters were fully dressed, bustling around their shared room while they muttered comments about lazy layabeds.

Charlotte rushed to catch up with them, stuffing herself into her clothes without even taking time to brush her hair. She rarely bothered to enhance her appearance in any way—her looks had been the cause of enough resentment as it was—but she preferred to present herself neatly, at least. She'd slept too late for that on this occasion, however.

But as she finally escaped into the forest, she acknowledged there was no need for tidiness. She wasn't likely to see anyone else all day. Especially since she was alone for once. Despite their father's reassurances, her sisters hadn't been brave enough to venture away from the house so soon after sighting the bear.

Her mother had looked once between her elder daughters and her youngest and declared she had plenty of tasks to keep Elizabeth and Odelia occupied inside. And this time Charlotte felt nothing but gratitude for her mother's instinct to separate them.

She breathed in the fresh air deeply, glad to be free of the confines of the small house. But as she walked, she glanced back at her home and sighed. The only thing that had reconciled her sisters to their move was the promise that the family would be better off once they had land of their own in a region with plentiful resources. Her father had been full of stories of the wealth of the valley folk, as relayed by his sister.

But so far that wealth had failed to materialize. According to their father, it would be unlocked soon. He often claimed they just needed more time—time he gave cheerfully—before they would reap all the rewards the valley had to offer. But he was never clear about the source of the promised wealth, and the rewards had assumed a mythical status in Charlotte's mind.

For the moment, they were significantly worse off than they had been in the village. And this reality had likely only exacerbated the recent return of her sisters' resentment and ill temper. After days of celebration at the home of their much wealthier cousins, it had been difficult for all of them to come back to their own house, but her sisters had been the most affected. Elizabeth and Odelia might have directed their resentment toward Charlotte, but she was far from the only cause of their unhappiness.

Charlotte herself occasionally gave in to bouts of resentment, although she never seemed able to hold onto her irritation for long. She certainly didn't care about being wealthy—their family's needs were always met and that was enough for her. But she missed her old home and her friends there, and those feelings had grown hugely since the wedding and the subsequent alienation from her sisters. Would it have been so bad to stay in a village where they were known and valued, even if they were not among its wealthier inhabitants?

She tried to shake off the thoughts and instead enjoy her surroundings. Spring was finally shedding winter's grip on the landscape, buds poking up everywhere she walked. She watched them with pleasure, keeping a careful eye out for anything edible.

After a winter of dried and preserved food, she was longing for greenery on their tables. She wouldn't be able to gather as much without her sisters, but she was determined not to come home empty-handed. Now that the last of the snow had melted, everyone was looking forward to a greater variety of meals again.

A flash of white once again caught her eye, and the jolt of excitement that shot through Charlotte made her admit what she had really been looking for. She froze, a distant part of her mind screaming to flee for the safe walls of home. Her feet didn't move, however. She knew she should feel fear, but curiosity burned more strongly. Despite everything, she had to know if she had imagined the expression on the bear's face the day before.

She barely breathed as he lumbered between two trees, moving in her direction. He hadn't seen her yet, and she rose on her toes, ready to run if he responded to her presence with aggression.

His large white head swung in her direction, his dark eyes fixing on her. Instantly he froze, reacting just as she had at the sight of him. It was such an unexpected reaction that the breath whooshed from her lungs, her muscles relaxing. More than anything, his surprise seemed so...human.

"You came back." The words were low and gravelly with a wild edge that hinted at their origin.

But even so, the sound was too shocking to be immediately understood. She opened her mouth, intending to exclaim in surprise, but only a squeak came out.

The bear blinked, still not moving closer.

"When I saw your father searching the woods with his bow this morning," the bear said, "I thought I had surely frightened you all away." Seeing his mouth move in time with the words made it impossible to deny the reality of what she'd heard.

The animal was speaking—and in perfectly intelligible words.

"You...you can talk," she said, her voice trembling.

The bear made such a terrifying rumbling sound that she

nearly ran, but a certain brightness to his eyes gave her pause. Was he laughing?

"I'm sorry," he said. "I didn't mean to startle you, but I couldn't think of any other way to communicate."

"No," she said blinking, "I suppose not."

Silence fell as she tried to think what else to say. While she had never been excessively talkative like some children, she had rarely been at a complete loss. But what sort of conversation was one supposed to have with a bear? The entire interaction was inconceivable.

Or was it? Her thoughts stopped in their wild spinning as she remembered a story Daisy used to tell. The tale had been about a girl from a kingdom across the desert—a girl who had become a princess with the help of a talking cat.

According to the story, the cat had come from the High King's lands. It made sense, of course. Something as fantastical as a talking animal had to come from the Palace of Light. In fact, hadn't one of her cousins claimed to hear stories of a talking horse who had spent some time in Rangmere? Her cousin had never met the steed himself, but he had insisted the story was true. And in that tale, the creature had come from the Palace of Light as well. If the High King's lands contained a talking cat and a talking horse, why not a talking white bear?

She relaxed. It still didn't explain what such an animal was doing here, in their valley. But at least she was in no danger from a companion of the High King. However long his claws and sharp his teeth, no animal from the Palace of Light would eat a human.

At least, she didn't think one would.

She considered how to phrase a query about the bear's origins. She didn't want to offend him by appearing too suspicious.

"Aren't you afraid of me?" he asked while she was still debating the matter internally.

"Should I be?" she asked back, still marveling at the way his head cocked to the side in curiosity and at the intelligence in his dark eyes. It was no wonder she had sensed from the first that he was no ordinary bear.

"You have nothing to fear from me," he said promptly, and somehow his words comforted her, despite the deep, gravelly tone.

"Thank you." She offered him a small curtsy. She wasn't entirely sure if you were supposed to curtsy to anyone from the Palace of Light or only to the High King himself. But it seemed better to be safe than risk offending such a very large creature.

The bear dipped his head in response, seeming pleased with her action.

Silence fell again as she considered how she was going to tell this story to her family. She could already hear her sisters' ridicule. They would never believe the bear was friendly, let alone that it could talk. Especially not after their excessive—and apparently unnecessary—fear the day before.

She bit her lip.

"Does something trouble you?" The bear took several steps toward her before halting abruptly, as if he had suddenly realized she might not welcome his approach.

She smiled, touched by his thoughtfulness.

"It's nothing of importance," she said. "Merely that my sisters don't like me, and that's hardly new."

She blinked, surprised by her own words. Whatever had led her to blurt out her problems? She had to be badly starved of companionship if she was turning to a bear as her confidante.

He gazed at her with such quiet patience that somehow her mouth opened and more words poured out.

"I do nothing to antagonize them. Quite the opposite! But the two of them are so close in age and temperament, and they've always been willing to close ranks against me at the smallest perceived slight." She sighed heavily. "I thought we were making progress when we moved out here. I even began to think of them as friends. I guess that's why it hurt so much more when they turned against me this time. I've been doing my best not to provoke them, but it makes no difference when they're in this mood. They see fault in everything I do and say." Her voice dropped. "I suppose they don't need me. They have each other. But that leaves me all alone."

The day before, she would have said it was impossible for a bear to frown. But there was no denying his frown in response to her words. His intense gaze fixed even more closely on her face.

"I've been watching you all for days," he admitted after a moment, making her start. "Even I, a stranger, have been able to see your sisters' feelings toward you." His eyes narrowed, and his voice dropped so low it was practically a growl. "Shall I teach them some manners?"

Her eyes widened, a strange rush washing through her—half fear and half imagined delight at the thought of the bear confronting her sisters. But she couldn't encourage the dark turn of his mood.

"Oh no!" she exclaimed. "You need to stay away from them! They're already afraid of you as it is. If you frighten them too badly, they'll never leave the house again."

"And then you'll have to gather food on your own," he said in a milder tone, looking disappointed. "I suppose that will only make everything worse."

She tried to hide her smile and didn't quite succeed. He sounded almost like a child denied a favorite sweet. But a moment later, he brightened, as if struck by a new thought.

He didn't speak, however, and her thoughts returned to his earlier words. He had been watching her and her sisters as they gathered food. Why?

She opened her mouth to ask him, but he spoke at the same time.

"What are the local wedding customs in this area?"

His unexpected words made her forget her own question

entirely. She stared at him, unable to fathom what interest a bear could have in such matters.

"You want to know about our marriage customs?" she repeated, sure she must have heard wrong.

He shook his head slightly. "I don't care so much about the marriage itself, just the wedding. I know the customs differ in different regions."

She wasn't sure if his clarification made the question more or less strange.

"You really want to know how the people of the valleys do wedding ceremonies?" she asked, still unable to believe she'd understood correctly.

"Very much so," he said. "I've come here especially for that purpose."

She gaped at him. The bear had come all the way from the Palace of Light to research how different regions conducted wedding ceremonies? Was he traveling the entire Four Kingdoms, or only the remotest parts? Would he want to know about other ceremonies and celebrations as well?

She hoped he wouldn't ask her to explain a local funeral because she hadn't been to one since they moved from Northhelm. In fact, she only knew about weddings because of her cousin's recent marriage for which they had spent three days at her aunt and uncle's to join the celebrations.

Perhaps that was why the bear was asking her about weddings in particular. Had he overheard talk about a recent one in the area?

"Since the people of the valleys live so far apart," she said hesitantly, "we welcome reasons to gather together. Because of that, an occasion as joyous as a wedding is usually accompanied by a celebration of several days. That also gives the opportunity for young people to meet each other." She gave a small chuckle. "Otherwise there wouldn't be any future weddings."

The bear didn't smile in response, though. Instead, he looked disappointed. "The local weddings last for *days?*"

"Not the wedding itself," she rushed to assure him. "Just the celebration around it. The actual ceremony is short and simple. Valley folk work too hard to waste time and effort on weighty or expensive traditions."

The bear took another step forward, not seeming to notice he was doing so.

"A simple ceremony? What does it involve?"

She shook her head slightly, still utterly bemused. "The bride and groom hold hands in front of their family and friends and make their promises. They promise to support each other through life's joys and disappointments and to remain loyal. Then the parents each speak a blessing. And that's the whole thing. I know it's nothing like the elaborate ceremonies they hold in the cities, but it's accompanied by just as much joy and love."

"What if the parents don't approve?" he asked. "Or they're not able to be present? Can the ceremony happen without their blessing?"

Her forehead wrinkled. "Since the bride and groom have to be adults, it can still go ahead without the parents. It is merely customary to include them."

"An exchange of promises," the bear muttered to himself. "So simple."

Charlotte straightened, reading an insult in his words. "The people of the valleys might be simple folk, but they are good folk, for the most part. And they're certainly hardworking. Fancy gowns and elaborate speeches aren't the mark of good character."

The bear blinked at her, as if he was just as bemused by her as she was by him. Perhaps he hadn't meant his words as an insult after all?

"I know that well," he said in his rumbly voice. "It is merely the simplest wedding ceremony I have yet encountered. But I can assure you I am pleased to hear it."

He spoke as if he was well-traveled. Had he already been all around the Four Kingdoms for his research? Perhaps he had even been to the kingdoms across the desert or the ones across the sea. Although she couldn't imagine the white bear lumbering up a sand dune beside a camel string, nor could she picture him on the deck of a ship. Just the thought made her lips twitch upward.

But then an inhabitant of the Palace of Light probably had other means of transportation.

The bear seemed transfixed by the movement of her lips, and it occurred to her that he might think she was laughing at him. A twinge of guilt reminded her that she had been, in a way.

"Would you like to know about other local ceremonies?" she asked, contrite.

"Oh, uh, no, this is fine." He stumbled over his words for the first time since initiating the conversation. "I think," he added, "that there is someone else I need to speak to now."

"Oh, of course," Charlotte said, surprised at the strength of her disappointment. "I suppose I won't see you again, then. You'll be moving on to some other place soon." She peeped across at him, a little embarrassed, but not able to stop herself adding, "Won't you?"

"Yes," he said. "At least I hope so. I hope I may soon return home."

She nodded, telling herself she should be pleased for his sake. The note of longing in his voice told her he missed his home, and she could hardly blame him, given the tales of the Palace of Light.

"I hope your journey is smooth and swift," she said, giving a deeper curtsy than she had at the beginning of their conversation.

"And I hope all your troubles are soon resolved," he replied.

She smiled at him, once again touched. "Thank you, White Bear. It is kind of you to think of the troubles of an insignificant girl from the valleys."

"Insignificant?" He sounded thoughtful. "Are you? I wonder…"

For what felt like the hundredth time since meeting him, she was left in confused surprise at his words. But this time he moved before she could respond or question him further. With a final dip of his head, he swung around and disappeared back into the trees, moving faster and more quietly than she would have thought possible for such a large animal.

She stood watching the spot where he had stood far after the last glimpse of white fur had disappeared. Had she really just exchanged an extended conversation with a *bear*?

And what a strange conversation it had been.

She finally shook herself and turned north. She still had searching to do if she didn't want to return home empty-handed. And since she wasn't sure it was a good idea to tell her family about the bear, it would be better if she didn't provoke questions by coming home with nothing to show for her day's effort.

GWEN

*G*wen stood in the doorway and surveyed the ballroom. It was full of people dancing and talking, and she wondered how it was possible to feel so alone while surrounded by so many people. Perhaps it was a special talent of hers.

"Gwendolyn." The sound of her full name on her mother's lips made her back stiffen.

She had vague childhood memories of liking her name. Princess Gwendolyn. It had sounded so elegant. But it had long since become a word that reminded her of responsibilities and unpleasant duties. And loneliness.

She knew all about how to behave properly as Princess Gwendolyn, but it felt like a role she slipped into in her mother's presence rather than something that actually belonged to her. And it was a role she always did alone. Was it really too much to ask that in this whole sea of people she might have one true friend?

She suppressed a sigh and pasted a smile on her lips. If she took any longer to enter the ballroom, her mother would say her name again but with an edge. And Gwen never liked what happened after Queen Celandine spoke to her with that edge.

If Easton had been there, he would have looked up at her from the mass of faces and smiled and just that would have been enough to drive back the loneliness. Gwen balled her hands into fists, hiding them in her skirts. Why was she thinking of Easton?

Usually she kept her thoughts under better regulation, but the errant memories of early childhood had brought him to the front of her mind. It wasn't that he ever completely left it, but she knew she had to keep him walled away from the surface of her thoughts. Otherwise she wouldn't be able to continue the grind of daily living without her mother throwing around phrases like *unnecessary melancholy* and *childish dramatics*. All said with the edge, of course.

Apparently, Princess Gwendolyn was not only not allowed to have friends, she wasn't even allowed to miss the one friend she used to have.

But now that Easton had pushed himself to the front of her mind, he wasn't easy to banish. She imagined the face of her lone childhood friend among the courtiers who smiled and bowed at her. She had to use her imagination because the last time she had seen him he had been only thirteen—on the cusp of manhood, but not yet with his adult face.

She had spent many solitary hours turning her memory of his childish features into an imagined adult face, and now it was haunting her. She should have listened to her mother and used her time more productively.

Except the responsibilities that fell to the princess of the mountain kingdom seemed to be universally dull. Her mother liked to talk of her duty and the position she would one day hold, but she never relinquished any actual power to Gwen. Any decisions of note or consequence were made by the queen, and if she wanted to discuss them with someone, she always turned to one of her courtiers, usually Count Oswin, the most senior of her advisors. She would never ask Gwen's opinion—the princess wasn't even permitted to accompany her while she conducted royal business.

Which makes you wonder, what exactly is the point of it all? she thought, not for the first time.

At least Gwen was circulating in the crowd now which meant her mother was no longer looking in her direction with an expression that managed to convey expectant pressure without breaking a smile. Gwen had attended enough of these functions that she'd long ago mastered the art of moving through the crowd with an unhurried gait that still managed to convey a sense of purpose and direction. Not that she actually had anyone to seek out, of course. But looking as if she was moving toward a goal reduced the false pleasantries she was forced to exchange with people who would clearly rather have been talking to someone else. Anyone else.

She could hear their desire to escape the conversation in their strained voices and see it in the way their eyes darted to her mother after every few words. Even when her mother wasn't physically present, Gwen felt her specter hovering over every conversation she had with members of her mother's court. It was why she had long ago embraced solitude.

She passed a server circulating with a tray of drinks, and the briefest flicker of a smile from the older woman lightened Gwen's steps. She needed to remember that she wasn't entirely alone. She might not be able to talk freely with any of the courtiers, but they weren't the only people in the palace.

As if summoned by her disobedient thoughts, Queen Celandine appeared at Gwen's side.

"Would you like a drink, my dear?" she asked with a false smile.

Gwen gave a diffident response and accepted the drink her

mother handed her. Why did the defiance in her mind never manage to translate to her words? No matter what her mother did, Gwen just went along with it, no matter how much she hated her own compliance later.

How many angry speeches had she composed in her mind, only to have them wither on her tongue? She tried to remember the last time she had truly spoken her mind, only to wince. More memories of Easton—and the worst sort this time.

She had never managed to entirely stop thinking of him, but she always tried to avoid remembering those awful days after he had disappeared. She had confronted her mother then, and the punishment had been terrible.

Before that, her mother had responded to defiance by confining Gwen to her room with only the barest of rations. Gwen had quickly learned that continued defiance meant she would be moved to smaller and smaller places of confinement and given less and less food, so even back then she had usually backed down quickly. But after the awful confrontation over Easton's disappearance, her mother had gone straight to a pitch-dark closet so small Gwen couldn't even lie flat, and she'd provided no food or drink whatsoever.

Gwen had believed she would die in there and might have done so if her mother hadn't relented and sent her a single glass of juice each evening starting from the second night. After several days in the dark, her mother believed she had succeeded in breaking Gwen's spirit, and sometimes Gwen thought her mother had been right. In the years since, she had certainly always capitulated at the first stage. Being locked in her room over a mealtime brought back too many memories of the closet for her to brave further escalation of the punishment.

But still, hidden deep inside, she protected a small flame of defiance. As long as it continued to burn, she could tell herself that Easton's Gwen still remained, not yet entirely subsumed by her mother's dutiful Princess Gwendolyn.

24

"You were late," her mother said, again without breaking the smile.

Gwen dared to give a small, audible sigh. Perhaps it was the effect of the memories.

"Why must we always have the balls in the afternoon?" she asked. "In the books I read, they happen at night. It would give everyone more time to prepare if we had them later, and they wouldn't interfere with the day's activities."

Her mother's eyes sharpened, and Gwen knew she had gone too far. Talk about nighttime always brought out the edge.

But her mother's response remained light. "But, my dear..." She ran gentle fingers over the frothy blue material of Gwen's gown. "You look so beautiful. Everyone does. What a waste to hide such magnificence in the darkness. You deserve to shine in the afternoon sun."

This time Gwen didn't let her sigh sound aloud. "Of course, Mother," she said dully. "I wouldn't want to prevent anyone gazing on their beautiful princess."

Her mother either didn't pick up or chose to ignore her irony. And when a courtier approached the queen, Gwen was able to escape entirely, considering herself to have gotten away from the interaction lightly.

Conversations such as those were the reason she couldn't indulge in thoughts of Easton. He had always brought out her true self—had made her feel brave—and there was nothing Queen Celandine hated more.

As soon as a small crowd gathered to talk to her mother, Gwen allowed herself to escape to the fringes of the room. She was tempted to hide behind one of the elaborate ice sculptures that decorated the edges of the ballroom, but it was safer if she remained in her mother's view. The queen always watched her most closely at this sort of event.

"I couldn't risk bringing my mother, of course," one of the courtiers said to another, catching Gwen's ear. "You know what she's like these days. She can't remember what she should or shouldn't say, and she keeps reminiscing about how things used to be before we were all—" He cut himself off.

His companion tsked, shaking her head. "Poor woman. You won't be able to bring her anywhere the princess might be now. Just imagine if she let the truth slip to Princess Gwendolyn! The queen would throw you all to the bears."

The original speaker winced. "One word on what has happened to this kingdom, and I tremble to think of the consequences. No, Mother will have to stay safely at home from now on."

Gwen stared at them transfixed. She knew the courtiers were uncomfortable speaking to her and that her mother was the reason for their discomfort. But it had never occurred to her that they might all be actively collaborating in keeping a secret from her. Or was it more than one?

What did the courtiers know?

She almost started forward, questions trembling on the tip of her tongue. But another courtier joined them, glancing at Gwen as he did so and giving a small, formal bow. The movement made the original two turn to look, expressions of horror transforming their faces when they saw how close Gwen stood.

They hurried into their own bow and curtsy, exchanging worried looks as they did so. Gwen attempted her warmest smile, trying to convey that they need not fear her. If they told her their secrets, she would never betray them to her mother.

Both of them responded to her expression, relaxing and shooting each other relieved looks. But her momentary swell of triumph died as they quickly turned back to their own small circle. Her smile had achieved nothing except to convince them she hadn't overheard after all. And from the alacrity with which they started another topic of conversation, she guessed they would never again risk saying something so revealing inside the palace walls.

As always, Gwen was left standing alone. But it felt different this time.

She looked slowly around the ballroom, heat bubbling up inside her. It started low in her belly and reached toward her throat. She had always been alone in crowds like this, and she had always wondered what was wrong with her to make it so. But suddenly she saw the scene in a different light.

What if the problem had never been with her at all? She had always known the palace held secrets, but she had never grasped the magnitude of the deception. It wasn't just the queen keeping things from her daughter but a conspiracy by the entire court. For so many people to keep a secret must have required a concerted effort of extreme proportions. No wonder the courtiers feared being caught in even a moment's conversation with her. They must have been living in fear of slipping up and saying something revealing.

Gwen had thought herself incapable of connecting with the people of her mother's court, but the fault hadn't been hers after all. It had been the courtiers who were actively working together to exclude her completely—from their friendships, their lives, even their simple conversations. Gwen might have lived in the palace and attended all the court events, but she existed in her own bubble, firmly outside the court itself. It must have been the only way to keep a secret so large.

She slowly turned to look toward her mother. She had no doubt about who had orchestrated her exclusion. But why? What was she hiding?

For a horrible moment, her stomach roiled as she wondered if it was because of her weakness and failings. The queen didn't want the court to know about the depth of her heir's flaws. But the face of Easton, which had plagued her since her arrival, flashed before her eyes again, and she stubbornly rejected the thought. Easton would never have befriended her if she was so terrible. Gwen might have faults, but she wasn't such a shameful heir that the queen would be forced to such lengths. Whatever secret lurked in the court, it was a secret being kept from Gwen, not from the courtiers.

Her feet kept walking as her mind worked, considering many things in a different light. Most of the courtiers had apartments in the palace as well as homes in the city, but she rarely saw children within the palace walls. She had always assumed the courtiers wanted to avoid bringing their youngsters to her mother's attention until they were old enough to be properly trained in respectful behavior. But perhaps they had a different reason for keeping them in the city where Gwen wasn't permitted to go. Children were notoriously bad at keeping secrets.

And the same explanation might account for why she never saw any of the mountain kingdom's regular citizens. The palace was surrounded by a large city, but of its many inhabitants, only the courtiers ever visited the palace. Among her future subjects, Gwen knew only the courtiers, and her mother's guards and servants who lived inside the palace itself. She had always accepted that fact—initially because she was too wrapped up in Easton to care about anyone else, and later because she knew it would anger her mother to question anything. But the strangeness of it burned in her mind now.

Had her mother excluded her subjects from the palace because she feared what might happen if Gwen ever had a conversation with someone not utterly loyal to the queen? Did that mean Gwen was the only one of the mountain people not to know her kingdom's secrets?

The heat of fresh anger washed over her. What secret was so important that her mother had completely isolated her in order to keep it?

It's because you're too weak. It was her mother's insidious voice in her mind. *You're too weak to be trusted.*

But again, another memory swooped in to override it. *Come*

on, you can do it! If I can do it, so can you! Easton's youthful voice was as clear as if he was speaking the words in her ear at that moment. She could even picture his easy smile, and the challenge in his eyes as he called her to match every feat of strength or dexterity that he attempted in the castle corridors. Gwen had sometimes doubted herself, but he had never done so.

Voices swirled around her, their words indistinct but alluring. The ball, which had seemed unutterably dull only minutes before, now sparked and fizzed. How many of the conversations hinted at truths she didn't know?

And most importantly of all—how was she going to uncover those secrets? She felt almost as alive as she used to when she ran, laughing, through the palace corridors, Easton always two steps ahead, and Nanny waiting for them with hot chocolate and warm cake. Discovering the conspiracy against her was the first step to laying it bare.

But for all Gwen's determination, and for all the conversations she sidled close enough to overhear, she learned nothing of note. No one else let any unwise words fall, and the topics that occupied them seemed even more dull than usual. She heard conversations about the weather—spring had started to reach the lower valleys, but it would still be a while before winter released their own vast basin, ensconced as it was by the deeper mountains. And she heard more than enough about who was dancing with whom and what gowns everyone was wearing.

Frustration filled Gwen, unalleviated by the frequent comments on her own beauty of both face and dress. It brought her no comfort to know the people of her kingdom admired her physical appearance even while they were afraid of speaking to her.

For once, the end of the ball brought disappointment instead of relief. Maybe if she had been able to hear more conversations, she might have stumbled on one of note. But at the same time, she was exhausted. Attempting to listen without appearing to do so was more straining than she had expected. Especially given how closely her mother watched her whenever she was among others. Gwen had always thought the queen was afraid of her daughter disgracing her, but that assumption, too, appeared in a different light now. Her mother wasn't afraid of Gwen—she was afraid of everyone else.

Had anyone ever tried to give her a hint? Gwen sifted back through a lifetime's worth of conversations, but nothing came to mind. In the early years she remembered only Easton, and in the last ten, her focus had been on avoiding her mother's disapproval. No one had broken through to her—she didn't even think anyone had tried. She wasn't the only one who feared crossing the mountain queen.

All through the evening meal—eaten in state with only the queen and her daughter present—Gwen racked her brain, trying to think of how she could uncover more information. Asking her mother outright was out of the question. Not only would that approach fail, but it would be far too dangerous. It had been years since she had been confined to the closet and left to starve, but she didn't consider herself safe from such treatment. Her mother would consider questions such as the ones that burned inside Gwen to be defiance of the highest order.

Gwen knew it would make no difference to her mother that she had officially been an adult for some years now. Gwen's age had never affected the punishments her mother meted out. And always there was the added horror of the unknown. Gwen still didn't know what had happened to Easton, and no one in the palace had ever been willing to speak of it. The queen had punishments Gwen didn't even know about.

No, talking to her mother was the last thing Gwen would consider.

And since the courtiers avoided conversation with her whenever possible, that left only one option. The servants.

Gwen shook her head in silent, stubborn denial of the title her mother gave to the people who served in the palace. In the privacy of her own mind, she would name them as they really were—captives.

She vaguely remembered a time when the palace had employed regular servants from families in the city. But she could no longer remember any of their faces, except for Nanny who had been more family than servant. After Easton had left— when she had emerged from those terrible days in the closet, weakened and dazed—they had all been gone.

When she asked after them—dully, and without great interest —she was told they had been sent back to the city. But the palace couldn't function without servants, and so others had soon begun to appear. It was obvious from the beginning they were different. They spoke with unfamiliar accents, for one, and their faces shone with desperation and fear. It hadn't taken much to discover they were captives, valley folk snatched from their lives and carried off into the mountains to work for the mountain queen.

Gwen, cowed by her days of imprisonment and lost in grief at Easton's unknown fate, waited for someone else to protest this strange new state of affairs. But no one ever did. At least not anywhere that Gwen could hear.

Instead, the court buzzed with the news that a path had been found through the mountains. After generations of isolation, Queen Celandine's guards had forged the way, led by Count Oswin's youthful son. They had traded with the valley folk, bringing back delicacies and medicines that were entirely new to the mountain people, and the whole kingdom celebrated their success.

But as time passed, Gwen noticed it was only ever the guards and those most loyal to her mother who went on the trading trips, and it was only the queen who benefited from the new wealth coming into the kingdom. And every time her people returned, they brought new servants with them.

The mountain people traded with the valley folk in the open, but in secret they stole something from them worth more than goods and gold. Gwen could only assume the valley folk hadn't made the connection, since they continued to trade with her mother's people. Or perhaps there were so many valleys the mountain delegation could visit a new one every time? Gwen couldn't be sure, since the distant valleys were one of the many topics she was discouraged from asking questions about.

Thankfully the number of new arrivals had dwindled over the years, and there had been no new faces for the past two. As a consequence, Gwen knew all the captives by name and personality, but she still shied away from the idea of questioning them.

As captives, they could know nothing of her mother's secrets. There was no point in even asking. But even as she thought it, she knew it wasn't true. Servants had ways of discovering information never meant for their ears. She was making excuses to herself to cover her true fear. She didn't fear their ignorance, but rather the opposite.

It was one thing to think the courtiers had been conspiring against her—they were her mother's people and had been for as long as she could remember. But Gwen privately thought of the captives as her people. In a life of compliance, befriending the queen's captives was the one major defiance Gwen had managed to preserve, a secret that had escaped her mother's watchful eye. In the unwelcoming environment of the palace, Gwen had found the only people who had more reason to hate and fear her mother than Gwen herself did. And while she never openly defied her mother, it had comforted her to know that she had allies of her own.

If she found out now that her allies had been siding against Gwen and keeping their captor's secrets, it might break what little will she still had left.

So, even knowing the truth of her motivations, she still

turned her mind to the courtiers instead of the captives. She determined to spend the whole night coming up with avenues of conversation that might trick the courtiers into revealing what she wanted to know.

But, as always, despite the most earnest resolutions, she had barely laid her head on the pillow before she was waking up to bright morning sunlight.

Groaning, she drove her fist into her soft mattress. Was the secret they were all hiding that their princess was gravely ill? She had always slept deeply, even as a child, and Nanny had assured her it was normal for children to be shut in their rooms before it even got dark and expected to stay there until morning. But what sort of adult still needed as much sleep as they ever had as a child? Was it even healthy?

She had tried raising the matter with her mother, but no topic related to nighttime was ever acceptable to the queen. She expected Gwen to sleep and to not ask questions about it. Given all the other things Gwen wasn't allowed to question, her mother's insistence had never seemed especially odd. But now it made Gwen even more suspicious.

On the other hand, if she really was ill—even dying perhaps—what purpose could her mother have in hiding it? If it was any other mother, Gwen might have suspected she was motivated by compassion. Nanny might have kept such a secret in the years before her passing. The elderly woman had been the kindest soul Gwen had ever met, and she wouldn't have been able to bear delivering such news to her beloved charge. But it was impossible to consider her mother in such a light. The queen considered compassion a failing. At least, she had always seen it as such in Gwen.

Which led her back to where she started. If the whole of the kingdom was keeping a secret from her, there must be a reason for it. And if she was to discover that reason, she needed to find someone who could be tricked or cajoled into sharing it with her.

But after spending the daylight hours prowling the corridors of the palace, searching for people to gently interrogate, Gwen was forced to rethink her plans. She had spent so long doing everything possible to avoid the people of her mother's court that she had never realized how skilled they were in avoiding her.

It hadn't only been her melancholy talking when she bemoaned the emptiness of the palace halls. They truly were almost deserted. And when she did manage to corner someone, they slipped away like water between her fingers. She had planned some conversation gambits over breakfast, but she never even got as far as attempting them.

The stark gray stone of the walls and floor mocked her, reminding her inescapably of her mother as she walked dejectedly back toward her room. Gwen would have chosen to alleviate the cold bite in the air with warm colors and soft materials—both on the walls and underfoot. But the queen preferred an austere look.

"Are you all right, Your Highness?" a timid voice asked from behind her.

Gwen ceased her contemplation of the empty wall and swung to look at the newest addition to the palace captives. Not that Miriam could really be counted as new after being at the mountain palace for almost two years. But she still felt new since it had taken the girl over a year to work up the courage to address the princess. And, even now, she still looked around like a startled rabbit before daring so much as a word.

Not that Gwen could blame her. She sometimes felt like a startled rabbit who had wandered into the palace herself. But Gwen had been willing to persist because Miriam was the closest captive to her own age, only a few years younger by her estimate.

"I'm fine," Gwen said by habit before remembering she wasn't fine at all. But it seemed too late to take the words back, so she let them stand. "I was just contemplating how lovely this wall would look with a large tapestry hanging on it. And perhaps a carpet underfoot in matching colors? What do you think?"

Miriam cocked her head, examining both the wall and the floor with due seriousness.

"It would be more work to clean," was her eventual conclusion, the words delivered simply and without rancor.

Gwen blinked. "Yes, I suppose it would be. I didn't think of that."

She watched the younger girl vigorously scrub the window on the opposite wall for a moment before speaking impulsively.

"Miriam, am I ill?"

Miriam's rag stopped moving. "Ill, Your Highness? Are you not feeling well? Should I call for the royal doctor?"

"No, no." Gwen shook her head impatiently. "I feel fine right now. I mean something bigger."

Miriam stared at her as if she'd lost her mind, and Gwen couldn't help laughing at herself. She must sound unhinged. She started again, trying to talk with more sense.

"I feel perfectly healthy. But I'm concerned that I sleep so deeply every night and for so long. I'm wondering if it might be a sign of some illness of which I'm unaware? Perhaps everyone is keeping the truth from me in order not to upset me?"

Miriam's eyes widened. "Surely not, Your Highness! Could you really be so ill and not know it?"

Gwen shrugged. It was clear from Miriam's reaction that she had no idea what Gwen was talking about.

"I don't know." She sighed and slumped onto one of the chairs lining the inside wall. "Never mind. It was probably a silly thought anyway. I just hate the feeling that I've lost so many hours. I'm sure someone could steal into my chamber in the night and make off with every one of my possessions, and I wouldn't rouse."

Miriam frowned, her expression concerned. "I would offer to watch over your sleep, but..."

Gwen grimaced, feeling instantly guilty for her complaints. It was rare for one of the servants to speak of nighttime—it would be bad enough if they were caught talking to the princess, but much worse if it was of forbidden topics—but Alma had explained the full situation to Gwen once. The older woman had been among the first captives and had been the first to take pity on the numb, bewildered girl who had taken to roaming the corridors alone once she had lost both Nanny and Easton.

Alma had explained in a hushed whisper that the captives were given free rein of the palace during the day—they needed it to complete their duties, and it wasn't as if there was anywhere for them to run. Tall mountains encircled the deep valley that held the mountain palace and the city that surrounded it. No one in the city would hide the captives, and only the queen's people knew how to find safe passage through the mountains. Even Gwen herself didn't know how they had succeeded when previous generations had failed, and Alma said the captives were all drugged for the journey in, so they didn't know either. Without knowledge of the route or even appropriate provisions, the mountains would be a death sentence.

And yet, despite the natural forces that kept the valley folk captive in the palace, at night they were locked into a small group of connected storage rooms—ones that were built into the basement level of the palace and lacked even windows. Once the sun was down and the court was abed, the queen didn't want her captives roaming free.

During the day, the queen liked to pretend her captives were regular servants—a charade she expected them to uphold as well. But at nighttime, they were reminded of their true status. Perhaps it was why Gwen had always felt so connected to them. Since Easton's disappearance, she had often felt like a captive in the palace herself. But still, she felt bad to have compared her own experience to Miriam's, however unintentionally.

Miriam resumed polishing the window, but she continued to

throw worried glances at the princess. And when she spoke, her words echoed Gwen's own thoughts.

"I wish I could help you at night, but I suppose we're both captives in the hours of darkness—me to a locked door and you to sleep." She paused, shivering. "Perhaps it's for the best, given the rumors."

GWEN

*G*wen bolted upright, her eyes fixed on Miriam. "Rumors?" she cried, only just remembering to modulate her volume. "What rumors?"

Miriam froze, her eyes widening and her expression growing terrified. "Wh...What? Rumors? I don't know anything about any rumors!"

"Miriam!" Gwen hissed. "You know something! Clearly you do! Tell me at once!"

Miriam stared at her, looking more like a startled rabbit than ever, except now she was caught in the gaze of a predator.

Gwen had the grace to feel ashamed, but she wouldn't let the dropped hint go. She couldn't. She needed answers, even if she had to press Miriam into giving them to her.

But footsteps around the corner shattered the moment. Their approach was rapid, and she barely had time to throw herself back into her chair before the newcomer appeared. Gwen smiled and nodded to the courtier, even as she watched Miriam out of the corner of her eye. Miriam had resumed polishing the glass at a feverish pace, her back to the princess, but Gwen still caught the telltale flush in her cheeks. Her eyes narrowed. Miriam definitely knew something she didn't want to tell the princess.

But the courtier paused, shifting uncomfortably as his eyes flashed from Gwen to Miriam. He might not have been comfortable in the princess's presence, but he clearly knew his duty. He obviously wasn't going to continue on, leaving the princess adjacent to such low company.

Gwen tried to wait it out, but as the man blustered through a series of increasingly terse attempts to get her moving, she gave up, putting all three of them out of their misery by agreeing to accompany the man in search of her mother. But once they found her, Gwen couldn't free herself again, and before she knew it, the evening meal had begun.

This time they ate in the presence of a select group of courtiers, including both the man who had *rescued* her and Count Oswin. Since the count was her mother's most senior advisor, he was always present at such affairs, but the other man was a surprise. Lord Rafferty, as he was apparently called, was a junior enough member of the court that Gwen couldn't remember ever meeting him before, although his face was vaguely familiar.

He had certainly never eaten with them before, and she could only assume his sudden inclusion was a reward for his meddlesome surveillance of her. The thought stung, although it shouldn't have come as a surprise given what she now knew about how her mother had been using the court against her. It wasn't much of a step from alienation to surveillance.

Gwen stuffed down her resentment, squishing her feelings away until there was no outward sign of them, as she had so often done before. She had no desire to attract her mother's attention, especially in the presence of guests. At least with the others present, she would be excluded from the conversation and could thus avoid having to converse with her mother.

As the meal progressed, her mind turned to more helpful topics, and she found herself extra grateful to be left to her own thoughts. In the corridor, she had been focused on Miriam's mention of a rumor—a topic she intended to pursue again at first opportunity. But in the time since, something else had occurred to Gwen, and as she ate, she was free to consider it from every angle.

Miriam had said they were both captives at night, and she was right. For the hours of darkness, neither the queen nor her courtiers watched them, believing both the princess and the valley folk to be safely shut away behind doors. But what if they were shut behind the same door?

If Gwen snuck into the storage rooms with the captives for a night, they could help keep her awake. Behind a locked door, they would have hours to talk freely without fear of discovery or notice.

The idea captivated her. Why hadn't she thought of it sooner? All she had to do was stay awake past sundown when the captives were locked away. Once darkness fell, she could creep through the palace to their prison. Given she and Easton had secretly appropriated a master key for the palace—to enable them to roam it freely—getting past the locked door shouldn't present a problem. Even if she eventually fell asleep—which she inevitably would, she was sure, even with assistance—Alma or Miriam could wake her before dawn so she could sneak back into her own room.

The hardest part of the plan would be staying awake long enough to sneak through the palace. She sometimes remained awake for a few minutes past her normal bedtime, but to succeed with her plan, she might need to last as long as half an hour.

As she considered the difficulty, she pushed her food around on her plate. How little could she get away with eating? A full stomach always made her drowsy, so perhaps hunger pangs would help keep her alert.

It wasn't as simple as not eating, however. She had long ago learned that her mother wouldn't permit her to boycott a meal altogether. She needed to walk a fine line—consuming just enough to satisfy her mother without coming close to filling herself.

Thankfully the guests took enough of the queen's attention that she didn't notice her daughter's tiny mouthfuls or how much of her movement was just shifting food around on her plate. And somehow the small amount she ate only made Gwen hungrier than she had been when the meal began.

She even limited the amount she drank, knowing the rich drinks favored by her mother would fill her stomach as easily as food. In a further stroke of luck, Alma was serving that night, and she seemed to pick up that Gwen was eating lightly on purpose. She whisked each plate and glass aside quickly before the queen could notice how full they remained.

Gwen wished she could whisper something of her plan to Alma, but she didn't dare try even the most subtle communication when she was at her mother's table.

Her fingers tightened around the handle of her fork, squeezing until her knuckles whitened. It didn't matter how many years passed. She might be a woman in her twenties now, but she was still trapped as a child beneath her mother's watchful eye.

But the surge of anger was accompanied with a familiar impotence. Her mother wasn't merely Gwen's parent but the queen, and there was no one in the mountain kingdom who would gainsay her. The princess really was just as trapped as the captives, hemmed in by the same mountains that restrained them.

When the meal finally reached its end, Gwen surged to her feet and gave the necessary curtsy to her mother. The queen's eyes narrowed slightly at her daughter's hasty exit, but she let her go unchallenged. Gwen made it two corridors over before she put her back against the wall and sucked in several deep breaths.

Closing her eyes, she continued to breathe slowly, reminding herself that the walls of the palace weren't closing in on her. They remained exactly where they had always been. And her mother wasn't all-seeing. It might feel like it on occasion, but Gwen had successfully kept her connection to the captives a secret from her. She could keep other secrets too. She could defy her mother's iron reign.

A tug on her dress made her eyes fly open, her heartbeat skyrocketing with the irrational fear that her mother had somehow sensed her thoughts. But the girl tugging on her was unfamiliar, and she immediately fell back when she saw Gwen's wide-eyed expression, her own face flushing a deep red.

"I...I'm sorry, Your Highness," the girl stammered. "I didn't mean...That is, I didn't..." Her words grew so tangled that she stopped altogether.

"Who are you?" Gwen asked as her heart returned to a more normal rhythm.

The girl didn't look much older than fourteen, and Gwen didn't think she'd ever seen her before. She wasn't one of her mother's courtiers, but neither was she one of the captive servants.

With a start, Gwen realized she must be one of the mountain kingdom citizens—an inhabitant of the city who lived in one of the houses surrounding the palace but was never invited inside it.

Curiosity spiked inside her. The queen sometimes paraded through the city streets, her daughter in tow, and the populace obediently lined the streets to see their ruler pass by. But Gwen had never been permitted to walk through the city or interact with any of its inhabitants. Often she forgot about their existence altogether, except as a vague concept.

The girl shook her head, swallowing visibly as she began to back away. "I'm sorry," she said in a tumbled rush. "I'm sorry. I shouldn't have come. Of course I shouldn't have. I didn't mean any harm. I—"

"Stop!" Gwen surprised herself by producing the same commanding tone her mother employed so effectively.

Sure enough, the girl froze, her eyes somehow growing even larger and her face even redder.

Gwen softened her voice. "I won't hurt you." She added a stern note of warning. "But the palace isn't a safe place for you. You mustn't approach anyone else, and you mustn't let the queen see you. Can you do that?"

The girl nodded, her lips pressed together, and her eyes fixed on Gwen.

"What's your name?" Gwen asked gently.

The girl shook her head this time, still not speaking, and Gwen sighed. Given the warning she had just delivered, could she blame the girl for not wanting to identify herself?

"Very well," she said. "Don't worry about a name. I'm Princess Gwen."

"Gwen," the girl said, as if testing it out and liking how it sounded.

Gwen smiled at her. "It must have taken a lot of courage for you to come here. Surely you didn't come to find me?"

"Mother always told me stories about the mountain princess who lives in the palace and is more beautiful than any other. The one who will someday save us."

Gwen laughed uncomfortably. "Well, some of that is true, at least. I am a princess, and I do live in the palace."

"I thought...I thought surely a princess would have the power to help us," the girl whispered. "Mother doesn't know I'm here, but I had to come. Can't you help us?"

She stared at Gwen pleadingly as Gwen tried to make sense of her words. First the girl had spoken of being saved, and now she was asking for help. But for whom? Did she mean her family specifically?

"I...I would like to help you," she said cautiously. "I would like to help any of my people who are in trouble. But what exactly is the problem?"

"We've barely made it through the winter." The girl's voice trembled. "Spring will be here soon, but it will still be a long time before any crops can be harvested. And now the taxes are to be raised again? If the queen truly means to go through with it, we'll all of us starve!" She finished on a crescendo, only to look up and down the corridor nervously, her expression sheepish.

From her reaction, Gwen guessed she was dramatizing the situation, in the way that was common for children her age. From the look of her, she wasn't on the edge of starvation. But at the same time, it seemed equally clear that the people faced genuine hardship. The girl wouldn't have mustered the courage to sneak into the palace in search of the princess if that wasn't the case.

"Will you really starve?" Gwen asked, testing her.

As she asked, the small amount of food she had consumed roiled in her belly. It might have been the end of winter, but there was no shortage of provisions for those who lived in the palace. To her shame, she couldn't have even said when the new season's harvest would arrive. Autumn, winter, or spring, their tables were laden just the same.

"Maybe not," the girl admitted. "But soon we won't be able to afford mother's medicine."

"Your mother is ill?"

The girl nodded. "It's a chronic condition, and the medicine comes from the far lands."

It took Gwen a moment to realize she must mean her mother needed the medicine brought back by the queen's traders. It wasn't hard to guess that her mother charged the people high prices for anything that came from the valleys.

"I see." Gwen stared at the girl for a moment before reaching a sudden decision. "Come with me."

She led the girl down the corridor and into her room, moving quickly. It was best for the girl to be gone from the palace as soon as possible.

Rummaging through her cabinet, Gwen found the small leather pouch she had hidden at the back. For a few seconds, she hesitated, feeling the meager weight of it in her hand. The coins inside were few given how many years she had been collecting them—hoarding them against her dream of one day leaving the mountains. She had saved the first coin the year Easton disappeared, but her stash had only grown slowly.

But it was a hollow dream. In the depths of her heart, Gwen had always known that. She was never going to escape. Never. So there was no point in the coins gathering dust in her cabinet.

She held the pouch out to the girl, a swift movement, as if she feared her hand might disobey her and snatch them back. The girl squeaked, staring at the pouch hungrily before reaching out tentatively to accept it.

"Thank you, Your Highness," she breathed. "You are as generous as my mother's stories always claimed."

Gwen smiled, but it was a tired expression. "I'm sorry I can't do more. I'll see what I can do about the taxes but…"

Even as she was speaking the words, she knew the dispiriting truth. There was nothing she could do. She hadn't even known her mother was planning to raise them—or that she had apparently done so several times before by the sound of it. She wasn't included in those sorts of decisions. She was powerless.

The girl curtsied deeply and thanked her again before moving to the door. Her hand was on the knob when Gwen called for her to stop, an idea striking her.

She hurried over to join her. "I'll help you leave. If someone spots you on the way out…" She trailed off, reading in the girl's face that she didn't need a reminder of the danger she was in.

What Gwen didn't add was that accompanying the girl out would benefit Gwen as well. Despite the late hour, she didn't feel in the least sleepy. Usually, her eyelids would be drooping by that point, but the surge of energy from the girl's unexpected appearance had driven away the fatigue. And surely creeping through the corridors and grounds would only continue that effect.

Gwen gestured the girl back and opened the door, peering outside into the corridor. There was no one in sight, so she slipped through, signaling for the girl to follow. She obeyed, tiptoeing behind with a thrilled look on her face that made Gwen want to laugh. How many of the girl's childhood imaginings were being fulfilled in that moment?

But Gwen was no longer prone to the dramatic swings of emotion that plagued children on the edge of youth, and she had a clearer idea of the danger. If the son of courtiers could disappear without a trace, how much more easily could the queen dispose of a girl from the city? Gwen couldn't let herself forget it wasn't a game.

They had almost made it to the closest exit when she heard voices. Sweeping the girl along with her, she fled through a nearby door. It led into a small storage space filled with cleaning supplies. Gwen knew the closet was there because she had seen the captives use it—she was just glad it hadn't been locked.

With the door closed, it was completely dark inside, and Gwen stood with her hand over the girl's mouth. It was probably an unnecessary move, but she couldn't help the tension flooding her. She had already been afraid for the girl, but being enclosed in the dark closet sent fear flooding through her at unmanageable levels. Only the contact with another person was keeping her from falling off the edge and plunging into uncontrolled panic.

Somewhere, distantly, she registered that the voices had faded. But her limbs remained locked in position, her mind too occupied with holding back the panic to manage proper thought. It was so dark, and she could feel the shelves pressing in tightly on her.

But she wasn't alone. She clung to that thought, hearing the scrape of the girl's breathing in the darkness and feeling the warmth of her presence. She wasn't alone. She wasn't being punished.

The girl pulled away, startling Gwen from her stupor. A crack of light appeared as the girl inched the door open, and Gwen's panic receded, leaving her feeling foolish.

"We need to keep moving," the girl whispered, sounding nervous. "I have to be home before dark."

Gwen nodded, hoping the girl hadn't noticed anything odd in her behavior. Shaking herself, she pushed the door the rest of the way open, taking the lead again.

The corridors stayed clear the rest of the way to the external door, and when she pulled it open, the girl rushed through. She paused to wave farewell to the princess, but Gwen shook her head and followed her outside. The girl wasn't safe until she was out of the extensive gardens that surrounded the palace. And the cool air of early evening would help drive away the sleepiness that had settled in the wake of Gwen's earlier panic.

As they walked along gravel paths between carefully sculpted bushes and beds of flowers, she glanced back at the building. Everyone always referred to it as a palace, but it had none of the lightness of the palaces in the storybooks of her childhood. It had the necessary size and turrets, but no bright flags waved at the top of them, and the dour gray stone gave it a stern look she had always hated. It seemed better named as a castle—or even a fort—than a palace. But her mother called it a palace and everyone else followed suit, playing into the fantasy her mother liked them all to enact—the one where she was a beloved monarch, her servants had chosen their positions, and Gwen was her loving, cosseted family.

Distracted by her thoughts, she nearly didn't hear the crunch underfoot as a patrol of guards neared their position. They were so close to reaching the palace boundary, but they weren't quite there, and there was no time to conceal them both.

Acting without thought, she shoved her companion hard. Caught by surprise, the girl staggered sideways and fell between two bushes. The greenery grew close enough together that the shadows covered her in the darkness. Turning in the same movement, Gwen reached for an early rose bud, a smile fixed on her face.

The guards came into view, both halting for the span of a breath before hurrying toward the princess. Their hands rose to their sword hilts only to fall away again when they got close enough to confirm her identity. But their expressions didn't relax.

"Your Highness!" the older of them said, sounding disapproving. "You shouldn't be out here."

"But the first of the roses are starting to bloom," Gwen said as innocently as she could.

"Your Highness, you need to go inside," he said more firmly.

A slight rustle from the bush beside them made the second guard start to turn. She grabbed his arm, smiling inanely up at him.

"How could I sleep on such a beautiful night?"

The young man threw his superior a panicked look, and the older man pulled Gwen off more roughly than she had expected. But at least his firm hold on her arm drove off the sleepiness that had started to weigh her down.

She still threw him a shocked look, however. "Captain!"

He didn't loosen his hold. "It's nearly dark, and you need your sleep."

A stab of excitement sharpened her senses, driving the sleep even further away. They had strayed onto the topic of nighttime, and though she was sure to suffer for this episode later, it would be worth it if she could reveal another piece of the puzzle.

"There's nothing dangerous about darkness," she said boldly. "I'm still within the palace grounds."

"Your Highness has no idea," the man said gruffly. "Nowhere is safe at night."

Gwen raised both eyebrows. He talked as if there were rabble at the castle gates waving pitchforks. Although given what she had just learned about the taxes, perhaps there soon would be. Gwen had helped one family today, but she was painfully aware there had to be many others with equally compelling needs in the city.

She pushed that thought down, however, focusing on the guard. "Please," she said as sweetly as she could manage, "enlighten me."

The younger man threw his superior another panicked look, this time encompassing the rapidly darkening sky in his glance.

"We have to hurry," he said, not speaking to her.

"Whatever for?" she asked brightly. "I don't feel at all sleepy yet. And I know the way well. I wouldn't lose my way even in pitch black." She smiled from one to the other. "And you two brave soldiers can accompany me to keep me safe."

They appeared not to hear her, too busy conducting a silent conversation comprised of their eyes and several expressive grimaces. At the end of it, they seemed to reach a consensus.

Still not addressing her, the other guard took her remaining arm in an equally firm grip as they hustled her along the path. When she exclaimed and tried to break free, they only tightened their hold, almost lifting her feet from the ground to hurry their passage.

Gwen managed a single glance back over her shoulder and caught sight of the girl slipping out of the bushes and running for the castle boundary. At least she had succeeded in distracting the guards. But she was going to have bruises to show for it in the morning. She had never expected castle guards to dare manhandle the princess in such a manner.

She swallowed down a lump of actual fear. Whatever had

spooked them, it had to be more serious than she had realized. Just what happened in these grounds at nighttime?

She ceased struggling, but they didn't slow or even loosen their grip. Her fear increased, and she wondered if they meant to haul her straight to her mother. If so, she would need an excuse for going outside that was more believable than a sudden desire to see the roses.

But Gwen's mind had stopped working, frozen in a state of confusion and fear, as it had done in the closet. The morass only lifted when it became clear they were heading for her bedchamber. By the time they shoved her inside, she had gathered herself enough to at least recover her balance before she fell.

She turned, meaning to protest, but the door was already being firmly closed behind her. Angry, she stomped over and pulled it back open. The guards, already part way back down the corridor, didn't pause or even look back. Despite their cowardly retreat, Gwen didn't risk stepping out of the room. Instead, she contented herself with glaring fire at their backs.

When they had disappeared around a corner, she reluctantly closed the door. At least the trip outside had used up much of the wait before she could enact her plan. But it was still too early to leave her room—especially given what had just happened. The guards might yet be fetching her mother.

She waited, sitting bolt upright on the edge of her bed in expectation of the queen sweeping into the room at any moment. But as the minutes passed without the door opening, she couldn't maintain the alert expectancy.

She tried to hold onto the earlier thrill of creeping through the palace, but it had faded beyond her reach. She pulled up her anger instead, gently exploring the burgeoning bruises on her arms. But even the anger felt distant and hard to reach.

Her blinks became longer, the weights on her eyelids making them harder and harder to open. Her thoughts grew muddled, no longer following logical threads but jumping erratically and chasing down nonsensical tracks. Several times she jerked, her whole body jumping as she pulled herself back from the verge of sleep.

Defiantly, she forced herself to her feet, crossing over to open the curtains as wide as they would go, letting in a wash of moonlight. She pressed her cheek against the cold of the windowpane, the shock of it driving back the heaviness for a moment.

But the sensation lost its effectiveness too quickly, her limbs growing as heavy as her eyes. The sweet lure of sleep was harder and harder to resist with each passing second. Giving in to it would feel so blissful.

She slipped down to curl on the broad window seat, her hands reaching instinctively for one of the cushions and putting it under her head. Despite everything she had tried, she couldn't fight the sleep that always overtook her. It was a river, and she was drowning.

She woke with a start and the certain knowledge that something was different. It took her a moment to realize what it was. She had slipped off the window seat, landing on the floor with enough force to pull her out of sleep before the sun rose. Gwen couldn't remember the last time she had woken when it was still dark.

Excitement flooded her, fighting against the pull that tried to drag her back beneath the waves of sleep. There were still hours of the night left. She could still seek out the captives.

It was difficult to keep her eyes open, though, and she let them drift most of the way closed as she wrestled her sleep-heavy limbs into compliance. She felt as if she were fighting for control of her own body, but her determination drove her forward, and she crawled toward the door on all fours. By the time she reached it, her eyes had drifted shut again, but she was still forcing herself to move. It was too warm in her room. If she could just get out into the cold corridor, she would wake up enough to get to the captives.

Feeling blindly up the wood of the door, she found the handle. But it wouldn't turn. Her door was locked.

She slumped against the floor, despair filling her. Had the guards returned to lock her in? Was this the result of her small defiance?

A worse thought flashed through her mind. Had her door always been locked, and she had simply never noticed?

Following on its heels was another thought that rapidly grew into certainty when she combined it with the strange behavior of the guards. She had feared that everyone was keeping a secret about her, but whatever was happening was bigger by far. Something dangerous was happening in the palace at night. Something big.

She tried to hold onto the thought as sleep claimed her again.

CHARLOTTE

*I*n the end, Charlotte did cut her foraging short but not because of her encounter with the bear. As the day wore on, gray clouds rolled in, and the afternoon became darker and darker.

She turned for home much earlier than usual, unnerved by the way day appeared to be descending into night hours too early. She was glad for her forethought when the heavy clouds released their wet load just as she ducked through the front door.

To her relief, her father was there ahead of her, although he had also planned to be out all day. He had probably read the change in the weather more quickly than she had and known what was coming. Even after five years, the sudden storms in the valley still took Charlotte by surprise.

"Charli-bear!" he exclaimed. "I was about to put my jacket back on and go out to find you. It looks like this will be a bad one."

She slipped her own jacket off and hung it on the hook by the door. "I should have turned back sooner, but I'd just found a pocket of wild mushrooms, and I wasn't sure I'd remember where to find it again."

She unpacked her load, laying it across their large wooden table. Her mother made several pleased sounds as she began to sort the delicacy, muttering to herself about what dishes she would make. Watching her made both Charlotte and her father smile.

"You turned back soon enough," he said. "All is well. And now we may enjoy a few snug hours together." He beamed, looking delighted at the prospect. While he never shirked the endless list of tasks waiting for him and seemed to genuinely love the valley, his favorite moments were ones like this, where the weather trapped them all together inside their cozy home.

Charlotte tried to feel the same enthusiasm. A few months ago, she would have at least been glad for the extra time with her father. But her sisters' frosty reception—they still hadn't even greeted her—reminded her that the painstaking ground she had won with them had all been lost, and her home was no longer a comfortable place.

Thoughts of her relationship with her sisters reminded her of her conversation with the bear. She knew she should tell her father about it, but she couldn't bring herself to speak of the strange meeting. Better her sisters be silent than speak up in ridicule.

She moved toward her mother, intending to help her with her food preparation, but Elizabeth leaped in before she could get there. Odelia followed with a contemptuous look at Charlotte, as if she had been lazing about all day instead of working hard like them.

Something bubbled up in Charlotte, and for once she wanted to speak up to defend herself, even knowing it would do no good. But her mother threw her a sympathetic look, clearly pleading with her to keep the peace, and Charlotte subsided, remembering they were all stuck inside together for the foreseeable future. As much as she would have liked to hear her mother defend her aloud for once, she was probably right that it wouldn't be worth it.

Sighing, Charlotte turned to the sewing basket instead. At least she had enjoyed her solitary wanderings, so maybe she really had enjoyed a nicer day than her sisters. She took a seat by the fire and was soon joined by her father, a block of wood and a carving knife in his hands.

He smiled at her, the quiet scene clearly filling him with contented joy. And glancing from him to the three women working in harmony on the other side of the large room, Charlotte could understand his feelings. She only wished she could share them. But while her father seemed not to have noticed the divide that had returned to his family, Charlotte felt it as a constant ache inside, a reminder of the pain of her childhood and their current isolation.

The sound of the wind grew, an eerie note to go with her melancholy thoughts. Her father had already fastened the shutters, but it was obvious the sky had darkened further. Night truly had come early, and the thunder of raindrops against the roof soon joined the wind. She usually enjoyed the sound of rain—as long as she was safely inside, preferably tucked in her bed—but the intensity of the storm turned the comforting noise into an assault. She kept glancing at the roof, wondering if it would hold.

"Don't worry, daughter," her father said softly, drawing her eyes. "It was stoutly made and will hold against storms worse than this."

She managed a tight smile and a nod. Her mind knew he was right, but deeper instincts couldn't help responding to the ferocity of the storm. She was glad now that she had taken the extra time to harvest the wild mushrooms. Even if she could have found the spot again, who knew if they would have survived the downpour. It might be many days before she found anything worth harvesting now.

Her mother and sisters were just laying out the completed meal on the table when a sound made all five of them look up.

"What was that?" Elizabeth asked, sounding afraid.

"Probably nothing," her mother said quickly, but her voice was uneasy.

"It sounded like a knock," Odelia said doubtfully. "But it must have been a loud one to be heard above the storm."

"How could there be someone out there in this?" Elizabeth snapped, clearly wanting to believe her own words but struggling to do so.

"We shall have to look before they beat the door down," her father said, cheerfully. He stood, and Charlotte couldn't tell if he was really unbothered or if he was just pretending in order to reassure the rest of them.

She stood as well, and since she was closer to the door than he was, she moved toward it. Whatever her misgivings, she wanted to prove to herself that she wasn't like her sisters. She wouldn't give way to fear.

Taking a deep breath, she threw open the door in one smooth movement. A hard sheet of rain angled through the opening, carrying a gust of freezing wind with it. She gasped at the sudden assault, and before she could recover herself, her father leaped forward, thrusting her behind him.

Grimacing at her poor exhibition, she stepped to the side, looking past the rain to what stood outside. She gasped again.

Standing in the doorway, apparently impervious to the rain and wind, was the White Bear.

Her father raised the staff that had somehow appeared in his hand, his expression no longer calm. He looked equal parts afraid and determined, his gaze wavering only once, when his eyes flicked to his wife and daughters and then to his bow, still hanging to one side of the door.

"No!" Charlotte cried. "He isn't dangerous!"

"Not dangerous?" Elizabeth shouted in a half-scream. "It's a bear!"

"Quick, Father! Kill him!" Odelia called from where she was cowering behind their mother.

Charlotte leaped forward, placing herself between her father and the doorway, arms outstretched to hold him back. It was a futile gesture if he was truly determined. She was much too small to physically restrain her tall father. But surely he would turn away from any rash action once he heard the truth about the bear.

She stood with her back to her father, her face toward the doorway. Her eyes immediately locked with the bear's, and the expression on his face was hard to read. At least he didn't look angry at the outburst of her sisters. If anything, he looked... pleased.

"He isn't an ordinary bear," she said, the words tumbling out. She twisted her head to look back at her father. "He can speak."

"Speak?" Elizabeth's shrill cry was laden with disbelief. "You've lost your mind, Charlotte! Bears can't speak."

"This one can," she said stubbornly, keeping her eyes on her father. "We had a conversation in the woods this morning, and he showed no aggression toward me."

She turned back to throw a pleading look at the White Bear. It would be the perfect moment for him to say something.

He gave the same rumbling sound she had earlier determined to be his laugh. "It's true I was raised to be polite in all circumstances," he said. "I wouldn't dream of offering any of you violence."

His eyes strayed toward her sisters, and for a fanciful moment Charlotte remembered his words in the forest and the moment when it had seemed he did want to threaten her sisters. But whether that desire had been real or imagined, he was firmly in control now, looking as civilized as it was possible for a bear to look.

"He...he spoke," Odelia gasped, the words barely audible above the wind and rain.

Charlotte rolled her eyes. Hadn't she just told them that?

"You conversed with him this morning?" her father asked in a slow, halting manner.

Charlotte lowered her arms and angled herself so she could see both her father and the White Bear. Her father's words didn't sound aggressive, and he had relaxed his stance, but his tone still made her frown. It was almost as if he was more concerned by her earlier encounter with the creature than by the appearance of a talking bear in the first place. Did he think she had been in danger? Surely her father must see the bear was a creature from the Palace of Light and therefore not a danger to her.

"I came to speak with you, sir." The bear was looking at her father. "Perhaps you might step outside so we can converse in private?" He glanced once more at the women by the table.

Charlotte squashed down a ridiculous feeling of hurt that he wished to exclude her from the conversation. It was foolish of her since the bear had already had the chance to ask her questions. Why would he wish to talk to her again?

"Outside?" Her father raised an eyebrow as he looked at the sheets of rain and the darkness beyond the house.

The bear grimaced. "Perhaps I do not have the best timing. I spent the day searching the forest for you but failed to locate you before the weather changed. Once the storm hit in earnest, I realized you would have returned here. Waiting for tomorrow might be more sensible, but I confess to a strong degree of impatience." He looked once at Charlotte, his gaze fleeting, but somehow the glance soothed her earlier hurt, although she couldn't explain why.

"I wouldn't dream of keeping you waiting," her father said respectfully, bowing his head briefly.

Charlotte expelled a breath of relief, glad her father had grasped the nature of their visitor after all. She would hate for her family to cause him any more offense than they must have already done.

"Wait!" her mother cried softly as her father stepped toward the open doorway.

He paused and glanced back at her.

"I must go, my dear. Surely you see that." He spoke only just loud enough to be heard over the storm. "We have no choice. But I believe all may still be well."

Her mother wrung her hands together before nodding reluctantly.

Charlotte frowned. There had been something strange in her father's manner since the first mention of the bear, and she now couldn't escape the certainty that whatever her father knew was also known to her mother. What secrets were they keeping?

She stood in place as her father took a waterproof wrap from a hook and swathed himself in it. Only once he had stepped outside and closed the door firmly behind him did she move.

Racing forward, she placed her ear against the door. But there was no use in attempting to overhear the conversation. The noise of the storm was too great to allow any other sounds to permeate the solid wood.

Rushing over to her mother instead, she gripped her arm, ignoring her sisters who both appeared to be in too much shock to speak.

"Who is the bear?" Charlotte asked in an urgent voice. "Why has he come here?"

"I have no idea," her mother said in such bewilderment that she couldn't doubt her. "I never dreamed such a thing would happen."

"Who would?" Elizabeth finally managed to say. "It's a talking bear!"

"Daisy used to tell stories about a talking cat," Charlotte said. "And our cousins were telling us only recently about a talking horse. Is a bear so different?"

"Horses and cats don't eat people," Odelia said firmly, and Charlotte had to admit she had a point. There was no denying it would create a very different impression to meet a talking cat.

The thought only made her feel sympathy for the White Bear. How often was he met with distrust and fear just because of his form? It wasn't as if he was an ordinary bear who might attack a human.

The door swung abruptly open, and all four of them jumped. But it was only their father striding inside, shaking off water like a dog. Their mother raced to him, her eyes roaming over his body, as if checking for signs of injury.

"Is he gone?" she asked.

Her father hesitated and then shook his head. "Not yet."

"Oh!" Her mother clasped her hands together. "What does he want?" She sounded terrified.

Her father didn't answer for a moment. Instead, his gaze lifted and pinned itself on Charlotte. Her heart began to race, a strange feeling suffusing her.

"He wants Charli." Her father's words were almost too quiet to be heard.

"Charlotte?" Elizabeth screamed, sounding actually worried for her sister. "What can you mean, Father?"

"Does he wish to eat her?" Odelia asked, sounding ghoulishly curious.

"Of course he does not," their father said sharply, his face losing color. "Do you think I would talk with him if he wished to eat any of us?"

Odelia subsided, looking sulky.

"But what does he want, Father?" Charlotte asked in a much quieter voice that nevertheless drew her father's attention immediately.

"He wants...*you*," he said again, as if struggling to know how to communicate the bear's request. "He wants to take you away with him."

"Take her away?" Her mother gasped and rushed over to wrap a protective arm around her daughter. "How can you be sure he won't eat her later, once he's away from us?"

Charlotte stood motionless beneath her arm, unable to think clearly but free of the fear that gripped her mother and sisters.

"I'm certain he doesn't wish to eat me," she said in a faint voice, earning another sharp look from her father.

"Do you know his intentions, Charli?" he asked. "Did he speak of it this morning?"

She shook her head. "No. I am as surprised as any of you. I merely feel certain he doesn't wish me harm."

Her father nodded, a strange and almost calculating look coming across his face. "That is a good start," he said. "Perhaps it is not impossible after all."

"Does he wish…" Charlotte hesitated, trying to make sense of it. "Does he wish me to go with him somewhere? Does he need a companion?"

Her father glanced once at her mother, seeming to stumble over the word.

"Yes, I suppose it is a companion of sorts. He wishes to make you…part of his family."

"Part of his family?" Elizabeth asked, still sounding incredulous. "But he's a *bear*!"

"He may be a bear," her father replied, "but he is clearly also a person. Or do you think him a mere animal?" He spoke slowly, as if willing them to read between his words.

Charlotte nodded. It made sense to her. The inhabitants of the Palace of Light might not all wear human form, but surely they must all be considered people. They certainly couldn't be thought of as animals—not when they were thinking, feeling beings with as much intelligence and capacity for communication as she herself possessed. Probably more, in truth.

But even so, she couldn't help her thoughts mirroring Elizabeth's. How could she join the family of a creature from the Palace of Light?

"How could I do so?" she asked. "Surely it is impossible."

Her father cleared his throat, glancing once again toward his wife. "There is an established way."

For a second, Charlotte and her sisters merely stared at him, confused. Then Odelia let out a gasping laugh, one that hung on the edge of hysteria.

"Marry him? You want Charlotte to *marry* a bear?"

"Of course not," Elizabeth said with a repressive frown. "That's ridiculous."

Utterly and completely ridiculous. They must be misunderstanding their father.

And yet, the bear had asked her specifically about marriage ceremonies. It had been the only thing he was interested in. She had assumed he was conducting cultural research, but...

"Of course she couldn't marry him in the normal sort of way," her father said quickly. "But a legal marriage would make her part of his family. It would make it all right for her to leave with him. They have different rules in..." He trailed off without saying the words Charlotte knew came next. *In the Palace of Light.* Was being tied together a requirement for the bear taking her there?

The idea caught at her, making her breath lodge in her throat. She had heard tales of the High King's domain, of course, but they were all fanciful ones. No one had ever been there—or even knew of anyone who had. Rumor said Queen Ava of Rangmere had traveled there once, but everyone seemed to agree she was the only one. Was it really possible she was to be given that opportunity?

The thought of visiting the Palace of Light had never even occurred to Charlotte. She couldn't say she had dreamed of it, but it was a captivating idea nonetheless. But why would the White Bear wish to take her of all people to such a place?

"This is madness!" her mother cried, rounding on her

husband. "You cannot be considering this! We cannot give our Charlotte to a bear. He isn't…he isn't one of us!" Again Charlotte had the impression there was something more that her mother wished to communicate, but something was holding her back.

Her father cleared his throat uncomfortably. "The ceremony only requires that they speak the necessary words, so it is technically possible. As I said, all he wishes is to take her into his family. This is merely the mechanism of doing so. But of course I would never force Charli into it. That's why he's waiting outside. I said the decision belonged to Charli herself, as is only right."

"Decision?" her mother cried again. "What decision? You should have sent him on his way the moment he suggested such an outrageous thing!"

But even as her mother spoke, she looked uncomfortable, as if she knew the words were more easily said than done.

The suggestion was outrageous. Charlotte acknowledged that openly. But the strange request hadn't shaken her inexplicable certainty that the bear would never offer her any harm. And neither could she deny the strange pull toward him. He wished her to become his companion on a fantastical journey, and there was something enticing about the idea of leaving with him, of freeing herself from the valley's isolation and exploring places she could only imagine.

But at what cost?

"Even if it's only a legal marriage," she said slowly, "it would still turn me into a married woman. I would be barred from entering into a true marriage. I would never get to fall in love."

Her father looked pained, and she expected her mother to speak again in protest against the idea. But instead she was looking at her husband through narrowed eyes.

"What have you not said?" her mother asked. "Why would you even consider such a proposal?"

Her father looked from Charli to the older girls and then back again, looking more uncomfortable than she had ever seen him.

"Of course I couldn't entrust my daughter to just anyone," he said. "He's not an ordinary bear, that much is obvious to us all, but it's more than that. He has power and position. There is much he could do for her...and for us."

"Do for us?" Elizabeth asked, catching at his words immediately. "Whatever do you mean?"

Her father looked from his older daughters to his wife. "I know you've all been disappointed in our life here," he said softly. "You agreed to the move at my assurances, and so far it's not lived up to our expectations. It is a burden I bear daily. And while we are close to a turning point that will bring us greater prosperity, it will likely be a gradual change. However, if Charlotte agrees to undertake the wedding ceremony, the White Bear will reverse our fortunes. We will soon be as rich as we have been poor."

CHARLOTTE

"*R*ich!" Elizabeth cried. "Are you certain? He's just a bear."

Her father gave her a stern look. "I think we have firmly established that he's not *just* a bear. We would not be having this conversation if he were."

"A rich bear." Odelia's wondering tone didn't match the hard light that came into her eyes. She cast a quick, conspiratorial glance at Elizabeth before turning to Charlotte with a sickly sweet smile. "He must be in great favor with the High King. Perhaps he even has a title. You might discover after you marry him that you are Lady Charlotte!"

Her father threw a glance at her mother that Charlotte couldn't read. Did he believe Odelia's words and think the bear had some kind of official title? It sounded unlikely to her. Did anyone at the Palace of Light have a title other than the High King?

"A bride price?" Her mother frowned. "That isn't a common custom in any of the Four Kingdoms."

"I have told you," her father said quickly. "They do things

differently in…" Again he trailed off, giving her mother a significant look as if she would understand his meaning.

Charlotte frowned. Was her father awed at the idea that his daughter might one day dwell in the Palace of Light? Was that why he wasn't speaking of it directly?

Charlotte herself certainly felt awed. But not awed enough to agree to the bear's unexpected proposal. As much as she longed to escape her isolated life, she wasn't willing to entirely give up on the hope of romantic love in order to achieve it.

She had seen enough households in their old village, as well as here among the valley folk, to know that the happiest and most fulfilling lives were those built on love. It was clear that even the High King agreed since he had decreed that the kingdoms would prosper when ruled by love. It was the reason he sent out his godmothers to help the royal families to find true love. Not even the most powerful king or queen would deny their heir the chance to marry for love, so why should she be asked to marry a stranger—and one who could never truly be a husband to her?

She knew there were other types of love than romantic love, and that a life could be happily built on them. She even felt a connection with the White Bear that she couldn't explain. But it wasn't enough to give up her hopes of something more.

"I can't." She shook her head rapidly, feeling a little sick. "I'm sorry, but I can't. I don't want a legal binding but a real marriage."

"A real marriage?" Elizabeth scoffed, although Charlotte knew both her sisters dreamed of being swept off their feet by an eligible young man. "What man might you be thinking of? There's no one who wants to marry you!"

"I didn't mean anyone in particular," Charlotte said, saddened rather than offended by her sister's words. "Just that I would like to meet someone one day." It was painfully clear that Elizabeth was projecting her own disappointed hopes onto Charlotte, and her sister's next words only confirmed it.

"And who would you meet here?" Elizabeth asked poisonously, once again triggering a wave of sadness in Charlotte.

After hearing the tales of her aunt's success, her father had expected to find prosperity in the valleys. And in the early days, her mother had talked of future visits to the Rangmeran capital after Elizabeth turned eighteen. Given the proposed timing, Charlotte had always known what the purpose of such trips would be. But the expected prosperity had been slower to come than expected, and in the years since Elizabeth turned eighteen, there had been no trips forthcoming.

Elizabeth was right that it would be a struggle for any of them to meet a man they might be able to love here. But their father claimed change was just around the corner. It wouldn't take much of an improvement in their circumstances to allow the promised trips to happen. Couldn't they be patient just a little longer?

"We will none of us find husbands here," Odelia said on a sigh, echoing Elizabeth. "Is there even a point to being rich if we have to stay here, away from all society and comfort?"

Their father coughed. "Actually," he said, "the bear spoke of helping us establish ourselves in Arcadia." He sounded dispirited at the idea, and Charlotte knew what it would cost him to give up his dreams of forging a new life in this remote region. But he was clearly willing to accept a move for the sake of his family.

"Arcadia?" Her mother couldn't keep a longing note from her voice. "Everyone talks about what a wonderful kingdom Arcadia is! The people lack the sternness of the Rangmerans and the formality of the Northhelmians, you know. And their royal family has led them to great prosperity. I've heard the old king is even thinking of retiring, as King Richard did recently in Northhelm. Everyone adores Crown Prince Maximilian and his wife, Princess Alyssa, and they say they will make excellent monarchs. It is better by far to have someone young and vital on the throne than someone declining in capacity. It seems a most sensible move."

Charlotte swallowed, trying not to feel betrayed by her mother's words. She could understand the appeal of riches and a life in Arcadia, but surely her mother wouldn't sell her own daughter to achieve it?

"Of course if you say no, it is not to be thought of, Charli," her father said, cutting through her sisters' excited exclamations.

He met her eyes across the room, and she told herself she was imagining the faintest shadow of disappointment at her resistance. It was merely exhaustion, and she couldn't blame him for that. Her father, at least, was always on her side.

"I only repeated the offer because I thought it might be of interest to you," he said, confirming her thoughts. "Someone so rich and powerful would change your life as well as ours, Charli-bear."

For the first time in her life, Charlotte winced at her old nickname. "I cannot trade love for riches, Father," she said softly.

He nodded quickly. "I will tell him."

As soon as he said the words, Charlotte felt a pang. She barely knew the White Bear, and yet she couldn't help but feel pain at the thought of disappointing him. But she comforted herself with the assurance that he would easily find a better companion than her. Plenty of people would be willing to sacrifice anything for the chance to travel to the Palace of Light.

Her father stepped outside, carefully closing the door behind him. Charlotte already knew it was futile to try to listen through the door, so she hurried to the window beside it and peered outside.

The storm still raged although she had barely noticed the wind and rain since the bear's arrival. The early darkness of the storm clouds made it hard to see far, but the whiteness of the bear's fur stood out, even through the driving rain.

She couldn't hear the words her father spoke to him, but she saw the moment the bear's demeanor changed, his shoulders slumping in a way that looked strangely human. Her stomach clenched, and she almost wavered. But she shook herself, remembering what was at stake. Something strange and magical was afoot, clearly, and she longed to embrace the strange adventure before her, but she could not sacrifice the chance of love and children and a home of her own one day. Not for adventure and certainly not for riches.

When her father slipped back into the house, unwinding his waterproof wrap, he looked subdued.

"He is gone?" Charlotte asked in a small voice. "I suppose he's already on his way to ask the next girl."

Her father shifted uneasily, pausing before answering. "Actually, he refused to give up hope. He said his offer had been sudden, and he could understand your hesitance. He asked me to assure you that he would never harm you and that anything you could wish for will be yours. He said he will return in a week for your final answer."

Charlotte gulped, her head spinning slightly. It had been a struggle to fight her impulse for adventure and escape, but she had succeeded and thought the matter finished. And now it wasn't finished after all? She could still prove weak and make a mistake that might throw away her life.

"No, no!" she cried. "You must tell him I do not mean to accept!" She ran to the door and pulled it open, poised to run out into the rain despite her lack of covering.

But there was no longer a patch of white in sight. The bear was gone, and she would have no hope of finding him in the downpour.

She slumped, slowly closing the door. As she turned, her eyes caught on her mother who had joined her older sisters by the stove. Her mother looked uncomfortable—as if caught between conflicting emotions—but Elizabeth and Odelia were openly exultant.

Charlotte's gut tightened again, but this time it was a dark, squirming feeling as if she might be sick. Her sisters had exclaimed in disbelief and even outrage at first, but the mention of riches had changed their minds completely. If there had ever been any doubt in her heart, she now knew for certain that they would sell her to the bear without a moment's hesitation.

The discomfort at her mother's reaction hit hardest, though. Since the wedding, her mother had been doing her best to smooth the way between her daughters, keeping the peace by separating them whenever possible. Charlotte had believed she was doing it for all of their sake because she didn't want the family marred by disharmony or to be forced to side with one child over another. But looking at her mother now, Charlotte saw her mother's silences and placating looks as something else entirely. By keeping the peace when Charlotte was being wronged, she had always been siding with her older daughters, even if she wasn't willing to admit it.

And now, despite her mother's bustling efforts to finish preparing the table for their meal, she couldn't hide her true feelings. She might feel guilty for it, but she was almost as tempted as Elizabeth and Odelia. She wanted a different life.

Just as she had chosen peace and an easier life over defending Charlotte in the past, now she was once again tempted to put her own comfort ahead of her daughter. Charlotte knew her mother loved her, but she didn't love her enough to choose her, and the pain of that constricted her chest.

A shiver ran through her, and she knew she couldn't possibly sit and eat the evening meal with them all as if nothing were wrong. Her family had shown their true colors, and although she had thought herself inured, it cut deep.

She managed to coax her legs into moving, pausing briefly

beside the laden table. Snatching up a piece of bread, a wedge of cheese, and an apple, she hurried to her room.

Her father called after her, but she shut the door on his voice. She felt a pang of guilt for shutting out the only family member on her side, but her emotions were running too high, and the house was too small for all of them. Removing herself was the only way she knew to prevent an eruption.

She would eat, and then she would hide herself in bed. If she hadn't fallen asleep by the time her sisters came in, she would pull the blankets over her head. She couldn't face them. Not tonight. Not when she knew what they would say.

Tomorrow she would have new reserves. And surely a whole night would give her enough time to come up with a strategy— some way she could resist her sisters' blandishments without turning her life into a misery.

It turned out one night was not enough. Despite many sleepless hours, lying still beneath her blanket and listening to the wind, Charlotte could come up with nothing of use. That her sisters would try to convince her to accept the bear, she was certain. What she didn't know was how to hold firm in her refusal without stoking her sisters' enmity toward her.

Given how late it was before she fell asleep, it was no surprise that she woke late yet again. But this time she was greeted with bright smiles of welcome and two cheery greetings.

"We have breakfast laid out for you when you're ready," Elizabeth said in the warmest tone Charlotte had heard her use in months. "You must be exhausted after the terrible night we had. The wind was so loud! And that rain! I'm sure none of us slept a wink."

Charlotte managed a forced smile, remembering the gentle snores of both sisters, just audible above the storm.

Odelia nodded vigorously. "And of course you must not think of going out gathering today. Everything will be mud! We'll stay inside and have a comfortable time together. Perhaps you can advise me on the new dress I've been making?"

Charlotte struggled to come up with a response. She had expected some sort of campaign from them, but this was excessive. Did they really think she would find it sincere?

In the end, she remained silent, merely joining them at the table. At least she felt up to eating in company with her family which was an improvement on the night before.

The rest of the day progressed in much the same way. Her sisters were sickeningly kind to her, and every instance of their consideration felt like the twist of a knife blade in her gut. Even her mother's effusive kindness was hard to take, although in her mother's case it didn't feel entirely false. But it still made her feel tired, small, and sad. Her mother might love her, but her love hadn't been enough to make her stand up for Charlotte in the past, and it wasn't stopping her thinking of a new life in Arcadia now.

When she managed to escape outside with her father on the second day after the storm, she felt nothing but relief. Stretching, she sucked in a long breath, lifting her face toward the clear sky.

Her father chuckled. "Relieved to escape, hey?"

Charlotte threw him a grateful look. At least one of her family members understood her. Her father had always sensed when Charlotte had reached her limits, responding by inviting her to spend the day with him in the forest. And in the past, a day away from her sisters, with her father for company in their stead, had always set her right again. He was her solid foundation. He would never turn against her, and that knowledge enabled her to endure her sisters' pressure.

"Do I dare ask what you're thinking, Charli-bear?" her father asked with another chuckle.

She winced. It seemed the old nickname was ruined forever

now. The thought dulled her enjoyment of being outside. Ever since their cousin's wedding, life had been growing increasingly insupportable, but how much worse was it going to get in five days' time when she stood firm and refused to sell her future for her sisters' enrichment?

But she didn't want to ruin the day with her father before it had even begun.

"I'm hoping there's still some edible greenery left after that storm," she said, forcing herself to respond lightly. "We've already eaten what we gathered from before, and I'm loathe to go back to a diet of only preserved food."

His smile grew. "If anyone can find something, it's you. You're almost as attuned to these forests as I am."

Her father was trying to compliment her, to buoy her up, but his words hurt. Did he really not know that it was a desire for escape that drove her from the house as much as a love for the forests themselves? In the face of her sisters' childhood dislike, she had aligned herself with her father from the beginning, always seeking his validation and approval. Had she taken it too far, leading him to believe she possessed the same love of the unclaimed wilderness as he did?

Charlotte did like the natural beauty and space of the valley— it was almost the sole positive in their second home—but it didn't light her up the same way it did her father. She explored because it was better than sitting at home with no break from her tense relationship with her sisters.

A cold, uncomfortable feeling swept over her. Did her one true ally in the family not actually understand her at all?

She shook the thought away violently. Her father loved her. Her father was loyal to her. He was the only one she had, and she wasn't going to undermine their relationship by focusing on hurtful imaginings.

She pinned a bright smile to her face. "I'll do my best."

They separated not long after, each off to pursue their own

tasks for the day, and Charlotte tried to push all other thoughts out of her head. She really did want to find something edible to forage, and given the damage to the fledgling plants, it would take some concentration to achieve.

By the time the sun was seeking the horizon, she had succeeded better than expected. At the height of spring, she'd be able to fill the basket to overflowing, but given it was still the tail end of winter, half a basket was doing well.

Distracted by her success, she nearly missed the white among the brown trunks. By the time she noticed the bear, he was already nearly close enough to touch.

Startled, she leaped back, only to freeze, staring at him. He remained carefully motionless, gazing back at her.

"I'm sorry," he said in his rumbling voice. "I didn't intend to startle you, but I wanted to speak with you directly." He shook his head. "Clearly I should have spoken to you from the beginning. I apologize for that as well. I thought it would reassure you if I went about everything in the proper, formal way, but I can see now that…"

He let out a great whuff of breath. "I am aware it's not a small thing that I'm asking. But I wanted to assure you of my sincerity, both toward you and with regard to the promises I have made. If you will agree to bind yourself to me, I will never harm you. Once we reach our destination, you need never even see me unless you wish it. And your family will live lives of comfort."

She bit her lip, the thought slipping through her mind that perhaps the bear had come to carry her off by force. But looking into his eyes, she couldn't believe it. Now that she was once again in his presence, she felt the same certainty as she had at their first meeting—he would not hurt her.

She felt something else too. The pull she felt toward him, the one that had made her consider running from her family to seek a grand adventure and the one that had made her sad at the thought of disappointing him, was even stronger than before.

"Thank you for your words, White Bear," she said slowly, trying to work out how to phrase her objections without disappointing him further.

"You may call me Henry," he said, cutting into her thoughts.

"What?" she asked, too surprised to formulate a more coherent question.

"Henry," he repeated. "It's my name. You may feel free to use it."

"Your name is...Henry?" she asked, still a little dumbfounded. She hadn't considered the matter of his name, but if she had, she would have expected something grand and foreign. "Are you sure?"

As soon as she asked it, she wanted to pull the words back. What a foolish question!

He made the rumbling noise that indicated his laughter.

"It is one of them," he said.

She nodded quickly, eager to make amends for her unthinking words. "It's a lovely name."

He laughed again. "I have always liked it well enough. It's a family name."

She raised her eyebrows. Did he have parents, then? Were they talking white bears like himself? Family was another thing she had never considered in conjunction with him. She didn't know how the magical creatures that dwelt with the High King came to be, but she had always imagined them springing to life at his command rather than being born in the ordinary way.

If he had once had a family and lost them, was that why he was so desperate for a family again—in any way possible? She softened, once again regretting the necessity of saying no.

If only he could have adopted her. But she was already eighteen, making that impossible. And she didn't think there was a single family in the valley that would send their minor child off with a bear, regardless of the promise of riches.

"I'm the one who is sorry," she said in a rush. "It's not that I mistrust you or am unwilling to accompany you. It's just..." She hesitated. "Are you sure the wedding ceremony is necessary? Could I not just travel with you as your companion without it?"

He winced. She had become so used to impossible expressions on his face that she barely even noticed the strangeness of it.

"Unfortunately, the binding is crucial," he said. "But of course I understand your reluctance." He gazed at her longingly. "I would assure you with every bit of sincerity I possess that your future is safe with me, but I understand the heart isn't something that can be so easily governed."

He slumped down, hopelessness in every line of his fur.

Alarm at his extreme reaction made her start forward. "Does something ail you?" she asked. "Surely your life cannot be in jeopardy and requiring this binding to save it?"

He hesitated, as if considering her words. Did he know that he only had to say yes to compel her to agree to his bargain? The inexplicable connection between them was strong enough that she didn't think she could abandon him to die.

Eventually he sighed. "I fight for much," he said softly, "but not my life. There will be no blood on your hands if you refuse."

Charlotte knew she should have felt relieved, but she felt almost regretful instead. Had she wanted him to provide her an excuse to say yes?

She shook herself. She could not allow her thoughts to stray in that direction. She couldn't allow the impulse of a moment to destroy her whole future. She had to stay strong.

"I'm sorry," she whispered again. "I wish I could give you a different answer."

"Once again, it is me who owes the apology," he said, seeming to gather himself together. He bowed his head even lower than he had on the previous occasion. "Even your sympathy is more than I might reasonably expect."

He turned as if to depart, only to hesitate and look back. "I told your father I would return in five days. I will be true to my word, but know that I will not pressure you. My offer, however, remains open until then."

She nodded, unable to summon the right words, and he disappeared into the forest. It was going to be a long five days.

CHARLOTTE

The five days proved even more difficult than Charlotte had expected. Her sisters grew more and more blatant with their hints and nudges. Their conversation was full of the possibilities of future wealth and luxury, and they exclaimed often over how they wished they were the ones being carried off to live like a princess. If Charlotte dared to comment, they quickly assured her that *of course* they weren't seeking to change her mind.

When it became obvious that they weren't, in fact, changing her mind, their syrupy blandishments grew sharper and sharper. By the day the bear was due to reappear, the knives were fully out.

Both sisters snapped at Charlotte, wielding their words as weapons and berating her for her selfishness and stupidity.

"Just know that every time we break our backs in hard labor in the days to come, we will be thinking of you," Elizabeth hissed. "For it will all be your fault."

Their mother looked up from where she stood over the stove on the other side of the room, her brows drawing together. Had she heard Elizabeth's words? Charlotte couldn't be sure. She told herself her mother couldn't have heard. If she had, she would have said something—rebuked her oldest and defended Charlotte.

Wouldn't she? Charlotte wished she felt more sure.

"Every time we're lonely," Odelia added, "and if we find no suitors, we will know you are to blame. We could have had everything, but you threw it away for the sake of a foolish dream. It's hard to comprehend such selfishness."

Their father stepped into the house in time to hear her final words. Both girls fell silent, looking at him guiltily. He frowned, giving them a sharp look.

"All three of my daughters are welcome under my roof for as long as they wish to say," he said sternly. "None of you will ever be forced out while I am alive."

Gratitude rushed through Charlotte, only growing stronger when he turned to her. "Why don't you join me in the forest today, Charli? I don't expect the white bear to come until evening, as he did last time."

She stepped outside, embracing the familiar feeling of escape. Smiling at her father, she fell into step beside him, pleased he was allowing her to accompany him. He rarely did so when he was off to cut wood, since he worried about her safety. But he must have recognized Charlotte's need for comfort and companionship today. It was getting harder and harder to bear her sisters' dislike.

They walked in silence, and Charlotte relished it. No one was berating her or trying to convince her to change her mind. Utter bliss.

Once they were well away from the house, her father cleared his throat.

"Are you sure, Charli-bear?" he asked, the nickname once again setting her teeth on edge.

She forced herself to respond calmly. "About what, Father?"

He cleared his throat again. "About the white bear's offer."

She stiffened, disbelief filling her. Was this why he had invited her to come with him today? She had thought he was offering her a reprieve, but instead he was joining in the chorus?

He kept his face forward, his voice uncomfortable. "I don't mention it because of what the bear is offering us. He also wishes to offer you a life of luxury. I know you aren't swayed by the lure of worldly goods in the same way as your sisters, but I can't help wondering if you might still benefit from what he can provide."

She stared at her father, still too shocked to speak, and he finally turned to look at her.

"I do believe we are on the verge of turning around our fortunes here," he said earnestly. "Your aunt and the other senior valley folk are finally going to—" He cut himself off, shaking his head. "Never mind that. The point is that I haven't been lying to you all when I said better times are on the horizon for our family. But it's taken too long. I've taken too long." He looked so crest-fallen that her instinct was to comfort him, but for once, she remained silent.

"With or without the bear's assistance, I think we're going to have to move," he said after a moment. "Your mother and sisters have been very clear about their feelings on the matter. I have to give Elizabeth a chance to..." He trailed off, grasping her arms as a new light came into his eyes. "But you don't have to come with us, Charli! The White Bear is offering you a chance to stay. And not just stay but seek out new frontiers." He looked in the direction of the mountains, his eyes still shining, and she wondered if he was seeing the Palace of Light in his mind's eye.

"You can have adventures the rest of us can only dream of," he whispered. "And perhaps, one day, when your sisters are settled, I'll be able to come and visit you."

Charlotte pulled herself free, stepping back. "Adventure?" she asked. "You think I should choose adventure over love?"

Her father frowned, as if confused at her reaction.

"There are different kinds of love," he said. "You can have a full life without romance. And your sisters might well be right.

Even if we move, you might not find someone to match your girlhood dreams. With the bear you can have both security and new adventures. That is not a combination to be considered lightly."

He continued to speak, dropping his voice even lower, as if he was ashamed of his own words. But she couldn't hear him, the buzz in her thoughts drowning out his whisper, one line echoing over and over in her head.

Your sisters might well be right.

She had thought she had one ally in the family. One person who saw her and thought she belonged—who loved her for her and would never try to send her away. But she had been wrong. Her father didn't know her at all.

And what had he said earlier? That one day he might visit her at the Palace of Light? He might not have been motivated by riches, but he was still thinking about how Charlotte's marriage could benefit him, saving him from the future her sisters were hemming him into.

Tears rose up, clogging her throat and threatening to spill from her eyes. She stopped, desperately trying to hold them in long enough to get away.

"I should have known you would want to send me away, too," she managed to choke out. "How could you not when you have so much to gain? This is a rare opportunity, and I guess I am selfish to stand in all of your way."

Turning, she nearly tripped over her feet in her haste to run. She had to get away from him. She had to escape before she started crying in earnest. She couldn't bear to let her tears fall in front of him.

"Charli!" he called after her. "Charli, wait!"

But she didn't slow. She fled without thinking, horror over-taking her when she realized her steps were leading her home. But maybe it was a good thing. If she lost herself in the woods, the white bear wouldn't know where to find her.

She wrenched open the door, clearly startling the three women inside. Her mother exclaimed, speaking her name, but Charlotte ignored her. Brushing past them, she rushed into the bedroom she shared with her sisters, firmly closing the door behind her.

They got the message for once, and none of them attempted to follow her. She could hear them whispering to each other, no doubt speculating as to what had happened. Did they know the reason her father had invited her out? Had they been waiting with bated breath to see if he could succeed where they had failed?

The thought filled her with rage. How dare they all conspire against her! She was as much a part of this family as any of them. And yet, they would *sell* her for their own comfort!

She flung herself on the bed and cried until no more tears would come. Still no one tried the door. Eventually she heard her father return, the distant murmur of his voice deep and concerned.

His arrival provided the final bit of certainty to her decision, compelling her to action. Hurrying around the room, she took only what she most needed, wrapping the items into a makeshift bundle.

She would not stay where she was neither understood nor valued. She had reached her limit. Her mother and sisters thought she should be motivated by wealth and her father by adventure. But her true motivation—as it had been on so many previous occasions—was escape.

After years of sharing a home, not one of her family members saw her true self. And yet, with the bear, she had felt seen in only two interactions. Foolish it might be, but she would trust her future to the one person who actually wanted her around.

Several exclamations were heard from the main room, and then the front door opened. Charlotte drew a deep breath. The moment had come.

A tentative knock sounded on her door.

"Charlotte?" her father called through the wood, not attempting to open it. "The bear is here and wishes to hear your refusal from your own lips." Silence for a moment. "He will not hurt you."

Was he reassuring her that she need not be afraid of a brief moment of interaction, or was he making one last attempt to convince her? Charlotte didn't know, and she no longer cared.

Pulling the door open, she swept past her father without looking at him. Striding through the house, she continued straight out the open front door. The bear stood at a respectful distance, his eyes focused on the doorway. When she appeared, his gaze met hers, holding her eyes for a moment before his attention moved to the bundle over her shoulder.

She saw the moment realization hit him, his whole face lighting up. Peace swept through her, settling the frenzied desperation that had driven her this far. Here was someone who thought she belonged with him. There was one family in which she was welcome.

She was making the right choice.

Moving more slowly, she walked to him. Previously she had curtsied to him, but now she was to join his family. She nodded respectfully instead.

"I will come with you," she said in a voice loud enough to be heard in the house. "I will complete the ceremony."

The bear—Henry, she should think of him as Henry, as strange as it seemed—smiled, radiance emanating from him.

"I am honored, Lady Charlotte," he said. "And I will do everything in my power to ensure you never regret this decision."

"Thank you," she said more quietly.

"You're going to marry him?" her mother gasped from the doorway. "Are you sure?"

She nodded, not turning to look at her parents. "If you wish to see the ceremony, you should follow us to Master Harold's." As the only official across their valley and the two neighboring ones, Harold conducted all ceremonies. She was only fortunate he happened to be their closest neighbor.

"You mean to be married immediately?" her father asked, clearly shocked.

Was he upset at the thought of her departure or horrified about how it would look to Master Harold when she arrived unexpectedly and demanded immediate marriage to a bear? It didn't matter either way. Her decision had been made, and she had no desire to linger.

"Of course." Charlotte still couldn't bring herself to look directly at any of them. "Henry has asked me to go away with him, and I see no benefit in delay."

"Henry?" her mother asked faintly.

"It is my name," the bear said in a deep voice.

Distracted by her swirling emotions, Charlotte hadn't noticed him moving. But at some point he had come closer, positioning himself protectively beside her.

Another band across her chest loosened. He wanted to defend her, to protect her from them. And he could clearly do it. She would be safe with him.

"We should leave immediately," she said. "The afternoon is already drawing on, and it's a long walk."

Henry looked at her, a considering light in his eyes. "If you would like to ride, we could get there faster."

"I don't own a horse," she said stiffly. And even if her father offered her one of his, she wouldn't accept it. She refused to accept their bribes, offered only to assuage their own consciences.

"I meant on me," he said with a smile. "But I understand if the thought is unpleasant."

"Ride you?" She stared at him, taken by surprise. People didn't ride bears, magical or not.

"We would get there much faster." He sounded apologetic.

A slow smile spread across her face. Her determination and sense of betrayal had been buoying her up, but she was dreading the long walk and the awkwardness of arriving in the middle of the night with such an odd request.

"If you really don't mind, that would be lovely," she said, already moving toward him.

He lowered himself as much as he was able, but he was still very large. She paused, unsure how to ascend.

"You can grip my fur," he said, the amusement in his tone reassuring her.

"I won't hurt you?"

"I will do my best to bear it," he said gravely although the amusement still leaked through.

She smiled at him and grabbed handfuls of his thick fur, using it to scale his side. The fur was soft—much softer than she had expected—and it was surprisingly comfortable sitting just behind the shoulders of his front legs.

"Charlotte!" Elizabeth's voice cried, her sisters both tumbling from the house to stand with their parents. "You can't get married without us!"

"We're supposed to have new gowns for a wedding," Odelia moaned. "And where is the bride price? We were promised a bride price!"

"You will have it," the bear said, all amusement gone from his voice. "Once the ceremony is completed."

"If you wish to be there, I can't stop you," Charlotte added stiffly. "But there is no time for new gowns. You will have to ride if you want to make it in time as it is."

Taking her words as a sign, the bear began to move. She had thought she would need to direct him, but he didn't ask any questions, moving with confidence in the right direction. She remembered that he had spoken of being in the region for some time. Perhaps he knew the homes of everyone who lived in the valley.

In what felt like an impossibly short time, Charlotte spotted the wooden house of their closest neighbor in the distance. And moments later they were lumbering to a stop in front of the door.

She hadn't expected him to move faster than a horse. Did bears usually move so quickly, or was it just the magical ones? She glanced over her shoulder, checking for her family, but there was no sign of them.

Her last glimpse of them had been of all four of them rushing toward the small stable attached to their house, so she assumed they were on their way. But their horses couldn't have kept up with the bear. With a brief pang of guilt, she wondered if she should wait for them. But a moment later she swept the feeling aside. She was doing what they so desperately wanted her to do, and they deserved no further consideration in the matter.

She still climbed down slowly, however, her courage wavering now that the moment had arrived. Not that she was reconsidering her decision, but explaining it to near strangers was another matter. What would Master Harold and his family think of her?

"This is the correct house, isn't it?" the bear asked when she stayed motionless beside him.

Charlotte shook herself and nodded. "Yes, Master Harold is the official who conducts all the local ceremonies. Hopefully he doesn't mind being disturbed without warning."

She made herself move forward and knock loudly on the door. Movement could be heard inside, and then the door opened. The tall man on the other side looked from her to the bear standing beside her, his expression going slack.

Charlotte tried to think how to word her request and came up blank.

But Harold recovered himself more quickly than she expected, looking down at her with concern, rather than confusion, in his gaze.

"Good evening, Miss Charlotte," he said gravely. "I can't say I thought you would actually come."

"You were expecting me?" she asked, surprised.

He nodded. "Your pa came to talk to me yesterday. Explained the whole situation. Just in case..." His words trailed off as he looked back up at the bear, a crease between his brows.

"Father came yesterday?" Charlotte repeated in a breathless voice, struck anew by the sense of betrayal. Had he been so sure he could convince her?

"Aye, that he did." Harold ran a hand over his head. "He explained the whole situation and received my agreement to conduct the ceremony, but..." He hesitated again. "I believe it is incumbent on me, given my position, to speak to you alone for a moment first."

Charlotte glanced quickly at the bear, her first thought for him. Would he be offended by the implication of Harold's words? But the bear merely smiled, gesturing with his head for her to follow Harold into the house.

She swallowed and trailed him inside, giving a subdued greeting to his wife and young children as he closed the door behind them.

"You really came?" his wife gasped, making it clear Harold had already shared his neighbor's odd story. "You're a brave girl! Your family will owe you much. If the bear's claim is true, that is."

Charlotte gave her a tight smile. She wasn't doing it because of the rewards promised to her family, but she couldn't say that to this woman, who had always been kind to her.

"But are you sure about this, girl?" Harold asked. "It's not a light thing. You aren't being...coerced?" He winced as he said it, clearly as uncomfortable as she was but still determined to do his duty. "I can't conduct the ceremony if I think you're being forced into it."

A sudden influx of warmth made Charlotte soften. Harold was a good official, one who took his responsibilities seriously.

He was attempting to protect her, as much as he was able, and she appreciated the efforts.

"It was my decision," she said softly, struggling to keep tears from her eyes at the look of sympathy on the face of Harold's wife. They had been at her cousin's wedding, like the rest of the valley, and must have some idea of Charlotte's position in her family.

"I understand, lass," he said quietly. "Although this seems a drastic step to take. Allying yourself with a white bear..." He shook his head. "I know his people have brought us great prosperity, but we know little about them, and there are some who think..."

He trailed off as his wife put her hand on his arm, her eyes wide as she shot a warning look toward the door.

Charlotte frowned. When people spoke of the High King and his servants, it was only to praise the great prosperity they had brought to all the Four Kingdoms. While it was true no one knew many details about the Palace of Light itself or the godmothers and creatures who dwelt there, that was hardly a matter for concern given all the good they had brought to the kingdoms. For herself, she couldn't believe the High King or his creatures wished any of them malice—especially given the inexplicable certainty she felt in Henry's presence.

"Of course it's unknown," she said, "but I don't fear the Palace of—"

"Hush!" Master Harold's harsh whisper cut her off. He glanced back at his children who were watching them with rapt expressions. "Of course I can see that you would need to know all about it given this unusual situation, but surely your father warned you of the necessity of discretion. It has been pressed upon him often enough. You shouldn't speak of such things aloud. Not around the valley folk, at any rate."

Charlotte blinked, utterly bewildered. In Northhelm, the people had spoken openly of the Palace of Light. She couldn't think why they would have a different custom here in the valleys. Unless there really were some people here who opposed the High King?

She frowned, wanting to ask the identity of such dissenters, but the sound of horses in the distance caught her attention. Her family was about to arrive to watch the wedding ceremony—her wedding. Did it really matter what the valley folk thought of the Palace of Light? She would soon be gone from among them anyway.

"Thank you for your concern," she said, "but I've made up my mind."

"I'll need a minute to gather the necessary papers then," he said. "Would you like to wait in here or..." He glanced at the closed door.

Harold's house was large, one of the oldest in their valley, and it was filled with cozy warmth. For a moment she hesitated, wanting to linger in the familiarity of ordinary valley life. But she straightened and shook her head. Her place was with Henry now and in whatever adventures awaited them outside the valley. She should wait with him.

Harold made no protest when she slipped back outside, leaving the door open behind her. All his children rushed to look, coming no further than the doorway despite their eager faces as they gazed at the enormous creature in front of their house.

"Has he talked you out of it?" the bear asked, saying it like a joke, although she could hear a hint of real concern behind.

"Of course not," she said. "I gave you my word, and I won't be so easily dissuaded."

"Thank you." He touched his great head lightly against her.

Her family's three horses pulled to a stop beside them, making her stiffen. Her sisters looked uncomfortable squeezed onto the sturdiest horse together, but at least all four of them had come. She couldn't help a sense of relief at their arrival. For all her bravado and hurt, it felt wrong to be married without a single family member by her side.

By the time Harold came back outside with a book in his hand, they had dismounted and stood awkwardly beside her and the bear. Charlotte's father moved quickly forward to greet Harold, and the two men exchanged some quiet words she couldn't catch. She kept her face steady, refusing to guess at what they might be saying. The only thing that mattered was that Harold had agreed to conduct the ceremony, which meant Charlotte was about to escape.

Harold's wife emerged, having somehow wrangled her children into staying inside, and she soon had Charlotte's family arranged to one side while Charlotte herself and Henry—she had to start thinking of him by his name, however hard it was—stood side by side facing Harold.

As she had promised the bear back in the forest, the ceremony was a simple one. He lifted one enormous paw, and she placed her hand on it as Harold led them through an exchange of promises. She knew the solemnity of their words, and she wanted to take it seriously, but she was feeling strangely weightless and detached. Her mouth repeated the words whenever she was called on to do so, but she couldn't focus on what she was saying. Was this really her wedding? It was nothing like she had imagined as a girl.

When it came time for the parents' blessing, everyone kept tactfully silent about the bear's parents, and Charlotte wondered again if he had any. When Harold turned to Charlotte's family, her mother instantly broke into gasping tears that left her unable to speak. But her father repeated the traditional blessing, sounding sad and broken in a way that twisted Charlotte's heart.

But she refused to soften toward him. His crimes against her had been the least, but they had hurt the most because she had trusted him.

His face crumpled when she wouldn't meet his eyes, but he

finished his part, completing the ceremony. Harold would already have recorded their names in his book, along with those of all the valley couples who had been married before them. The next time he traveled to the capital, he would record them in Rangmere's official registries, but it might be years before that happened. It didn't matter, though. By valley law and social custom, Charlotte was married.

GWEN

$\mathcal{F}$or the second time, Gwen woke to find herself on the floor. This time she was slumped by her door, and the warm sunlight bathing her had driven away the sleepiness. But the exhaustion had been replaced with stiff muscles and aching bruises. This was why she usually slept in her bed, no matter how frustrating she found her long slumbers.

Standing slowly, Gwen gingerly tried her handle. It turned without resistance. Had she dreamed of the door being locked?

But Gwen refused to believe the night's discovery had been only the muddle of sleep. She could still feel the lingering indignation and fright at finding herself locked in. So why had she so tamely fallen back asleep? She had succeeded in waking in the night, but it had gained her nothing.

No, Gwen corrected herself. *It gained me knowledge.*

She had hoped to gain even more knowledge from an open conversation with the captives, but at least she had learned something. Between the guards and her locked door, she was now certain that something went on in the palace grounds at night—something she was being deliberately excluded from.

Gwen's eyes fell on her cabinet, now bereft of its small treasure. Other memories of the night before flooded back. Why had she never considered the regular citizens of the mountain kingdom? She had spent years pitying herself and the captive servants while overlooking a whole city full of people suffering at her mother's hands. Why had she never spared them a thought?

She could only conclude it was because she had no contact with them. To her, the people of the mountain kingdom were her mother's court—perpetual strangers who shut her out and kept her mother's secrets.

She knew better now. The regular people wore the face of a fourteen-year-old girl, full of the dreams of a child and the courage of youth. But while Gwen had gained knowledge the night before, she had acquired no extra power.

Still, she couldn't shake the thought of the girl all through breakfast. She ate well, hungry from her small meal the night before, but when she finished, she looked at her mother.

"I'm planning to go riding this morning," she ventured, holding her breath while she waited to see how her mother would react.

From the queen's calm behavior through the meal, she didn't seem to have received a report of Gwen's misbehavior the previous evening. But it was possible she knew and was just waiting for an opportune moment to bring down the hammer.

"Not today, my dear," her mother said, and Gwen's heart sank.

The only time she ever escaped the palace grounds was on horseback. Usually, she rode alongside her mother, but on occasion she rode with only two guards as companions. In the past, she had always headed to the edge of the valley on such rides, wanting to get away from everyone and as close to the wilderness as possible. But she had a different plan in mind this time. She wanted to ride toward the city and see if she could glimpse the ordinary life of its inhabitants.

But it seemed the guards had reported her after all.

Gwen could barely suppress her trembling as she looked at

her mother, but Queen Celandine's smile didn't fade. And while it didn't reach her eyes, that was normal and not any cause for particular concern.

But somehow Gwen only felt more afraid. She almost wanted the punishment to fall just to escape the limbo of waiting.

"Really, my dear," her mother said, her voice sharpening. "Must you always look so diffident and uncertain? How many times have I reminded you that you're my heir and will one day rule the mountain kingdom? How can our people be expected to follow a girl who can't even string two words together in the presence of her own mother?"

Gwen swallowed. She knew she needed to answer, but she couldn't think of the right words. Her mother certainly didn't show any appreciation if Gwen ever spoke with strength or confidence. In that case Gwen was unattractively defiant and impudent and needed to learn respect for her elders and monarch.

"Yes, Mother," she said finally.

Easton would have known what to say—how to tread the exact line between diffidence and insolence—but Gwen's mind all too often froze in her mother's presence.

The queen sighed, as if she should have known it was futile to expect better of Gwen. "This is why you need me. Without me, you would be nothing. But you needn't fear. I will always be here for you."

The words should have sent a chill down Gwen's spine, but they were too familiar to warrant a reaction. Her mother rarely commented on Gwen's many deficiencies without saying something similar.

The queen surveyed her silent daughter and spoke again. "It's been too long since we spent time together."

Gwen stared at her, speechless. *Spend time together?* When had they ever done such a thing?

"I have some things to speak to you about," the queen continued.

When Gwen still didn't answer, the queen's brows contracted. She looked nettled by her daughter's obvious confusion, so Gwen schooled her expression and nodded obediently.

The effort satisfied her mother somewhat, so Gwen relaxed slightly. But as she trailed behind her mother all the way up to her room, her mind raced, even as she kept her face placid and calm. Was this some elaborate scheme to enable a new form of punishment? What was her mother planning to do to Gwen in the privacy of Gwen's room?

Her mother had never physically hit her—although her words often felt like blows—but locked away in the dark as a child, Gwen had understood her mother was capable of anything. When they reached her room, however, the queen's false smile was still firmly in place.

As Gwen followed her mother's directions and sat at her dressing table, she had to fight against terror. Gazing into the mirror, she met her mother's eyes where she stood behind her, and the longer they held, the more terrible the queen's smile grew. Gwen dreaded her mother's anger, but somehow this pretense of friendly affection was even worse. What lay behind it?

When her mother's fingers pulled at her hair, Gwen had to use every ounce of her self-control to hold herself still. With a few swift tugs, her mother released the hasty arrangement Gwen had managed before breakfast. Once her hair was flowing freely down her back, her mother picked up a brush and began to run it through her locks. While her hands moved, she smiled at her daughter in the mirror.

"You have grown into a lovely lady, my dear."

Was Gwen's panic showing in her eyes? She stared at her reflection, trying to see it the way her mother might. The face that looked back was strikingly similar to the life-size portrait of the previous king that stood in the line of monarchs that graced the throne room. Gwen might not have inherited the stunning, fair-haired beauty of her mother, but she still looked both beautiful and royal. A dark-haired princess with a pale, but otherwise composed, face. Her mouth was even curved slightly upward. The expression didn't touch her eyes, but perhaps her mother considered that normal.

The young woman in the mirror was Princess Gwendolyn, not Gwen. The reminder let Gwen breathe more freely.

"In truth, I've been remiss in my duties," her mother continued, not bothering to wait for a reply.

Gwen could barely keep her face still, unable to fathom what her mother could be referencing. The queen never criticized herself. She gave a laugh, a tinkling sound that never failed to grate on Gwen's nerves.

"I can see I've surprised you, my dear. I've been half-expecting you to ask me about it, but I'm gratified you're so content to remain here with only me."

"Ask you about what, Mother?" Gwen asked carefully, still with no idea what her mother was talking about.

"Why, your marriage, of course! You are old enough for it— and past age according to some." She laughed again. "But even the most impatient must recognize a mother's heart. What parent wants to give their precious child away to another?"

"You want to give me away?" Gwen asked, too dazed to filter her words.

The brush yanked downward, making her wince.

"Aren't you listening?" the queen asked, an edge to her voice. "I said I don't want to give you away."

"I…I apologize," Gwen stammered out, still lost. "But why are we talking of my marriage?"

"Because it is time, of course," the queen said calmly, her eyes meeting Gwen's wide ones in the mirror.

Gwen's mouth dropped open, not even fear of her mother

enough to suppress her shock. "You want me to get married? To whom?"

While she had always dreamed of escaping from under her mother's eye, she had never thought of marriage as the answer. Surrounded by no one but the servants and the cold court, there was only one person who had ever occupied her heart. And he was never coming. She had given up hope of that a long time ago. She didn't even know if he was alive.

Her mind raced through the various courtiers, but she couldn't think of anyone eligible enough to appeal to her mother. She certainly couldn't think of anyone she could stomach marrying.

"To a prince, of course," the queen said. "Only royalty could be worthy of the princess of the mountain kingdom."

"A prince?" Gwen frowned. "But there are no princes here." Slowly the truth broke over her, and her eyes flew up to meet her mother's in the mirror. "You want me to marry a lowlander?"

It was inconceivable. She knew the valleys existed, of course, and the captive valley folk had assured her the lowlands existed beyond them. But the valleys had always seemed a part of the mountains—if a distant part—while the kingdoms beyond were as distant as a fairy tale.

She started to rise to her feet, but her mother's hand tightened on her shoulder, pushing her back into place. Gwen slumped into the seat, her mind whirling. A lowlander prince? Did the lowland royals even know the mountain kingdom existed? Which of them would want to brave the mountains and make their home there?

Gwen didn't fool herself for even a second thinking that her mother might plan to release Gwen, sending her off to a far kingdom. The idea was appealing, but she knew it to be nonsense. Her mother would never let her go. Even if she had another heir —and she did not—she wasn't the type to relinquish anything that belonged to her.

"I don't like that term," her mother said stiffly, showing more restraint than she usually did when they were alone.

Gwen murmured an apology. Her surprise had betrayed her into using the term of her childhood, although she had never understood what issue her mother had with it.

"Are not all lands equal?" her mother asked. "What is high that cannot be brought low and what is low that cannot be made high?"

Gwen kept her eyes lowered, not wanting her mother to see the skepticism in them. Queen Celandine was the last person to believe in the equality of all. Whatever her true objection, it wasn't over some imagined slight against the lowlanders.

"We must think of them as an extension of our own people," her mother continued in the gracious tones she usually used in company. "Indeed, after your marriage, they will be as much your people as our own citizens are."

Gwen frowned. Her mother's words sounded conciliatory enough, but there was something predatory in her tone. Did she hope to use Gwen's marriage to extend her own influence? That would be like her mother, but it seemed pointless when the mountains created a barrier that would forever separate them from the other kingdoms. Passage between the mountain kingdoms and the lowland kingdoms was difficult enough to keep them apart forever. Gwen's marriage couldn't turn mountains into valleys.

"You need not concern yourself with the details," her mother said, as if reading her thoughts. "You need only prepare yourself for your marriage."

Gwen looked up again. "Is it that soon? Who is the groom?"

"He will be here soon enough," her mother said, ignoring the question about his identity. "And when your prince arrives, we must not delay. This afternoon, the seamstresses will attend you and take your measurements. You will need an entire new wardrobe before you're married."

Gwen nodded silently, her mind still whirling too fast to engage on such mundane topics as dressmaking. Her mother had plans—advanced plans—to marry her to a foreign prince. It didn't seem possible.

But her mother never spoke frivolously. If she said it was so, then she already had someone in mind. Knowing her, she must even have an agreement in place already.

Gwen wanted to press her to discover the name and kingdom of her supposed groom, but she couldn't shake off her unease from earlier. For some reason the queen was pretending affability, and Gwen didn't want to trigger overt anger.

She couldn't remain completely silent, however. "When?" she pressed. "How long before he's here?"

Her mother laughed. "So you are eager to be married after all. It is natural. But I cannot give you exact details on timing. We must wait for his arrival."

She finally put down the brush, meeting Gwen's eyes in the mirror in a way that told her they had finally reached the point of greatest importance to her mother.

"Once you are married, your duties and responsibilities will increase. You will find that the people look to you in a new way. But remember, the mountain kingdom is subservient to no one. Your future husband may be a prince, but that doesn't mean he'll be permitted to order matters here in the mountains. I am queen in this valley."

She held Gwen's eyes until she nodded. After all the years she had spent in her mother's company, she understood the underlying message. Marriage wasn't going to provide Gwen an escape. Single or married, she would still be under her mother's eye.

Her mother wasn't opening a gate and letting her walk free. She was merely luring another sheep into her pen.

Gwen felt a fleeting whisper of pity for the unsuspecting prince. But she couldn't hold onto the feeling in the face of her own discomfort. She had bowed her head and remained meekly in place for years in order to pacify her mother. But could she take it as far as marriage? Could she marry a stranger at her mother's order?

Everything in Gwen revolted, and she could no longer see her own reflection in the mirror. Instead, she saw curly brown hair and warm brown eyes with flecks of gold.

Was her mother leaving? She hoped desperately she was because Gwen couldn't lose her composure until her mother left the room.

Somewhere in the distance, she heard words that might have been a farewell. She must have managed a reply because she caught the sound of her door closing. Looking up, she confirmed she was alone.

Stumbling back from the dressing table, she collapsed onto her knees beside the bed, bracing her forehead against the soft mattress. Her breath rasped in and out too quickly, and she knew she needed to slow it down, but her body had stopped responding.

Tears leaked out, and the hands that gripped the bedspread shook. *Easton!* she cried silently. *Why did you leave without me? If you escaped from here, couldn't I have come as well?*

Her breath continued to rush in too quickly, and her head grew dizzy. What would she do when she didn't even have the sanctuary of her room? When the one space that was hers alone was filled with a stranger? Could she survive the palace when she no longer had even shreds of privacy left?

It was an unanswerable question, and she didn't try to count the minutes that passed until she finally steadied her trembling and took back control of her breath.

When she finally stood, she knew that even fear of her mother wasn't enough this time. She needed to find out the extent of her mother's plans, and then she needed to escape.

CHARLOTTE

The farewell exchanges between Charlotte and her family were stilted and awkward, and all she wanted was for them to be over. And yet, once they were, she hesitated. She knew it was too late to turn back, but her courage wavered in the face of departing everything she knew for a deep unknown.

She tried to remind herself of what was before her. The Palace of Light would no doubt be more glorious than she could even imagine. Her future might be unknown, but that didn't mean she needed to fear it.

Bolstering herself, she crossed to the bear, placing a hesitant hand on the soft fur of his shoulder. He stilled beneath her touch, but when she peered at his face, he seemed pleased. Did he still worry that she was afraid of him?

"Where do we go now?" she asked him, not quite managing to use his name.

"To my home," he replied, and she felt her first shiver of genuine excitement. Were they going to the Palace of Light immediately?

"Should I ride you again?" she asked, glancing toward the sky where the light was starting to fade.

"Yes," he said in his deep rumbly voice. "It is necessary if we are to reach our destination today."

She nodded. It made sense that she couldn't merely walk to another realm on her own feet. Murmuring an apology, she once again used his fur to haul herself into position on his back. From there, she sent a final glance toward her family who stood with Master Harold and his wife.

All four of them looked awed, and Charlotte allowed herself a moment of satisfaction. She was going to a bigger life, while they had merely made their world smaller. Then she remembered her family were to move to Arcadia and the feeling soured.

The bear took off with a lurch of movement that made her forget all about the people behind them as she clutched at his fur.

"Apologies," he called back to her. "But I will have to move faster this time if we are to make it before nightfall."

"Faster?" she gasped, remembering how swiftly they had traveled before. "Is that possible?"

He gave his gravelly laugh. "It is, indeed. If you lean forward and rest your head on my neck, you can wrap your arms around me in a more secure hold. You can even close your eyes and sleep if you wish. I will not let you fall, and we will be there before you know it."

Charlotte had intended to remain alert, curious about the journey itself, but as the bear picked up speed, she was forced to flatten herself or risk losing her balance. And pressed against his warm fur, it was easier to close her eyes than keep them open given the wind generated by their speed.

She wouldn't sleep, however. How could she sleep after all that had just happened and with all that was before her?

An unknown length of time later, she awoke with a start. It took her a disorienting moment to realize she was still clutching the bear's fur but they had come to a stop. When had she fallen asleep?

"We have arrived," the bear said in a deep tone she couldn't entirely read.

Shaking the remaining fuzziness from her mind, she slipped off his back and looked upward. The sight in front of her made her gasp.

An austere castle of gray stone had been built against a craggy mountain face. There were no lights in the windows nor any other sign of life, but it appeared to be in good condition and was by far the largest building she had ever seen. It had turrets but no flags—nothing to indicate which kingdom they were in. And given the rapidly gathering darkness, it didn't seem possible it could be the Palace of Light.

"Are we to stay here tonight?" she asked, bewildered, wishing she had stayed awake long enough to see the direction of their travel. The presence of the castle suggested they had moved westward, leaving the fringes of civilization and moving deeper into Rangmere. But the mountains that ringed them on three sides indicated they had rather gone east into the impassable mountains that bordered the Four Kingdoms.

"Of course," the bear said, sounding a little confused. "You would not want to sleep in the open."

"No," she rushed to assure him, despite the resurgence of her trepidation now they were truly alone in such a foreign place. "This is by far the grandest building I've ever seen. I will be honored to stay here. But…is this your castle?" She managed a small laugh. "Are you a prince among the bears?"

He hesitated for a moment, the air between them turning awkward. "It's true this is my home for now," he said at last, "but the castle doesn't belong to me."

She laughed again, trying to break the new tension. "Are you a squatter then?"

"More like a prisoner," he murmured, so quietly she almost didn't catch it. But when he looked up, he was grinning, and the coldness in the air had disappeared.

"Princess Charlotte suits you, though, don't you think? I'm sorry there isn't great fanfare awaiting you and a line of courtiers ready to pledge their loyalty."

She laughed back.

"I'm no princess, and I have no desire for such a scene. This is already far more than I expected."

Henry's face turned serious. "I hope that's true, and you didn't marry me because you thought I held some high position."

"Of course not!" she laughed. "And how could I complain when your home has turned out to be a castle? You said you would provide for me, and you're already doing so. It's clear you keep your promises." She said the last words with extra weight, and he nodded slightly, seeming to instinctively understand her sudden tension.

"You can be sure I will always endeavor to do so. And for now, you are princess of this castle, at least. Though I hope one day I may offer you more."

He spoke with a careful lightness that betrayed underlying tension.

"Truly, it isn't necessary," she rushed to reassure him. And even as she spoke the words, she realized she had no idea how he felt about their marriage. She had only ever considered the matter from her own perspective. Did it pain him to have to seek a human girl as a bride? What had driven him to do so?

"How long will we stay here?" she asked. "Before we continue on to your true home, I mean."

He looked shocked at her words, and his reply was slow and cautious. "My true home?"

Charlotte frowned. "The Palace of Light, I mean. That is where you are originally from, isn't it?"

Her clarification only seemed to shock him further.

"You thought I was one of the High King's creatures from the Palace of Light? And that I meant to take you there?"

"Aren't you?" She drew back, fear clogging her throat.

"Is that why you married me?" he asked, horror in his voice. "Is that why you trusted me?"

"Yes," she said in a small voice. But after a moment of heavy silence, honesty compelled her to continue. "Well, not entirely. That's the explanation I gave myself, but my instincts told me you were trustworthy and safe from the beginning. I was drawn to you from our first meeting in a way I can't explain."

She clasped her hands together, desperately hoping her instincts hadn't led her astray.

Henry drew back, his expression conveying a level of distress that shouldn't have been possible on the face of a bear.

"I'm truly sorry," he said. "I did not intentionally deceive you. If I had dreamed—" He shook his head abruptly. "No, I should have guessed it. It was a reasonable assumption. It is my fault for not foreseeing that you would—"

"No, indeed, you can't blame yourself!" Charlotte cried, moved by his concern. Clearly it had not been a duplicitous deception. Her heartbeat slowed again, the momentary panic receding. It might not have made logical sense, but she still trusted him.

Their current situation was another matter, however. Was this castle more than a temporary home for him? Had he really muttered something about being a prisoner? She stared at the castle with new eyes.

He wanted her to live here, in this cold and lifeless place, deep in the mountains? Who else lurked behind the castle walls? Were there others like him?

The thought filled her with horror, and she couldn't entirely keep the emotion from her face. The bear looked from the sky— which was clinging to only the last vestiges of light—to her face, desperation in his eyes.

"This is a truly terrible misunderstanding," he said, "but night is upon us. Shall we go inside at least?"

The pleading in his voice made her nod, and she followed him silently inside. There was certainly nothing to be gained by standing on the castle's doorstep as darkness descended.

The great double doors creaked as they opened, revealing a cavernous entryway that was as dark and cold as she had feared. From the outside, the edifice had looked lifeless, and inside it appeared no less so.

She tried to reassure herself that at least there were no fearsome beasts, but the shiver that rocked her made it hard to cling to any positivity. Was she really to sleep—to live—in such a place?

The bear still seemed concerned, but he moved quickly, his actions verging on frantic. Crossing to the mantelpiece over the vast and empty fireplace, he delicately lifted a silver bell, clasping the wooden handle in his jaws.

Shaking his head, he rang the bell, the sound echoing against the stone all around them. Instantly a roaring fire sprang to life in the dead fireplace, and all around her light bloomed as hundreds of candles began to glow.

Charlotte gasped, spinning to take in the whole entranceway. Filled with light and warmth as it now was, the space felt entirely different. Even welcoming.

But how was it possible? Even if the bear had been able to instantly start a large fire, it should have taken time to warm the air.

Her eyes fixed on the bell, and she spoke in reverent tones.

"Is that a godmother object?"

She had heard legends about such objects—gifted to worthy humans by the godmothers who served the High King, they were often passed down through generations.

"It is," the bear said, although he still seemed distracted and hurried. "And a powerful one."

"You have a godmother, then?" Charlotte asked, some of her earlier hope rekindling.

The bear hesitated before finally saying, "It wasn't gifted

directly to me. I...acquired it from someone else. I don't know how old it is."

Charlotte frowned. The tales she had heard included some that involved nefarious people twisting godmother objects to their own ends. Surely the bear was not such a person? His presence couldn't fill her with such a sense of safety if he was.

Unless that was part of the enchantment that surrounded him.

She drew back, trembling as she realized yet again how isolated and alone she was. She didn't even know how far or in what direction lay her home valley.

No, she thought miserably, *not my home any longer. This is my home now.*

It was a painful thought.

The bear had always been sensible of her moods before, but he didn't notice this time, approaching her without regard to her new emotions.

"Who are you?" she gasped, needing answers. "If you are not a creature from the Palace of Light, how can you talk?"

The bear halted abruptly, shifting from side to side. Placing the bell carefully on the flagged floor in front of him, he opened his mouth as if to speak but ended up groaning instead.

"Please, just tell me," she said, her voice shaking.

The bear glanced at one of the long windows that framed the doorway. "There isn't time now. I will explain it to you later—it will be easier then anyway. For now, you should hurry and take this." He gestured toward the bell with his head.

"The godmother object? You want *me* to take it?" Charlotte stared at him.

"Of course," he said. "It's my wedding gift to you. You need only ring it and anything you wish will appear. You can use it to turn this place into a comfortable home. Please feel free to make any changes to the castle that you desire."

He glanced at the window again before muttering something

hurried and dark. When he started to move, fresh horror filled Charlotte.

"But wait!" she cried, grasping for the first time that he meant to leave her. "Where are you going?"

"I'm sorry," he growled, not looking back in her direction. "There is no more time. Use the bell, and you will be able to sleep in comfort. I will explain what more I can...later."

"Wait! No! Stop!" she cried, but it was too late, he was already through one of the doors that opened off the entranceway.

Belatedly, she ran after him, pulling open the door that had swung closed in his wake. But although the door opened into a long corridor, he was nowhere in sight. He had already disappeared. Charlotte was truly alone.

She swayed for a moment, fearing her legs might give way. But despite herself, the warmth and light of the entranceway drew her back inside. Her eyes fell on the bell, discarded on the floor where they had been standing, and she hurried back to it.

When she reached it, she paused, gazing down at it. She couldn't doubt it was a godmother object—not after seeing its powers displayed. But did she dare pick it up—claim it? Who was she to possess something so rare and valuable?

Princess Charlotte. The echo of the bear's words made her chuckle, something she would have thought impossible only minutes before. Why shouldn't she claim it, after all? She was mistress of a vast castle now—empty though it might be. The bear had said it was a wedding gift. If so, it was the only one she had received, and she would not spurn it.

Drawing a deep breath, she wrapped her hand around the wooden handle. It was smooth to the touch, the whole thing weighing less than she expected. She laughed at herself. Had she thought its value would increase its weight? It was a small thing and should be light.

Holding it carefully motionless, she considered the world of possibilities in the bear's earlier declaration. By ringing this bell, she might have anything her heart desired.

Any material thing, an unwelcome voice whispered. *It cannot create love for you or companionship.*

She shook the thoughts away and considered what she wanted. She knew what her sisters would wish for. Gowns, jewels, chests of gold. Her mother might wish for a feast. Her father for sturdy walls.

Holding those thoughts in her mind, she rang the bell. Nothing happened. Or rather, nothing she could see. But she had been wishing for something far away. Was it possible the power of the bell worked at such a distance, and she had just gifted her family the bride price they had sought?

A vindictive part of her wanted to wish it away again, just in case. But for all her lingering resentment, she would gain nothing by wishing misery on her family. If the bell had done something for them—as impossible as that seemed—she would leave it be. Her thoughts were better spent on her own immediate needs.

Her eyes traveled the stone of the castle entryway. She had sturdy enough walls to keep out an invading army. And she doubted her ability to eat—not with her emotions in such turmoil. Fancy gowns and jewels would be equally wasted. Who was there here to see them?

She considered again. Her family's wishes would do her no good. What did *she* want?

The answer came immediately. After everything that had happened, she longed for nothing so much as the comfort of her bed and blankets she could pull over her head. She wanted to collapse into a soft mattress and enjoy the oblivion of a few hours' unconsciousness. Surely this strange new home would be easier to accept in the light of day.

Smiling at herself, she rang the bell. "My own room with a warm bed," she said, knowing it wasn't the sort of thing the bell could provide.

But to her astonishment, a door in the far wall swung immediately open, lights springing up in the corridor beyond it as candles flared into life along its length.

Charlotte hesitated for only a moment before picking up her discarded bundle and hurrying toward the door. Once in the corridor, she could see that the lit candles created a pathway, guiding her through the castle. She followed where they led until a second door swung open for her, creaking with a reminder that the castle was old and abandoned despite the lack of dust.

She paused in the doorway, peering inside. An enormous room emanated warmth and light. A large fireplace crackled with a cozy fire and deep, forest green carpet enticed her to step inside. The heavy brocade curtains were a lighter shade of green, while the green of the bedspread was enlivened with intricate gold embroidery. The curtains of the enormous four-poster were tied back with heavy gold cord and tassels, beckoning her to slip between the crisp white sheets.

"But it's huge," she gasped aloud as the door swung closed behind her. She had never seen or imagined such a large bed. "I'll be lost in that!"

She glanced dubiously at the bell in her hand, but another look at the room made her discard the idea of attempting to use it again. The enchantment might have miscalculated the size of the bed, but everything else was perfect, and she didn't want to risk changing anything.

Cautiously she placed the bell down on the walnut side table that was placed conveniently beside the bed. She didn't want to risk ringing it by accident. What if the bell attempted to make something out of her confused thoughts?

Although her meager things seemed laughably out of place in the room, Charlotte unpacked her bundle, changing quickly into the long nightgown she had brought with her. The material felt rough against the softness of the sheets as she crawled between them, and she suspected she would soon be requesting new clothes from the bell.

But she would wait for the next day. Surely the bear would return in the morning, and she would have the chance to ask more specifically about how the bell worked.

Wistfully she considered how he had run from her. What had been so urgent that he needed to abandon her like that?

A memory popped into her head of words he had spoken to her previously. He had said that once she reached her new home, she might choose never to see him. Surely he didn't think that was what she wanted? He didn't mean to abandon her alone in this enormous place?

She shook off the thought. He had promised her an explanation, so he hadn't left for good. She would have to hold on to that assurance until morning.

Sighing, she leaned over to blow out the candelabra sitting on the side table. She didn't relish lying alone in the dark, but the fire in the hearth would provide enough light for reassurance, and she didn't want to risk accidentally setting the bed curtains alight.

But the second the candle flames winked out, the room was plunged into complete darkness.

Charlotte gave a terrified cry, too startled to exercise restraint. Her heart pounded as she sat up in bed, trying unsuccessfully to peer into the black around her.

She told herself her reaction was unwarranted, but she wasn't convinced. What might be lurking unseen in this strange place? And what had happened to the fire? She hadn't made a request—she hadn't even been holding the bell.

The bell! Grasping blindly with both hands, she knocked over the candlestick before she finally felt the curved shape of the bell.

"Start the fire again," she gasped out, her fingers curled around the wooden handle as she made the bell peal out.

Nothing happened.

"Light the candles," she said in growing desperation, ringing the bell louder.

Still nothing happened.

She could feel the tears gathering, her panic threatening to take over and send her blindly fleeing. But where to?

She could try to use the bell to wish herself out of this room and back in the entryway, but it no longer seemed to be working. And what if the lights had gone out there as well? At least here she was snug in a bed, and she knew the room was empty and the door closed. Could she bear to be in the dark in the vast emptiness of the entryway? Or worse—wandering lost among the castle corridors?

No, it was far better to remain where she was. And her eyes would adjust to the darkness any minute, and she would see it wasn't as complete as she thought. There had to be traces of moonlight seeping around the curtains if nothing else.

But the minutes dragged out and nothing changed. No matter how closely Charlotte waved her hand in front of her face, she could see no flicker of movement. The darkness was absolute.

"It's still better to remain here," she whispered to herself. Morning would come eventually. Even the bell couldn't change that.

And at least she was alone in her room. She had even seen inside the wardrobe when she was putting away her clothes.

She slowly lowered herself back down to lie flat. But just as her heart was slowing to a more normal rhythm, the door to the corridor creaked open.

Charlotte only just bit back her scream, clapping both hands to her mouth. She felt sure she should do something—get up and fight perhaps, although she had no idea what she was facing and would be more likely to end up tripping over the side table than intimidating the unseen creature.

At the very least, she should call out to whoever had opened the door—assuming it had not been the work of the bell. But instead, she disgraced herself. Primal terror overcame her, and she scrambled beneath the bedcovers.

CHARLOTTE

*P*ulling the blankets firmly over her head, Charlotte lay there, trembling from head to toe. Her breath rasped in and out, the only sound in the heavy silence. She strained to hear footfalls, but the lush carpet absorbed any sound that might have reached her ears.

"Is…is someone there?" she mustered the courage to say, just as something tugged at the blanket.

For a second she feared it was being pulled off her entirely, and she gripped it harder. But it was merely rippling as someone touched the far side of it.

The mattress dipped slightly as someone climbed in beside her, although the size of the bed meant they were still out of reach of her arm. She scrambled away, nearly falling out of the bed before soft words made her freeze.

"Wait," the voice said. "I won't hurt you."

It was a deep voice, masculine and commanding, but it still had an edge of youth, and she would have guessed its owner to be only a few years older than herself. Strangest of all, the sound of it, although unfamiliar, filled her with the same sense of safety she always felt in the presence of the white bear.

Even so, she couldn't possibly accept the current situation.

"This is my bedchamber, sir!" she exclaimed, putting as much indignation as she could into her voice without making it waver. Better to show this stranger anger than fear. "This is my bed! You cannot be here!"

She remained poised on the edge of the mattress, ready to leap out if he came any closer. But there was no movement from his side, just words that carried a disconcerting layer of amusement.

"I think even the strictest matron would find it acceptable for a bride and groom to sleep beside one another on their wedding night."

"What?" Charlotte gasped. "What are you saying?"

"I am your husband," he said with more solemnity. "I am Henry in my true form."

"You're *human*?" Charlotte asked, dizzied. Part of her wanted to protest that it couldn't be true, but this latest shocking revelation was no more extraordinary than anything else that had happened to her in the last twenty-four hours.

"Yes, I am human," the voice that apparently belonged to her husband said. "I was once quite an ordinary human, in fact. But now I'm under an enchantment. At night I am allowed my true form, but during the day I become a white bear."

"You should have said as much!" Charlotte cried, and he was silent for a moment.

"That too is part of the enchantment," he said at last. "I cannot speak of my enchantment while in my bear form. I thought you would know of it anyway, however. From certain things your father said, he seemed aware of such enchantments."

Charlotte wanted to protest hotly, but the words died in her mouth. Her father had been so insistent that the bear was a person, and Master Harold had spoken of secrets that couldn't be shared. Clearly her father knew something—something he had been sworn to secrecy over.

"What is your business with the valley folk?" she asked, some of her anger at her father's secrets tingeing her voice. "What do they know of you?"

"Nothing," Henry said. "Your family is the first I ever talked to there. Whatever your father knows of my enchantment, he didn't learn it from me."

Charlotte frowned, but it was too late to pry the truth out of her father or Master Harold now. She felt the bed shift slightly and tensed, but Henry stilled again.

"In truth, I don't like to speak of my enchantment anyway," he said in a low voice. "It is because of my own foolishness that I've found myself in this situation, and though I hope to gain my freedom again, I cannot guarantee it. Even if I had been free to do so, I don't know if I would have spoken to you of my true identity. I needed a wife of strength and courage, and I didn't want to marry someone under false pretenses. After all, it is possible I'll spend our whole marriage as a bear."

"Except at night," Charlotte said softly, glad for the darkness that hid the warmth in her cheeks. Henry had promised her a legal marriage and nothing more, but now it turned out he became a man at night, and he had come here to her bed. Was he expecting a proper marriage between them after all?

"Don't worry," Henry said, once again picking up on her emotions. "There are other reasons for my silence. The same reasons that bring me here to this room. But while there are things I can't fully explain to you yet, I meant the promises I made. All I ask is for you to accept my presence beside you at night. I will not harm you, and neither will I impose any further upon you. You may go all day without seeing my bear form if you wish, and we can sleep side by side in silence at night. I ask only for you to stay true to the promises you have made and to endure it."

Charlotte let out a relieved breath. There was no doubt the

request was strange. But was there anything about the entire affair that hadn't been strange?

Even the bed they slept in was large enough that two could occupy it without ever coming into contact. It occurred to her that the size of the bed hadn't been a mistake by the bell, after all. Apparently her husband had gifted her the use of the silver bell, but ultimately it still belonged to him and obeyed the parameters he had set.

She wished Henry could have explained it to her ahead of time, but she couldn't help but soften now she knew he had done his best to consider her comfort despite the oddness of the situation. Touched to once again see the signs of her new husband's consideration, Charlotte spoke, her voice coming out quiet and shy.

"I thank you for your kindness, and I have no desire for you to stay away from me or to stay silent. I'm sure I should be lonely if you were to disappear." She gathered her courage. "In fact, if you give me a moment, I will relight the candles. I should like to see your true face, and we will be more comfortable talking with a little light."

"No!" he said so sharply that Charlotte started and nearly fell out of the bed. "You can never turn on the light. You will find, in fact, that you cannot. None of the candles or fires here will permit such a request."

Heavy silence wrapped around the room for nearly a full minute before Henry sighed.

"I'm sorry. I know this is a strange marriage, and I have done little to earn your trust. But I must ask that you give it to me anyway."

Charlotte lay there, her heart beating erratically in her chest. She couldn't even see his face? He did ask a lot.

And yet, did he really? So far, he had met every promise he had made. If she had carried different expectations, that was her error, not his. He had given her a vast mansion for a home and even gifted her the use of a godmother object that would grant her every whim.

And in return, he asked only that she allow him to sleep in the same room as her at night without the comfort of illumination. Technically, they shared a bed, but it felt wrong to think of it that way when he lay so far away. She could thrash around in her sleep, or even reach for him on purpose, and she wouldn't make contact.

No, his demands were strange, but not onerous. As her husband, he could have expected far more and provided less.

"I don't understand," she said at last. "But I can accept it." She hesitated. "You said you can't explain the situation to me yet. Does that mean one day you will?" *Once I have gained* your *trust,* she added in her head.

"If you will trust in me, it will be a greater gift than any I have been given," he said, not quite answering her question.

She sighed quietly. He had said he couldn't give further explanations, and obviously he meant it. Was the enchantment physically restraining him from speaking? At least one of her cousin's stories had included something of that nature.

Silence fell between them again, but it was laced with awkwardness, and Charlotte couldn't imagine sleeping in such a strained environment.

But just as her nerves were stretching taut, Henry laughed. A rich chuckle that pulled an answering smile from her, although she didn't know the source of his amusement.

"I know I said we could lie here in silence," he said, "but I didn't realize it would be so awkward. And yet, somehow, the harder I try, the less I can think of anything to say."

Charlotte laughed. "I'm glad it's not just me. I used to have an invisible friend, you know, but I've never had a stranger for a husband nor conducted any conversation in the pitch dark."

"An invisible friend?" he asked with another chuckle. "I didn't picture you as a fanciful child."

"Oh, she wasn't *imaginary*," Charlotte said calmly. "She was just invisible, although not to children. Of course that meant the adults all assumed she was imaginary, so you can guess how infuriating that was. But I'm sure my imagination couldn't produce someone like Daisy." She laughed again.

"You were friends with Princess Daisy?" Henry asked, clearly shocked. But after a moment, he added, "I suppose you would have been the right age. But I didn't realize you used to live in Northhelm."

"*You* know Daisy?" Charlotte asked in even greater astonishment. How did a man cursed to spend his days in the mountains in the form of a bear come to know a princess from across the sea?

"Not personally," he said hurriedly. "But I've heard the stories, of course."

"Oh, of course." Charlotte relaxed. "I suppose half the Four Kingdoms have heard the tale by now. It's a strange thought, even if I don't feature in the tale by name."

"I'm surprised the valley isn't abuzz about having a celebrity in their midst," Henry said, and she thought she could hear a smile in his voice.

"My sisters didn't like me to talk about it," Charlotte said heavily. "They didn't take it well when Daisy's true identity was revealed."

"Because she was more your friend than theirs?" Henry asked shrewdly. "And they didn't like that she turned out to be someone important?"

Charlotte nodded, only to remember he couldn't see her. "Yes, that was part of it. And beyond that..." She hesitated, loathe to reveal the extent of her sisters' behavior.

"You can tell me," he said in a gentle voice. "I'm your husband now, so you don't need to hold back any of your story. Your past is safe with me."

Lying beside him, she realized he was already far more her

husband than she had ever thought he could be. She had already pledged her life to him, so why would she withhold her past? She finished the thought she had held in.

"It wasn't just that I was closer to Daisy," she said. "Once Elizabeth and Odelia grew too old to see her, they sided with the adults, pretending they had never seen her at all and she was just a game I played with the younger children."

"They wanted to make you look foolish," Henry said with unexpected savagery in his voice. "Because even then they could see that you would outshine them both."

"I never wanted to believe that was the reason," Charlotte said softly, "but..." Given everything that had happened in the years since, it seemed almost certain. "It's a difficult time in those years between childhood and adulthood," she said softly. "We all make foolish choices we regret later."

"You're kinder to them than I would be," Henry said, still with that note in his voice.

It made her shiver, and she was once again glad he couldn't see her. Not that she was afraid of him. It was her own responses she feared. She was pleased enough at the way he leaped to her defense that she felt guilty.

She should try harder to understand her sisters, not delight in hearing them disparaged. But she couldn't help her pleasure at Henry's support. For some reason he seemed to genuinely care about how she was treated. Not since Daisy's friendship so many years ago had Charlotte had someone so actively on her side.

The cold, empty castle had frightened her, promising a future far different than what she had been imagining. But now Henry's words reminded her that she hadn't married him because of the Palace of Light. That had merely been an exciting possibility. She had married him because she wanted a place—a family—where there was space for her.

And here, lying in the darkness with a bodiless voice that

burned in outrage on her behalf, she had found that sense of belonging.

"Goodnight, Lottie," Henry whispered, the unfamiliar nickname seeming to slip out without him realizing.

"Goodnight, Henry," she whispered back, his name comfortable on her lips for the first time.

The silence that fell between them no longer felt awkward or tense. Instead, it was filled with warmth and connection. She couldn't see the man who had become her husband that day, but she could feel his unquestioning support. It cradled her in a feeling of comfort and security that enabled her to sleep as peacefully as she had ever done in her own bed.

But when she awoke, daylight glowed around the edges of the curtains, and the long stretch of bed beside her was empty and cold.

GWEN

Gwen endured hours of forced stillness while a team of seamstresses dressed her in gown after gown, exclaiming over designs and materials and measurements. She couldn't enter into their excitement, but they didn't seem to notice her lack of it, treating her more like a doll than a bride-to-be. Had they known of her mother's plans for a royal marriage before this? Had everyone but Gwen known?

She told herself it didn't matter, and she tried to use the time to make plans. Part of her wanted to run straight for the mountains to the west of the valley—the ones that eventually led to other kingdoms. Surely, with enough provisions, she could find the passage through that was used by her mother's people.

But she couldn't leave just as she was uncovering the mystery at the heart of her home. And she must still have some time, going by the number of dresses her mother had commissioned. If they were intended to be finished before the mystery prince arrived, he must still be a way off. She would uncover her mother's secrets first, and then she would devise a plan to flee. Maybe she would even find something that could aid in her escape.

By the time she was finally released from the dress fitting, it was almost time for the evening meal. And after her experience the previous night, Gwen knew she wouldn't be able to stay awake for any nighttime wanderings.

She had the secret master key that should let her out of her room, but the locked door wasn't her primary hurdle. A key was no use to her if she couldn't stay awake long enough to use it. And worse—if she made it out into the corridor and then fell asleep there, she would alert her mother to her possession of the key.

So Gwen endured a normal evening meal, even forcing herself to eat as usual, and when she grew sleepy, she went to bed. At least the mattress was soft on her bruises.

But the next morning she arrived at breakfast filled with determination. She wasn't getting caught up in meaningless activities for another entire day.

On the threshold of the dining room, she paused, however. While they often had guests for the evening meal, having anyone but her mother at breakfast was unusual.

Count Oswin rose instantly to his feet on seeing her, bowing respectfully. "Good morning, Your Highness."

He smiled and held out her usual chair, waiting for her to take a seat.

"I apologize for intruding on your remaining family time," he said once she had begun her meal.

Gwen's hand froze, the knife halfway to the butter. He knew about her mother's plans?

She shot her mother a look and caught the strain around her eyes as she held her smile in place. The count definitely knew, but the queen didn't like him mentioning it.

Count Oswin also glanced at the queen, hurrying into speech at sight of her expression. "Not that I mean to imply you'll be losing each other, naturally. But it will be different to have someone else join the family."

Seeing her mother relax, Gwen experienced again the familiar feeling that she was missing an underlying meaning in the words spoken around her. In the past, she'd allowed the sensation to wash over her, but now it sent energy crackling up her spine.

She could smell the secrets as clearly as she could smell breakfast. If only she could pluck them off the table as easily.

She forced herself to eat her toast, carefully chewing and swallowing each bite. But her ears were sharp, straining to catch any double meaning. The conversation had moved on to safer topics, however. The count and her mother discussed the weather and an upcoming picnic as if they were perfectly natural topics for a ruler to discuss with her most powerful advisor.

Gwen forced herself to drink her tea. This conversation couldn't be the real reason he had joined them for breakfast. And from the way he kept stealing glances at her, it was easy to guess that he wanted her gone so he could move on to his true agenda.

As disappointing as that might be, it was for the best. She wanted to escape as much as the two of them must want her to disappear.

Swallowing the last of her meal, she stood. When she tried to think of an appropriate excuse for her abrupt departure, her mind went blank, so she settled for a half curtsy to her mother before hurrying out of the room.

Alone in the corridor, she could finally breathe. And the further she got from the dining room, the more she recognized the unexpected windfall in the count's presence. Not only had her mother not given Gwen any tasks for the day, but she was likely to be occupied with Count Oswin for some time. The combination of those two things allowed Gwen to start her investigation somewhere she might actually find answers.

She forced her shoulders straight and her face into an expression of detached confidence as she approached her mother's exclusive wing of the palace. The guard who was always stationed at the door gave her a curious look but didn't stop her.

Apparently the queen's one family member was allowed into her domain.

Once past the guard, with a door shut safely between them, Gwen's legs trembled slightly, but she couldn't risk slowing down.

She considered the options open to her. She could search her mother's office, but her instincts steered her away from there. Her mother sometimes mentioned having meetings there, and Gwen suspected anything the queen had hidden would be somewhere more private. Somewhere like her bedchamber. Not even Gwen was ever invited in there.

When she tried the handle, it didn't turn. She had expected as much and come prepared.

Somewhat to her surprise, the master key turned in the lock. She'd feared her mother might have an individual lock for her own chamber.

Inside, she found a room that looked like a mirror image of her own, down to the location of the bed and coloring of the carpet and curtains. She frowned. The castle might have been austere, but what little decoration it had was tastefully diverse. She'd never seen two identically decorated rooms before.

The unexpected appearance of the room gave her a disconcerting feeling of familiarity and wrongness at the same time. She shook it off and began a methodical search.

It didn't help that she didn't know what she was searching for. It was ludicrous to think she might come across a paper titled *My Evil Plans for my Daughter Gwendolyn*, or *A List of the Secret Things that Happen in the Mountain Palace at Night*. But if she didn't do *something*, she might spend another day shaking and crying by her bed.

Her mother's possessions were as luxurious as you would expect from a queen, but it struck Gwen that they were oddly impersonal. Nothing in the room gave any real sense of the owner's identity.

When she had examined each piece of furniture without finding anything of note, she turned her eyes to the walls. It would be just like her mother to have a hidden door in her bedchamber.

Her gaze lingered on a pair of closed, floor-length curtains. They would have been unremarkable except for the fact they were positioned on an internal wall.

Gwen pulled them open with a sweeping movement, gasping at what they revealed. Rather than a door as she had hoped, they concealed a large and striking portrait.

A stunningly beautiful girl stared into the distance, her golden hair matching her gown of golden satin. But more impressive still was her hand, which rested on the shoulder of an enormous white bear.

The pose was affectionate on her behalf and protective on his, although Gwen couldn't have put into words what gave her that impression. The painter had placed them in a spring setting, in a forest, although Gwen could see the edge of a gray stone building that reminded her unpleasantly of the stone that always surrounded her.

She stood still for several minutes, taking in every detail of the painting and trying to make sense of its existence. Why did her mother possess such a portrait—it matched no one Gwen had ever met—and why was it concealed in her bedchamber?

Something about the fanciful idea of a girl with a bear as a companion reminded Gwen of a fairy story. And nothing could match her mother less. Her mother didn't waste time on imagination or stories for children.

Unless the portrait itself hid something? It wouldn't explain the subjects of the painting, but it could possibly explain the concealing curtains.

Gwen stepped close enough to touch it, hesitating for a moment before carefully running her fingers along the edge of the frame, feeling behind it. Sure enough, she found a small lever that she managed to pull upward with a single finger.

As soon as she touched it, a creaking sounded, and the entire life-size portrait swung forward. Gwen only just jumped out of the way in time, gaping at the dark space revealed behind. She had been looking for hidden doors but had only half expected to actually find one.

She stepped to the edge of the space, peering into the black. Just as she was considering going in search of a candle, her eyes adjusted. It wasn't completely dark inside after all—she could see the rim of sunlight around at least two sets of closed curtains.

Within moments, her eyes had adjusted enough to allow her to step inside without any further illumination. Whatever she had expected to find, however, it wasn't what awaited her.

Several chests rested against one of the walls, their lids thrown open to reveal the sort of riches you might expect to find in a secure treasury. But they weren't what drew Gwen's attention.

Scattered around the middle of the room were a series of plinths, each proudly displaying a single item. She had seen an illustration like this in a book once. It had shown a royal treasury, with the positions of honor reserved for godmother objects that had been passed down within the kingdom through generations.

Gwen gasped as her gaze roamed over the room. There were so many of them. And yet, she knew of no recent stories about the godmothers visiting the mountain kingdom. Where had they all come from?

She stepped closer, fascinated. Her fingers reached for the nearest object, but she pulled her hand back. These weren't like the treasures in the chests. They had power she didn't understand, and a single touch might be enough to unleash something.

She wanted hours to slowly look through the room, guessing at the powers and original purpose of each object. But she didn't know how much longer she had. Her fruitless search of her mother's room had already taken too long. She should have looked for a hidden door first.

Her attention was drawn to a plinth that held two items. They both appeared to be made of gold, but they had a soft, pliable look that didn't match the metal. She knew why she had been drawn to them—the miniature version of a halter and whip were unusual items to see molded from gold, but they were also familiar. Just looking at them brought back the sensation of wind in Gwen's hair as she galloped away from the palace.

Without meaning to do so, her hand rose, reaching to finger the halter. The whip made her shudder—she didn't like them and had never used one—but the halter felt like freedom.

As her skin touched warm, supple metal, the air pressure around her changed. Someone had just entered the room. She jumped, whirling to face Queen Celandine, standing in the doorway of her secret treasury.

Gwen's face and hands went cold, her breath catching. How had she been so careless? She should have noted what she could and already left. She should have—

"Well done, my daughter!" The queen smiled at her, and for once she actually looked pleased.

"I'm sor—What?" Gwen asked, caught off guard in the middle of her half-formed apology.

Her mother gestured for her to exit the hidden room, but Gwen hesitated. Was there some reason why her mother didn't want to unleash her anger in this room full of powerful objects?

But staying would only increase her mother's wrath. So Gwen stumbled out in her wake, watching numbly as the queen closed both the portrait door and the curtains, shutting the girl and bear from view. Gwen almost blurted out a question about the girl's identity, but she held it in.

When her mother turned to her, Gwen's surprise grew, however. She still had the unfamiliar look of actual pleasure. If it had been on anyone else's face, Gwen would have called it pride.

"I wondered when you would find your way here," the queen said. "Perhaps I should have had that conversation about your marriage with you earlier."

"You're...pleased I'm here?" Gwen asked, analyzing her mother's face for any hint of her true emotions.

"Soon you will be married," her mother said, "and to an outsider. Some spine and spirit will be necessary if you are to keep him in line. It is a skill you must learn because your husband will not be the last you must control."

Gwen swallowed. She was not only to have a stranger thrust on her as a husband, but she would be responsible for his subservience to her mother as well? And what was this talk of others? Her mother surely couldn't mean more lowlanders, could she?

The queen approached her, cupping Gwen's face in what might have been a loving, comforting gesture from a normal mother. From Queen Celandine, it sent a chill racing down Gwen's spine.

"Of course, my daughter," she said, dropping her voice low, "independence shouldn't be taken too far or else it might grow displeasing."

She emphasized the last word in a way that made Gwen want to shrink from her hand. She forced herself to remain as still as a statue, however.

"I understand, Mother."

The queen regarded her for a long moment more before giving a slow smile. "Yes, I think you do. My expectations were low when you were younger, but you have turned out well enough, after all."

With a satisfied nod, she let her hand drop and stepped away. Her eyes flicked to the room's door, and Gwen recognized the dismissal with relief.

Picking up her skirts, she all but fled into the corridor, not slowing until she had passed the guard and escaped her mother's wing entirely. She kept her face down on the way past, not wanting to see the man's expression. Had he let her past on her mother's orders? How long had the queen been waiting for her daughter to go snooping in her chambers?

When she reached her own room, she closed the door and leaned against it. But even with its support, her hands were still trembling. She thrust them both into her pockets, wanting to hide her weakness, even with no witnesses.

She instantly stilled, distracted from the lingering echo of her mother's words and manner. Her right pocket wasn't empty.

Pulling out the miniature golden halter, she stared at it. Running the events in the secret treasury back through her mind, she remembered the moment when her hand had reached— almost of its own accord—to touch the halter.

It had been just at that moment that the queen had appeared, surprising Gwen. She had no specific memory of it but, when startled, she must have instinctively seized the halter and concealed it in her pocket.

She stared at it, so innocent looking in her palm. Slowly her heartbeat picked up its earlier terrified rhythm.

She had entered her mother's rooms to look for information, but somehow she had stolen a godmother object. This was undoubtedly taking the matter to a level the queen would find *displeasing*.

But slowly Gwen's fingers closed over it in a gesture of possessiveness. She had acquired something of unknown power, and she couldn't let it go. Not now.

If Gwen was ever going to break free from her mother, the time had come. And she needed all the power she could get.

CHARLOTTE

$\mathcal{C}$harlotte considered trying to find a dining room of some kind, but her courage failed her. Instead, she rang the bell and requested a hot breakfast in her room. It would be easier to face exploring the empty castle with a full stomach.

At first she thought nothing had happened, and the bell really was broken, but then a delicious smell reached her nose. Turning, she saw a tray resting on a walnut table by the window, a padded chair in front of it and steam rising from the dishes.

Smiling, she rushed over and fell on the food. How many hours had it been since she had last eaten? She couldn't remember, and she didn't want to calculate it. Her life had changed so completely since her last meal that she didn't like to think how little time had actually passed.

She would have to thank the bear—no, Henry. She would have to thank Henry properly for the bell. It was clearly going to make life in an empty castle much more enjoyable.

Henry. She stopped eating and placed her hands against her warm cheeks. Her husband was a human, not a bear. It was a shocking new reality, one she still hadn't fully absorbed.

Who was he? And what was he doing living in this empty

castle? Surely he hadn't lived here alone before the enchantment? It was a strange enough home for a talking bear, but it would be stranger still for a lone human.

She'd never even heard of a castle in the mountains, but they couldn't be too far from the valley where her family lived. Even though the bear moved quickly, they had arrived at the castle before dark.

And now she understood the necessity of their speed. No wonder he had hurried them home given night was falling.

Thinking of her home made her wonder about her family. Had they received the bride price promised to them? Had her wishes from the night before reached them? It was strange to imagine her sisters and parents preparing for a move to Arcadia without her. It didn't really matter how close the castle was to the valley when her family wasn't going to be there anymore.

When she'd finished the food, she hesitated for only a moment before using the bell to fill her new wardrobe with gowns. When she flung open the walnut doors, she gasped at the array of luxurious material and beautiful designs. She could barely bring herself to touch them and choosing one to wear felt like an impossible task.

She had never obsessed over gowns and wealth like her sisters, but she still appreciated beauty, and she had never seen such dresses. Eventually she forced herself to choose one of the simpler ones, only to be delighted all over again at how easily she was able to get it on without assistance. Apparently the power that resided in the bell was of a practical as well as beautiful nature.

She blushed in earnest as she admired herself in the mirror, noticing how the folds of the dress enhanced the elegance of her shape. Here in the privacy of her room, she admitted that her request for new gowns wasn't solely about enjoying beautiful things. She had discovered her husband was really a man, and overnight she had become conscious of how she appeared to him.

Did Henry think her beautiful? Is that why he had chosen her? Or was it some other quality he saw in her?

The dispiriting realization that it might have been neither crept over her. She had quite possibly been the only girl in close vicinity who was miserable enough to consider such a proposal.

She didn't like that idea, but there was a good chance it was true. The valleys didn't offer a huge range of choice when it came to marriageable females.

Staring at herself in the mirror, Charlotte shook her head. It didn't matter what his reasons might have been. He was her husband, and he had already demonstrated his consideration and willingness to defend her against others. It was her turn to show him the same care he was showing her.

And to start with, that meant braving the castle that was his home. She cautiously opened the door of her new bedchamber, relieved to see that the stone corridor looked far less intimidating with daylight streaming in through a large window.

The overall effect was still stark and cold, though, and she remembered Henry's words from the day before. He had told her to restyle the castle to her taste, and with the bell, the task was simple. She didn't even have to worry about making mistakes, since she could easily fix them later.

Dashing back into the room, she retrieved the bell before gazing up and down the corridor, considering her options. Finally, she gave a decisive nod and rang it.

"Give all the corridors a central runner of thick red carpet, and add tapestries to the walls. Also some comfortable chairs."

Instantly, the space around her transformed. She gazed up at a stunning tapestry of geometric shapes in complementary shades of red and gold. It matched the carpet beneath her feet and the red upholstery on the elegant wooden chairs that had appeared beside the tapestry.

She smiled. Practicality and beauty. She could get used to having the bell at her disposal.

"Lottie?" The sound of her new nickname in the rumbly voice of the bear shot straight through her heart.

She had been afraid that in the light of day, seeing his enchanted shape, she would lose the sense of him as Henry. But the sound of the single word was enough to tie the two together. He might be wearing a different shape, but he was still her husband underneath.

"When I suddenly found myself walking on carpet, I realized you must be awake," he said with amusement in his voice.

"Do you like it?" she asked, knowing her tone made it clear she was proud of her initial effort.

"It's an instant improvement," he said promptly. "I don't know why I didn't do it a long time ago."

A draft sent shivers through Charlotte, and she lifted the bell again. "Warmth please, as well." She glanced at Henry as the crackle of a distant fire reached her ears and the air temperature rose around her. "I suppose you don't feel it with that thick coat. Please let me know if it gets too hot for you."

He shook his large head, his eyes intent. "I've taken you away from your home and your family. I want you to be comfortable here. Please don't worry about me."

"But how can I not?" she asked softly. "You're caught in a terrible enchantment." She straightened her shoulders. "I don't have any particular experience or skill, but we're family now. There must be some way I can help you."

"You are helping me. More than you know." His intent gaze speared into her, and she felt a flush of warmth that had nothing to do with the change in air temperature. Did her presence and companionship mean so much to him?

"I can do more," she said stubbornly. "Surely there's something more I can do."

Henry blinked and looked away, as if considering. Finally he nodded and turned back.

"If you really mean it, then there is something." He hesitated again, a smile spreading over his head. "Come with me. There's something I want to show you."

Holding back her curiosity with difficulty, Charlotte followed him down several corridors and up a flight of stairs. He stopped in front of a set of double doors that rivaled the front doors of the castle in size.

When he looked at her, she realized he wanted her to open them. Hurrying forward, she had to exert her full strength to pull them apart.

"I suppose having paws must make lots of things difficult," she said, breathless from the effort.

"I've worked out I can manage door handles. But it's difficult and awkward." He took several paces into the room and then turned to look at her. "But I can't handle books."

Charlotte gasped when she saw what filled the room inside. Despite her best efforts, a laugh burbled up inside her.

She turned to Henry. "That's a lot of books for someone who can't even pick them up."

Everywhere she looked, stacks of books were piled haphazardly, many of the piles taller than her. It was a large room—large enough she couldn't see its far reaches—but the entire thing seemed to be full of books.

Henry grinned ruefully. "I asked the bell to lead me to the library, and then I asked it to fill the room with a copy of every book found in any of the royal libraries. This is what I got."

If there was furniture in the room, it was too covered in books to be seen, with a single exception. The lone clear spot stood out like an oasis in the mess. A circle of lamps surrounded a small but thick rug, and the piles of books scattered around its edges were a much more manageable height. Realization filled her, followed by a pang of sorrow.

"This is where you usually spend your time at night," she said. "When you're a man."

The space was already cramped and unwelcoming, but she

could imagine it was even more so at night. It pained her to think of the many solitary hours he must have spent there.

He nodded. "As I said, large paws with even larger claws aren't ideal for holding books and turning pages."

"So you spend your nights reading and your days sleeping—or roaming the forest and valleys."

He nodded again. "I hope that somewhere in this vast trove of knowledge is a secret that will break my enchantment or aid me against the person who trapped me in it."

Charlotte raised her eyebrows at the mention of his enchantment—it was the first time he had spoken of someone else's involvement. But she was more immediately struck by a different aspect of his words.

"Except now you're spending your nights with me," she said. "You can't continue your research."

"Unless you're willing to help me," he said, sounding boyishly hopeful. "Not that you should feel any obligation to spend your days here. Even an hour or so would be an assistance."

"Of course I'll help you," Charlotte said quickly. "The bell meets all our practical needs, so there's nothing else demanding my time. Of course I should help my husband."

She gazed around the room again, her nose wrinkling. "But I think we need to make some changes first."

She paused, looking at him for permission, and he made a gesture of encouragement. Wrapping her hand around the bell in her pocket, she took her time shaping what she wanted in her mind. Once it was clear, she shook the bell.

From one blink to the next, the library in front of them transformed. The full length was now visible, the long space larger than any ballroom and stretching to enormous heights about them. Tall windows let in plenty of light, but every other inch of wall was covered in bookshelves, and at least three levels could be seen, accessed via a series of delicate stairs and layered balconies. The piles of books were gone, all the titles in neat rows on the shelves instead.

Charlotte's eyes lingered on the brocade curtains on the windows and the cozy reading nooks scattered around the main floor, many of them lit by lamps.

"That's better, don't you think?" she asked with satisfaction.

Henry's mouth had fallen open. "Infinitely!" He shook his head. "I think the godmothers like you better than me. Look what I got when I asked for a library, and you got this!"

Charlotte's lips twitched. "You should have been more specific in your request." She wandered to the closest shelf. "I directed that the books be arranged according to their piles, with the ones closest to your reading space at the front. So hopefully I haven't destroyed whatever organization system you were using."

"That was clever," he said approvingly. "I spent many weeks just finding titles of interest, so I'm glad all that work isn't lost."

"Do you know where I should start then?" she asked, gazing at the multitude of shelves and feeling overwhelmed at the task, despite the more welcoming environment.

Henry padded over to the closest shelf and examined it. "These are all the titles I had chosen to review next," he said with satisfaction. "We should start here."

Charlotte winced to see the number of books he was indicating.

The bear grimaced in response. "It's a wide range of topics. I didn't want to risk missing anything that might be of use." He gazed down the long room. "Although I'm sure I have. There are just so many books."

"To say the least." Charlotte ran a hand along one of the shelves before adopting a positive tone. "So it's a good thing you have me to take over for you." She glanced sideways at him. "Will you stay here with me?"

"If you'll have me." He gave her a look that seemed almost as uncertain as her own. "I don't wish to make you uncomfortable, but I would love to be part of the search still. Perhaps you could even read aloud if you find anything that might be of interest. Even if it's only distantly related. There might be some clue hidden somewhere that will mean something when combined with what I've already read."

Henry was clearly as uncertain as she had been as to whether his bear shape would change the rapport they had started to build the night before. She smiled at him as brightly as she could, hoping to convey that he was welcome to stay at her side no matter what his outside appearance was.

As she looked from the shape of the enormous white bear to the closest reading nook, her smile grew. Nothing about this scene fit her vague expectations from their wedding, but it was all so much more appealing than she had thought the evening before.

Logically, she was even more isolated than she had been in the valley—her company reduced to a single person. But it didn't feel the same. Being around Henry made her nerves fizz even as it filled her with a sense of contentment. There was no comparison with the presence of her sisters who had so obviously wished her elsewhere.

Soon they were settled in place, her in a comfortable armchair, and Henry curled up on the rug at her feet. He asked her to look particularly for any mention of people transformed into animals or the mythical mountain kingdom. She wanted to tell him that her cousins considered the mountain kingdom to be nothing but legend—as befitted a place that was supposed to lie east of the sun and west of the moon—but she couldn't scold him for seeking fairy stories when he was apparently living one. Those tales might be the exact ones that would hold a hint to his current situation.

The day passed easily, especially given the bell's prompt provision of requested food. It even cleared away the dishes.

"Where do you think they go?" Charlotte asked Henry from where she sat, her legs tucked beneath her.

He lifted his head from his place on the rug beside her.

"Are you afraid there's some hardworking soul somewhere receiving a steady supply of our dirty dishes?" he asked with a grin. "I'm fairly sure it's not anything like that. I think they just... cease to exist. They're not real plates. They're all part of the bell's power."

"Does that mean this isn't a real castle?" Charlotte wrinkled her brow. "That hurts my head."

"I recommend not giving it another thought," he said cheerfully. "Real or not, the castle keeps out the rain and wind."

"And it provides enough reading material for a lifetime," Charlotte added, gazing around them.

Henry gave a rumbling growl. "I don't have a lifetime."

Charlotte winced. "I'm sure we'll find something soon." She picked up another book. She had been skimming them, stopping when she found anything of potential interest and reading it aloud. But other than a story about eleven brothers who were turned into swans, there hadn't been anything that seemed relevant.

She had been excited by the story of the brothers, but according to the legend, they had been freed when their sister took a vow of silence and knit them all shirts from stinging nettles. The whole thing sounded hideously unpleasant, and she was afraid Henry might ask her to try it. But he rejected the idea before she even mentioned it, seeming certain it wasn't the answer to his situation.

As the light outside the windows finally began to fade, Henry excused himself. Charlotte didn't want to be left alone, but she was conscious that he had barely eaten all day, subsisting mainly on water which he had to lap from a dish. She didn't know what he ate in his bear form, and she didn't want to ask too many questions. Whatever practical life matters he needed to tend to, it was best he did them away from her.

She also could use some time to take care of the practical necessities, although she had never washed and changed into her nightgown so quickly in her life. Once again she was grateful for the bell's provision since the nightgown she found in her new wardrobe was far softer than anything she had worn before. Unlike the night before, she felt no discrepancy between her garment and the sheets as she slipped into bed.

This time, she didn't linger in bed with the candles lit. As cozy as the crackling fire was, she felt only eagerness to blow out her candle and be plunged into darkness.

CHARLOTTE

harlotte lay in bed, filled with anticipation, despite an entire day spent in Henry's company. And sure enough, within only a few minutes, her straining ears heard the sound of the door opening.

"Henry?" she called, the name slipping out before she could stop it. Despite her newfound knowledge, it was hard to shake the fear of such complete darkness.

"It's me," he said reassuringly. "I would never allow anyone else to come into this place and frighten you."

She felt instantly at ease, remembering that the darkness itself was a sign of the control he exerted over the castle thanks to the bell. Real or not, this castle was his domain.

During the day, they had spoken of the books and the things they discovered in them, their attention on his enchantment—although he had refused to give her details of how he had come to be trapped in it.

But she felt instinctively that those weren't topics for the night. Here, in their shared bed, they were just Henry and Lottie, beginning a marriage the wrong way round—getting to know each other after their vows instead of before.

Haltingly, she asked him about his childhood, and he spoke with warmth of loving parents and a younger sister. A pang of longing hit her at the way he talked about his sister. She had always dreamed of feeling that way about her sisters.

But she reminded herself that she had at least had Daisy, and when Henry returned her questions, she spoke of her old friend rather than her sisters by blood.

When their talking drifted slowly off, Charlotte lay there and listened to Henry's breathing shift to become slow and rhythmic as sleep claimed him. She had shared a room with her sisters for years but lying here beside her husband felt entirely different. Even if they were separated by the expanse of the bed, she could still feel his electrifying presence.

Only the previous night, the distance between them had felt safe, but now she found herself wishing she could roll closer. She could hear his breathing, but she wanted to feel the warmth of his body as well, as he lay close enough to touch.

She forced down the foolish thought. It was enough that she wasn't alone in this strange place. She would sleep, and in the morning, she would be reminded that far more than a stretch of empty blanket lay between them.

Eventually she slept, waking alone as she had the first morning. This time she hurried through her morning routine, however, eager to return to the library and Henry.

When she stepped into the corridor, he was waiting for her in his bear form.

"I wasn't sure if you knew the way to the library yet," he said in his deep voice, and she gave in to instinct and wrapped her arms around his broad neck, resting her cheek against his soft fur.

He stiffened for a moment before relaxing and pressing back against her, which she took as a bear's version of returning the hug.

"Thank you," she said, wishing she could find the words to

express everything in her heart. From the first moment of their meeting he had shown more consideration for her than her own family.

When she let go and stepped back, she wondered if she should feel embarrassed by her display. She couldn't muster the emotion, however. Somehow it was much easier to express affection to Henry in this form than in his true one.

They spent another companionable day in the library, although they found nothing of import. Charlotte knew she should feel impatient to free Henry, but it was hard to maintain a sense of impatience in the face of such contentment.

As on the previous day, Henry disappeared before the sun set, and she was able to watch him go without a qualm. Already the castle was becoming a warm and friendly place, and she struggled to remember why she had found it so unwelcoming at first.

Again he appeared quickly at night, and again they spoke of their lives and dreams, speaking as if there was no enchantment or mountain isolation. They might have been any two people getting to know one another.

He told her he had always dreamed of a big family, and although it made her cheeks furnace hot, Charlotte agreed. By silent agreement they kept the topic abstract—for all the intimacy of their nights together, the barrier of Henry's enchantment still lay between them. But it still thrilled her to know they agreed although their motivations were different.

Henry wanted multiple children because of the love he had received from his parents and sister—he wanted more of the warmth that had saturated his childhood. Whereas Charlotte wanted the chance to make a different family from the one she had grown up in. She was determined she would never stand by and see one of her children excluded.

Days and nights passed in the same manner—so many days that Charlotte was vaguely conscious her wedding had been weeks ago and spring had reached the valleys in earnest. Spring had certainly bloomed inside Charlotte.

She hadn't dreamed her strange marriage could bring such joy and contentment. From the beginning she had felt seen and known by Henry, but the nights of sharing their hearts in the darkness had deepened that sense into a surety. The only thing that marred Charlotte's happiness was her growing desire to be rid of the barriers that still held them apart. The gulf in the middle of their vast bed had never felt so large.

Eventually there came a morning when Henry waited outside her door with a different air from usual.

"I'm sorry, Lottie," he said without preamble, "but I can't read with you today. I'm heading into the forest, and I fear I'll be gone most of the day. Will you be all right on your own?"

Charlotte wanted to protest that she didn't want to be alone. For a second she even considered asking if she could accompany him. But no matter how comfortable she had become with him as a person, her husband spent his days as a bear. There were parts of his life she couldn't share.

"Of course I'll be fine," she said instead. "I don't want to risk missing anything important in the books, though, so I'll wait for you to return to resume the research."

He thanked her, but he seemed distracted and eager to be gone. After his departure, Charlotte wandered listlessly, realizing her feet had taken her along her usual route. But when she arrived in the doorway of the library, she couldn't bring herself to go in. The library was her haven within the castle—a place of comfort and enjoyment—but it felt empty without Henry.

"Stop this," she said aloud to herself. "Since when have you become someone uncomfortable in your own company?"

Many of her most enjoyable days in the valley had been the ones when she slipped away and roamed the forest alone. She refused to become a person who couldn't cope with being alone.

Turning her back on the library, she decided to go exploring.

With the bell safely in her pocket, she knew she could always find a way back if she needed one. But it was past time she discovered the extent of her new home.

Everywhere she went, she found the same red carpet underfoot, and the corridors were lined with variations of the same tapestry and sprinklings of identical chairs.

"Beautiful and practical, but limited," she muttered to herself after viewing the same tapestry for the fifth time. Apparently the bell's power wasn't as vast as it had seemed.

The carpet and decorations still achieved a positive effect, however. Even impersonal, repetitive decoration was better than a whole building full of nothing but stark, cold stone, so she was far from complaining.

"But why is it so large?" she mused as she looked into yet another empty room. "If Henry used the bell to create a home for himself after the enchantment, why did he ask for such an enormous one? Or had the castle sprung into being as part of the original enchantment? Did it mirror a real place, like when Henry had asked for a copy of the books that already existed in the royal libraries?"

The thought stilled her steps, and she gazed at the walls around her with new eyes. Was she roaming a copy of a real place that had once featured in Henry's life? If so, what had brought him to a castle? Was it the castle of his home kingdom?

She had always heard that both Rangmere's capital and its palace were austere places of gray stone. Never having visited them herself, she had no idea if she was now living in an enchanted version of Queen Ava's castle.

She continued her exploration, but everything she saw had a new fascination. It became a game to guess at the original purpose of the rooms. Bare of furniture, many of them looked foreign, but she could make guesses from their shape and location.

Opening another door, she stepped into the first room that

wasn't empty. Stretching along the length of the room was a long dining table of heavy, dark wood. It stood alone except for a single elaborate chair at its head.

Charlotte stood transfixed, but it wasn't because of the unusual presence of furniture or even from the mental image of Henry eating alone after sundown each evening, the long table stretching emptily before him. Her attention was caught by an enormous portrait hanging on the far wall, facing the head of the table.

The brunette woman was both young and beautiful, and she was dressed in a filmy gown of blue. Her face shone with a gentle strength that gave her an appealing quality that was hard to put into words. She evoked a protective instinct that was unfamiliar to Charlotte as the youngest in her family.

She wanted to shake off the feeling, to laugh at herself. After all, this woman looked several years older than Charlotte and from the quality of her dress, she didn't need anything that a girl from the valleys could supply.

But the woman wasn't so easily put aside. Her stomach churned as the image of Henry's solitary meals soured in her mind. Before her arrival, the entire castle had been unadorned. Henry hadn't added a single piece of furniture or decoration outside of the library—except for this table and this single painting.

How many nights had he sat here, gazing at the woman in the portrait? What sort of protective instincts had she roused in him?

Charlotte ran from the room, slamming the door behind her, her heart pounding. But the image of the painting had been burned into her mind. She might have closed the door, but she could still see it in front of her eyes.

Charlotte was playacting as a princess in this empty castle, but the woman in the painting clearly belonged in such a setting. The painter had captured a poise that Charlotte envied but also a light of kindness that only made her feel sick.

The woman in that painting was one it would be easy to love. She pressed her hand against her stomach, her nausea surging.

She knew something had compelled Henry to marry her. Even without knowing his secrets, he had hinted as much. There was something he needed from her, and it was more than mere companionship.

Had this enchantment separated Henry from the woman he loved? And then, even worse, had it forced him into marriage with someone else? Had he sat here, night after night, longing for his lost love and trying to strengthen himself to put her aside and marry another?

Before their marriage, Henry had been earnest in assuring her that it was a legal marriage only. And even after she discovered the truth of his enchantment, he had repeated those promises. She had assumed his words were for her sake, and they had been gratefully received. In the growing relationship between them, it had been easy to forget about their early intentions. She had even started gathering the courage to tell him she no longer needed such distance between them.

But now the words took on a different light. Was Henry's determination to keep his distance not about Charlotte's comfort but his own emotions?

She stumbled down the corridor, heading back to more familiar parts of the castle. But now everywhere she walked, she was followed by the specter of Henry's life. The curious interest from earlier was gone, replaced with a burning in her chest as she imagined Henry walking identical halls with the woman by his side.

She stopped in the middle of a corridor, recognizing the sensation for what it was. Jealousy.

"He's mine!" she growled at the empty air around her. "Henry is my husband, and I'm his wife."

The words brought her little comfort, however. Henry had committed his life to her, but she admitted to herself that she wanted more. She loved him, and she wanted his love. She wanted a real marriage. But Henry had never promised her that. They had never so much as touched each other while he was in his human form.

Her queasiness grew as she realized what she had to do. If he had only married her because of the enchantment, then once it was broken, she would have no choice but to offer him an annulment. She couldn't allow him to be tied to her for the rest of his life just because he had been trapped in an enchantment. She cared about him too much to do that to him.

She told herself she was overreacting and leaping to assumptions. But no matter how hard she tried, she couldn't shake the thoughts free.

All the time she had been exploring, she had been listening with one ear for Henry's return. But now she dreaded the sounds of the bear's arrival. She needed time to settle her emotions, to find a way to mask the sickness that swirled in her stomach.

She wandered slowly back to more familiar parts of the castle, running her hand along the small pieces of furniture that lined the way. The backs of the chairs somehow always remained dust free, although she never cleaned them, and the small side tables that paired with some of them remained equally spotless.

Still listless, unable to marshal her thoughts into a proper course, she slid out the small drawer in one of the tables. It would be empty, of course, but she couldn't keep her restless fingers still.

Except it wasn't empty. Charlotte froze, her heartbeat speeding up in contrast to the stillness of her limbs. Inside the drawer was a small oval frame protecting an unfamiliar painting. But while Charlotte had never seen that particular artwork, she instantly recognized the face and shoulders depicted. The woman from the full-length portrait in the dining room.

Slamming the drawer closed, Charlotte staggered backward, stopping only when she collided with the opposite wall. She wanted to scrub her mind clean and forget she had ever seen it lurking in there on the route between her room and the library—the route she had walked so many times with Henry and that he must have walked so often alone, coming to wait for her.

The full portrait had been painful enough, but it was a relic of a time before she came to the castle. Henry did not sit there alone at night anymore. But this was different. The side table had only appeared after she had requested it with the bell. And yet, secreted inside it was a remembrance of this woman.

Unable to help herself, Charlotte hurried down the corridor, making for the next side table. Was it really possible that of all the drawers in the castle, she had happened to open the one containing the picture?

As soon as she pulled open the next drawer, her nebulous fears crystallized. In this one, too, sat a small portrait showing a woman's head and shoulders. She slammed that drawer closed as well and hurried to the next one and the next. In every drawer she opened, she found the mystery woman's eyes smiling kindly up at her.

The sickness in her stomach surged, and she sank to the floor against the corridor wall, tears running down her face. Earlier that day she had recognized the castle must be a copy of a real place—it made no sense otherwise. But she had only thought of Henry at the center of it. She had been wrong, though. It was this strange woman who lived at the heart of the castle Charlotte thought of as home. Even now, she had to be out there somewhere in the castle's original.

Part of her wanted to confront her husband immediately and demand the truth of the woman's identity. But the rest of her shrank from the idea. Even in her head, she sounded shrill and ungrateful. He hadn't demanded she reveal her own painful past —he had merely provided a safe space and waited until she opened up of her own volition. She owed it to him to offer him the same courtesy. His past was his own until he chose to share it, and despite what her feelings shouted, there was no betrayal to confront him over. The fact he might once have had feelings for another woman—in the past before he ever even met Charlotte—indicated no act of disloyalty to his marriage. And how could she accuse him of loving someone else now, when he spent night and day by her side, doing everything possible for her comfort?

She would have to ask him eventually. She couldn't live not knowing. But she couldn't do it while her emotions were so out of control. If she did, she would say something she would later regret. She would hurt Henry and that thought was the most unbearable.

Even as a bear, he was kind, his gentleness only broken by the strength of his protective instinct toward her. He treated her with respect, valuing her taste and opinions, and seeking out her company. And despite the direness of his situation, he laughed and joked with her, making it easy to spend time in his presence. Of course she was in love with him. She'd been a little in love with him ever since that first night when she'd discovered he was a man.

In these past nights, when they had lain side by side and shared their hearts, she had secretly longed for more. If he had broached the expanse of bed that lay between them and reached for her, she would have reached back.

But he had not done so.

Charlotte had assumed it was his promises holding him back. She had taken comfort and joy in the camaraderie and understanding growing between them, assuming it would gradually lead to more. But now she faced the reality that her husband might have no desire for a true marriage between them.

Time passed although she didn't track it. Eventually the growling of her stomach roused her, and she managed to get herself back to her room, even forcing herself to eat as the sun began to set. But as the last of the daylight faded, there was no sign of a white bear, and for the first time, Charlotte faced the possibility of a night on her own.

The prospect pulled her emotions into line more effectively than anything else. She couldn't endure this life without Henry. Just the thought of it was horrifying. But if she was going to continue to spend her days and nights at his side, she had to talk to him about her discovery. And to do that, she had to first master her new emotions.

She crawled into the sheets with steely determination, but she felt her control tremble as she blew out the candle and solid darkness descended. Every part of her was tense, listening for the sound of her door opening.

And, sure enough, it came as expected, only minutes after she had extinguished the candle.

"I'm sorry I'm so late back," Henry's now-familiar voice said into the dark.

Despite Charlotte's resolutions, her eyes immediately over-flowed, silent tears tracking down her cheeks. The mattress moved slightly as Henry climbed into his side of the bed.

He said something else, but Charlotte didn't hear it over the beating of her heart. Her tears increased, betraying her into a small sob.

Henry instantly froze.

"Lottie?" He sounded worried. "Did something happen while I was gone? Are you hurt?" He shifted slightly toward her and then away again. "Curse this darkness!" he muttered with violent emotion.

More sobs escaped, Charlotte's emotions flowing out of control.

"Lottie," he said helplessly. "Talk to me! Please!"

She tried to form words, but the attempt only made her cry harder. Finally, with a muttered exclamation, as if driven past bearing, he closed the space between them.

Cautiously his hands reached out and, as she had predicted,

her own reached back of their own volition. His fingers found hers, and he squeezed them, seeming to take courage that she wasn't drawing back.

"Lottie," he said again, sounding almost as pained as she felt.

Her heart expanded, the fresh sign of her husband's care only making the pain worse. She sobbed more loudly.

With another exclamation, he closed the last of the distance between them, gathering her into his arms.

Shock stopped Charlotte's tears, although a few sniffles still escaped. The feel of his strong arms around her was like nothing she had experienced before, enclosing her in an immediate sense of safety. But at the same time, it also made her senses thrill, sensation running through every part of her.

"Don't cry, Lottie," he whispered into her hair. "It hurts me to hear you cry. I'm sorry that I left you."

She rested her head against his shoulder and tried to master the shudders that were all that was left of the sobs.

"Did something happen while I was gone?" he repeated. "Did you injure yourself?"

She shook her head against him, knowing it still wasn't safe for her to speak of either her feelings or the woman in the portrait. Her tears might have stopped, but her heart still raged out of control.

"It's just foolishness," she finally managed to say. "Please ignore it."

His arms tightened, and she was secretly glad he hadn't ignored her tears. After the revelations of the day, she knew it was wrong of her, but she couldn't help the way she thrilled at being held in his arms.

If she lay still, she could imagine for a moment that theirs was an ordinary marriage and Henry was truly hers.

"It's all right, Lottie," he murmured against her hair. "You're safe here. I won't let anything happen to you."

She didn't doubt his words. That was the character of her

husband. He might be full of secrets, but they were not ones of his making, and he would never swerve from the promises he'd made. He had promised to take her into his family and protect her, and he would never stop doing that. If he was ever going to be free, she would have to give him his freedom.

But still she couldn't bring herself to pull away from him. In that moment, there was no future, only the present. And in the present, she was his wife, she was in need of comfort, and she would accept the comfort he was offering. Perhaps tomorrow she would have gathered herself enough to speak to him safely.

Falling asleep within the circle of his arms was far easier than she could have imagined, and her sleep was deeper and more peaceful than she had anticipated after the upheavals of the day.

But, as always, when she woke, the bed was cold, and she was alone.

GWEN

*C*aution told Gwen she should wait at least until the next day before doing anything else that might draw her mother's attention. But that instinct was balanced against the object that seemed to burn in her pocket.

How often did her mother visit the secret treasury? And if she did visit, would she notice something was missing? Would she know Gwen had taken it?

The fear of discovery overcame her sense of caution.

Mother and daughter had never been in the habit of eating the midday meal together, and so Gwen took it on a tray in her bedchamber. She found sitting at the small table by one of her windows less depressing than eating alone in a formal dining room. And that meant a servant always arrived at midday to deliver the meal.

It wasn't always delivered by the same servant, so she waited by the window, shoulders tense as the minutes ticked by on her clock. She was much closer to some of the servants than others, and there was only one she wanted to see that day.

The door finally opened, causing Gwen's anxiety to peak.

Alma appeared, carefully balancing the tray as she closed the door behind her.

Gwen slumped down in relief before her eyes zeroed in on the closed door. Her eyebrows arched.

None of the servants ever shut the door when delivering the lunch tray. If Alma was doing so now, it was with a purpose. Which meant it wasn't coincidence that she was the servant who had appeared on this of all days.

"What did you hear?" Gwen asked as Alma approached and deposited the tray on the round table.

The servant woman looked briefly back at the closed door before sighing.

"You were outside? In the evening? What do you think your mother will do if she hears?"

"She hasn't heard?" Gwen should have felt relieved, but she already had larger misdeeds hanging over her head.

"Princess Gwen." Alma sighed, her manner more motherly than Queen Celandine's had ever been. "You are fortunate. If it had been different guards that found you…" She shook her head.

Gwen's brow creased. "Are you saying they had a reason not to report me?"

"Did I say they didn't make a report?" Alma snapped, only to rub a hand against her forehead as if overcome with exhaustion and anxiety. "How do you think I know of it?"

"I don't understand," Gwen said slowly, trying to make sense of Alma's cryptic words. "You said my mother didn't know of it yet, and now you're saying they did make a report."

Alma straightened and gave a rough chuckle. "Do you think the guards who patrol the grounds report directly to the queen? For someone who grew up here, you have an odd notion of how a palace works."

"Oh." Gwen frowned. "Yes, I suppose…"

The situation still didn't make sense to her, but Alma seemed irritated by the questioning, and she didn't want to put her in a bad mood before she got to much more important questions.

"My mother intends to marry me off," Gwen said, getting straight to the point. "Do you know of that too?"

Alma's eyes widened. "She told you about him?"

Gwen gasped, clutching Alma's arm. "You know who it is? She wouldn't tell me, except to say that he's from beyond the mountains."

Alma grimaced, her expression suggesting she had made a mistake. Gwen's suspicion hardened into certainty. The captive servants—her only allies in the palace—knew a great deal more than they had ever revealed to her.

She pushed aside the feeling of betrayal. There would be room for that later. For the moment, she had to make the most of this brief opportunity. She tightened her hold on Alma's arm, not letting go when the woman tried to gently tug herself free.

"What do you know, Alma?" she pleaded. "You have to tell me!"

Alma's expression of unease morphed into one of sorrow and compassion.

"Please, Alma," Gwen whispered, tears coming to her eyes.

She didn't have to dig for the emotion—it was already there. Her desperation for answers went deeper than even Alma could guess.

Alma opened her mouth and then closed it again, her eyes sliding away from Gwen's before coming back to her face. She was clearly torn.

"We didn't like to do it," she whispered, making Gwen's fingers dig tighter into her arm. "The few of us who know have often debated if we should..." She sighed. "But it's dangerous, and you're not the only youngster we have to consider."

"Youngster?" Gwen managed a smile although it felt distant and strange on her lips.

Alma smiled softly, finally removing her arm from Gwen's grip and taking her hands instead.

"To one as old as me, you're young still, Princess. But so is Miriam, and others like her. Surely you can understand our hesitance. We have seen all you endure, but you are still—"

"My mother's daughter." The words slipped from Gwen's lips, burning on their way out.

"That doesn't make it right!" Alma said with muted ferocity. "What sort of mother drugs her own child? It's almost enough to make the rumors about the mountain people seem true."

"What?" Gwen stared at Alma. "My mother drugs me?" Her voice rose on the final words, and she glanced guiltily at the closed door.

Alma bit her lip. "I didn't...You mustn't...Princess, you mustn't say anything! There's no one else who knows about it, so if the queen finds out you know the truth, she'll know who told you. You must promise me—"

"She drugs me!" Gwen repeated, at a quieter volume but with no less heat. "How often? Why?"

But even as she asked, she already knew the answer, at least to the first question. Her unnaturally deep slumber every night had seemed unnatural. But even knowing her mother, she had suspected illness rather than deliberate poison. Why had she never drawn the connection with the sleepiness that always overtook her after the evening meal?

She could only conclude it was because it had been her reality for so long. And she sometimes felt sleepy after a large lunch as well.

It was all excuses, though. She should have been able to feel the difference.

"Where is it?" she asked, new steel in her voice she'd never heard in it before. "Where does she have you put the drugs?"

Tears ran down Alma's cheeks. "I never wanted to do it,

Princess Gwen. I swear it. But if I refused her order, she would punish the others. You do understand, don't you?"

"Never mind that." Gwen still spoke in the hard new tone. "Where are the drugs?"

"In your drink," Alma admitted softly. "It's always in your drink."

Gwen groaned. All her efforts to eat less had been pointless.

"What else aren't you telling me?" she asked, suddenly remembering the rest of Alma's words. "You said something about a rumor about my people. What rumor?"

Alma hesitated, clearly nervous, but Gwen could see she was wavering. The fevered light in Gwen's eyes wasn't scaring her—quite the opposite. The longer she gazed at Gwen's determined expression, the more hopeful her own face grew. Gwen just needed to convince her old friend that she was serious this time.

"I have to get away from her." Gwen's voice came out hoarse, although she'd been aiming for strong. "I always dreamed of escape, but I always thought it was nothing more than a fantasy. This is different, though. This time I'll do anything to get away."

Alma stiffened, her face closing up. Whatever she had wanted to hear from Gwen, it wasn't that.

But it was too late for Gwen to take back the words, and she didn't know if she wanted to do so. She had made the declaration as much for her own sake as to convince Alma, and she had no idea what the woman had been hoping to hear instead.

Alma let Gwen's hands drop, stepping back and bowing formally. "I apologize, Your Highness. I hope you can forgive me for my role in this. And I hope you will see fit to keep our secret."

"Alma," Gwen cried. "Please! Will you not help me?"

Alma hesitated. "I think that's all the help I can provide. After all, I'm securely locked away each night. Just like you."

For a second she held Gwen's eyes, a message in her gaze that the princess didn't understand. Then she left, gently closing the door behind her.

Gwen stared at it for at least a minute, trying to make sense of the interaction. Her thoughts were too muddled to think clearly, and her emotions were even more of a mess. Should she feel gratitude to Alma for telling her about the sleeping potion or anger at her betrayal in keeping it a secret all these years? And why had she refused to tell Gwen anything further?

Or had she...? What had she been hinting at?

Gwen's circling thoughts slowed, focusing. Something in Alma's eyes had been pleading with Gwen to understand, but what exactly had she wanted her to grasp?

Just like you. The words echoed in her mind, and Gwen drew in her breath sharply as she realized she hadn't spoken of her recent discovery. Alma knew Gwen was locked in every night. Were the servants the ones to turn the key, just as they were the ones to place the potion in the drink they served?

Betrayal surged up again, but Gwen tamped it down once more. If they locked her room, it was at the queen's command. Her mother was the one hiding things from her, not Alma. Alma was locked up herself.

Gwen's mind circled around that thought. Alma had mentioned it specifically, although she knew Gwen was well aware of the captives' predicament. Almost as if she wanted to remind Gwen of their limitations.

What was it she had said at the start? She had mentioned rumors of the mountain people as if the servants didn't know the truth of those rumors—even after so many years in the heart of the mountain kingdom.

The two thoughts came together in Gwen's mind, making a conclusion that seemed so obvious she couldn't think why she hadn't seen it from the start. Alma hadn't been refusing Gwen information so much as goading her to go in search of it for herself. And she had been telling her where to start. Nighttime.

Everything pointed to the hours of darkness. And now Gwen knew why those hours were always lost to her. Which meant she could reclaim them. The answers were finally in front of her—she just needed to work out how to make it through an evening meal without drinking and without her mother noticing it.

Her fork clattered against her plate, and Gwen could barely restrain a wince. Years of discomfort during the meals she shared with her mother hadn't prepared her for her current level of tension. At any moment she expected her mother to stand up and accuse her of not drinking. Would she turn on the servants immediately or wait to order Gwen's punishment first?

A hundred times she had reconsidered her plan, wondering if she could truly put others at risk alongside herself. But no matter how many times she hesitated, she always returned to the same truth. Knowing what she did now, she couldn't sit there and drink the sleeping draft. She couldn't placidly accept a forced marriage and a lifetime of misery.

A curly-haired face appeared in her mind, the warm eyes laughing at her. She drew strength from Easton's encouraging expression, even if every part of his image in her mind was imagined. She hadn't dreamed up his personality and character, and she knew he would tell her to fight. He would never passively accept the queen's schemes—the evidence of that was in his disappearance.

But he also couldn't be dead. Gwen couldn't believe it—she wouldn't. If this worked, if she succeeded in escaping at last, she would find him, whatever it took.

The thought bolstered her as nothing else had done, and she lifted her goblet to her mouth, tipping it back against her firmly closed lips before taking another bite of food.

Her stomach roiled, but she forced herself to eat well, clearing her plate. If her mother saw how much she was eating, she was less likely to notice she wasn't actually drinking.

Alma appeared to remove the dishes after each course, taking Gwen's cup away and replacing it with another. She was protecting Gwen as she had on the night when the princess had attempted not to eat, and Gwen recognized it for the apology it was.

She didn't know which course's drink held the potion—maybe they all did—so she drank nothing. Her mouth was growing drier and drier, but she ignored the discomfort, intent on her purpose.

When her mother finally signaled the end of the meal, rising with her normal goodnight platitudes to her daughter, Gwen could hardly believe she had succeeded. Was she really about to experience the night hours?

Walking back to her room, she could already feel the difference. Her overly full stomach gave her a slow feeling that could be described as sleepy. But it was nothing like the irresistible pull to sleep that she usually felt. How had she mistaken that sensation for the ordinary response to a full stomach?

But she already knew the answer. Lack of experience. Gwen might have lived for more than twenty years, but she lacked experience in far too many things. Her life had been bound by walls of stone for far too long.

Waiting in her room felt impossible—at the lightest jump she might bounce off the walls or ceiling. But somehow she endured, even lying in her bed and feigning even breaths. She didn't know if her jailer usually checked on her before turning the key.

But when the grating sound of a key turning in a lock finally sounded, it came without the sound of the door opening first. After so many years, no one doubted the effect of the drugs.

Gwen leaped out of bed and laced on her boots, fumbling with the ties thanks to her trembling fingers. It only took seconds to retrieve the master key from her dressing table, but she made herself wait longer, peeking out at the darkening sky.

She preferred not to wait until full dark, but she didn't want to risk running into whoever had just come by.

Finally she let herself turn the key in the lock, slipping out into the corridor before locking the door behind her. She doubted anyone rattled the handle in the night, but if they did, they would find it locked as it should be.

She had thought her heart was beating fast when she snuck through the corridors with the girl from the city, but it was nothing to how she felt now. While it only took her minutes to reach the outside, it felt like hours, and she was surprised to discover the last of the light lingering in the sky still. It felt as if enough hours had passed that it should have been midnight already.

Hurrying down the familiar paths of the garden, she considered the best place to conceal herself. Recent experience told her the palace grounds were actively patrolled, even at this hour, and she needed somewhere to conceal herself until the early hours.

Deciding on a place where tall hedges hid a bench seat from view, Gwen settled herself to wait. With the sun beneath the horizon, the last of the light was leaving the sky fast.

An itch made her scratch her leg, but it was immediately followed by one in her other leg. She scratched at that one, too, but it did little to reduce the strange ache which lingered just below her skin.

Her left arm took up the sensation, followed by her middle, and Gwen jumped to her feet. Almost dancing in her efforts to scratch herself all over, Gwen writhed and squirmed until a deep tearing made her freeze.

She was coming apart—she could feel it—tearing all the way up her body in a horrible sensation no person should ever feel. Why wasn't it hurting? She should be in agony as her final moments passed too quickly.

But no blood appeared, and no pain either. Instead, she dropped to the ground, landing on all fours as her eyes involuntarily closed. Dizziness made the world around her grow distant, her ears ringing and skin tingling.

And then, just as suddenly as it had begun, it ended. All that was left was a strange feeling of being far too large for her own skin. She felt…enormous.

Her eyes snapped open. Sure enough, she was looking at the garden from an unfamiliar vantage point. She looked down at herself and would have screamed if shock hadn't robbed her of all sound.

She was white. And covered in fur. And a bear.

CHARLOTTE

*W*hen Charlotte left her room, there was no white bear waiting in the corridor, and her heart contracted almost as painfully as it had the day before. On trembling legs, she ran to the library, but when she pushed open the door, he was waiting there, one of his unnaturally human smiles on his face.

"It feels an age since we were here together, Lottie," he said, "instead of just a day. I hope your throat is feeling better for the rest. It must be tiring to read aloud so much."

She blinked away tears, trying to find the words to reassure him that she didn't mind the reading. But all she could focus on was the way her heart leaped and fluttered in her chest when he called her Lottie—the name that belonged only to him.

She had once responded warmly to her father's affectionate nickname for her, but that had been a feeling of familiarity and the comfort of family. For weeks she had told herself she felt similarly for Henry, but now she had accepted the truth. When he spoke her name, it was an entirely different type of warmth that she felt—all fast heartbeats and a flush that made her turn her face away in case he saw the red in her cheeks.

He was in his bear form now, but all she could think about was the way it had felt to have his arms around her, and she longed for darkness to arrive so he could hold her again. But would he do so?

He had responded to her pain with comfort—something she could see he had done from the beginning. She would be foolish to read more into it than that. And she didn't want to compel his affection through pity.

One thing was clear—if just hearing him speak her name could overset her so badly, she hadn't yet gained the equanimity she needed before raising the topic of his past and what it meant for their future together.

"You're still unhappy," he said softly, making her startle.

"How could I be?" she asked. "You give me everything I ask for." It was a non-answer, and they both knew it.

"My godmother object provides any physical item you desire," he said, "but can possessions make a person happy? It has never seemed so to me. The bell cannot provide you with friends or family. You are lonely."

He had seen her grief the night before after a day alone in the castle and come to the wrong conclusion, but she didn't deny the charge. He was right in one way—just not in the way he thought. She did feel an aching loneliness, but not for the lack of family and friends. It was a different relationship with him that she longed for. She was lonely for his love.

"It's my fault," he continued. "I brought you here and have kept you day after day in the library with nothing to do but read. It's not the life you thought I was offering when I proposed. The Palace of Light must be nothing like this castle."

She remembered with an effort that she had once thought her marriage would take her to the fabled home of the High King. It felt like a long time since her dreams had changed.

"I know you can't take me there," she said, needing to say something. "I don't hold it against you."

"No, I can't take you there." He sounded defeated and sad, and she wondered with horror if he'd lain awake the night before trying to think how to fix her sadness. "But that doesn't mean you can never leave here," he concluded.

Shocked, Charlotte stared at him, frozen in place. "L...Leave?" she asked, horrified. Was he sending her away?

"Certainly." He sounded even sadder, as if he had mistaken her horror for shocked delight. "Not permanently, of course. I need you yet a little longer. But I can see no reason why you couldn't visit your family for a short while." He managed a smile although it looked strained. "I understand it's a common practice for new wives."

Her heart slowed, no longer feeling as if it would beat out of her chest. He wasn't sending her away forever. But she couldn't be entirely easy either. He had said he needed her only a little longer. Was the time she could stay by his side already drawing to a close?

"I...I don't know," she said, her mouth dry and her thoughts tangled. "I...I should think on it."

"You don't need to feel bad about going," he said gently. "It need only extend our situation by a few days, and there's nothing in that."

A few days? She tried to make sense of his words. He spoke as if he needed her for a specific length of time. So if she left, she wouldn't be losing any time with him.

Her first reaction had been to reject his suggestion, fearing what might be behind it. But now that he'd explained more fully, it didn't seem like such a bad idea. She desperately needed to sort out her emotional turmoil so she could have a frank conversation with him. Wouldn't it be easier to calm the raging storm inside her if she could have some space from him?

"Yes," she gasped, meeting his concerned eyes. "Yes, please. I would like to go to my family."

He nodded slowly.

"Can we leave immediately?" she asked.

"Leave now? This morning?" He came closer, his expression growing even more concerned.

At the hint of pain in his eyes she nearly crumpled and said she wouldn't go. But she couldn't weaken. She had to leave. She couldn't stay near him while there was such a weight between them, but neither was she ready for the necessary conversation. This was the best option open to her. She would leave him briefly and when she returned, she would be honest with him, even if she still didn't feel ready.

"If it's possible," she said. "Will you take me?" She suddenly remembered they had to be in Arcadia already. "Or can the bell send me to them?"

"I will carry you to them," he said. "And we can leave as soon as you're ready."

"I'm ready now. There's nothing I need to take. If my family has disposed of the things I left behind, I can easily borrow items from my sisters."

He hesitated still, but after another glance at her troubled expression, he nodded. "Very well. Let us leave."

GWEN

The minutes that followed Gwen's transformation were hazy. But eventually reality intruded over the panic and shock that robbed her of coherent thought. As impossible as the situation seemed, she had to accept the truth. She was no longer a human but a white bear.

She had discovered the secret concealed by the darkness, and it was nothing like she had imagined. Her mother must have been concealing Gwen's condition from not only Gwen herself but the entire court. She wouldn't want the kingdom knowing her daughter and only heir transformed into a bear at night. And if Gwen herself had known, she would have told someone—it would have been her ticket to escape from the virtual prison of being her mother's heir.

Or perhaps she wouldn't have mentioned it to anyone. Perhaps she would simply have made for the mountains at sunset one evening. As a human, the snow-covered peaks promised only death, but in her new form, she could find a way across.

The thought stilled her involuntary pacing for a moment. Her huge gait and heavy paws made small work of the constrained section of garden, but she couldn't hold herself still for any length of time.

Her first assumption had been that her transformation was the secret. But if that was true, why did the captives need to be locked away at night? And why did the courtiers talk of keeping a secret from the princess? If she was the secret, why would a girl from the city speak with fear in her voice of needing to be home by sundown? And how had her mother's guards found a pass through the mountains when the generations before them had failed?

Gwen took off through the gardens, her new shape making subtle movement difficult. She lumbered down the paths no matter how delicately she tried to step, but she had to test her theory. If she was right, then...

Her new ears picked up the sound of footsteps far earlier than her human ears would have done. And her nose detected a scent she didn't recognize. Someone unfamiliar was approaching her down one of the gravel paths.

Pushing through several bushes, she retreated until she found a place where she could watch the path while keeping her giant frame out of sight. As she waited, fresh fear washed over her.

She felt entirely like herself, her normal mind and personality merely trapped inside a new body. But what if the instincts of a true bear lurked beneath the surface? How would she react to the sight of another person? Would she be overcome by a desire to attack them?

The sounds reaching her ears made her frown, her thick lips pulling strangely against uncomfortably sharp teeth. The footsteps didn't sound as she had expected. The gait was off and the sound too loud.

She surged forward, peering between branches as two shapes came into view. Sight of them froze her in place, her breath stopping as her theory was confirmed.

She had suspected what she would find, but it still took her breath away to see two white bears—looking just as she knew she must now look—walking toward her, one after the other.

The two bears stopped, the one in front twisting to frown at the one behind.

"Did you hear something?" he asked in a gravelly voice that still sounded strangely familiar to Gwen's ears.

"Just one of the other patrols," the second bear answered, and Gwen instinctively knew their identity.

The two guards who had forced her back into her room were now patrolling the grounds in the form of bears. The earth beneath her feet felt soft and unstable, and she looked down to make sure she wasn't sinking into quicksand. But the gravel beneath her feet was steady. It was only everything she knew of her world that was shaking.

It wasn't just the princess who turned into a bear at night. Others did as well. Potentially the entire palace.

This was how her mother's people had found a way to get across the mountains and why no one from the city could make use of the path they had forged. The trading delegations must have traveled at night, their frailer human forms using the day to sleep.

What had triggered such a terrible enchantment? And how long had it been in place? It couldn't have existed for generations or some hint of it would have found its way into the storybooks and the kingdom's lore.

Easton's disappearance. The answer appeared in Gwen's mind already fully formed and obvious. As a young child she had been fully human—she must have been because she had the occasional memory of waking in the night or staying up past sundown. And she had definitely been human that first night locked in the dark closet.

Gwen shivered. Memories of that night weren't easy to forget. She'd barely slept, and the hours had felt like days. When the glass of juice arrived on the second night, she hadn't known if her mother had given way to compassion or if she was merely prolonging Gwen's suffering. When she slept so soundly after drinking it, she had assumed it was due to the exhaustion and weakness from her long ordeal.

But it had been neither compassion nor malice that had driven her mother. Her mother had sent the drink because she needed a way to deliver the sleeping draft that would hide the enchantment she had just unleashed. Knowing her mother hadn't been motivated by emotion—either positive or negative—but by cold strategy made sense. Gwen should have guessed as much.

The rest of the timing fit as well. It was only after her days in the closet that she had begun to hear talk of a new mountain pass.

But was it coincidence it had happened just after Easton's disappearance? Gwen couldn't credit the idea. Before the court stopped speaking Easton's name entirely, she had heard whispers about his fury as he marched to confront the queen. If anyone had seen the confrontation and heard the source of his anger, they didn't speak of it, but he had disappeared immediately afterward. And the next day an enchantment had taken hold of Gwen and the court.

Gwen didn't need anyone to confirm what she knew in her bones. Her mother had been the one to unleash the enchantment —her mother with her hidden room full of godmother objects. Gwen just didn't know why.

Knowing her mother, she had reasons wrapped within reasons. Queen Celandine was a master at turning any situation to her advantage and always thinking two steps ahead of her enemies.

Whatever her intentions, she had ended up with an army of enchanted bears at her disposal. Did she send them out to patrol the city at night?

The fear shown by the girl from the city hinted at the answer. The people had to contend not only with large and fearsome beasts in their streets but with the reminder of a power that was both foreign and terrifying in its strength. What limits were there for a queen who could turn people into animals and then command their obedience?

Did the city's inhabitants all lock their doors and windows and stay inside from first dark until morning light? A part of Gwen wanted to join them, to go back to hiding from the enormity of the truth. But there was no going back. She had to face the reality her mother had been hiding from her.

After enchanting her own people, the queen had orchestrated an enormous deception to ensure her daughter's ignorance. She had done it to preserve total control over Gwen and to keep her a prisoner at her side. She had known the truth would fuel Gwen's escape. It had been true when she was fourteen, and it was equally true now. Whatever political games her mother was using her daughter to play, they would all end now Gwen knew about the enchantment.

But she still needed to confirm her theory that the whole palace was affected. Employing her newly heightened senses of smell and hearing, she crept through the gardens unseen. She dodged another two patrols before she reached one of the wings housing palace apartments for the courtiers. Many of the courtiers would be in their city homes, but some always remained in the palace overnight.

Most of the curtains were tightly closed, although the occasional one was rimmed in light. But finally she found one set that had been thrown open, the window wide to let in the night air.

Inside, the room glowed with warm light, making it easy to see the large white form pacing up and down. Despite her own shape, despite seeing the guards earlier, the image still sent instinctive fear through Gwen. There was something different about seeing the hulking shape of a bear inside a room decorated with fine furnishings, and it was even more unnerving to see the animal conversing with a young boy. Even knowing everything, her instinct was to rush in and pull the boy away.

She kept herself frozen in place, however, her ears straining to hear. The bear spoke in a low voice, but as his pacing brought him near the window, she caught a few words. It wasn't enough to follow the meaning, but it was sufficient to bring the same shock of recognition as had hit her with the guards.

The voice might have been lower and rougher, but she could still recognize the words of Count Oswin. Which meant the boy must be his grandson—the seven-year-old child of the son who had led the first team through the mountains.

Count Oswin's son was obviously a white bear as well given his mountain exploration, but apparently his son was not. Whatever enchantment existed, it didn't affect children born after it took effect. Perhaps it hadn't affected many children at the time either, since most of them were kept sheltered in their homes in the city.

Although Gwen had known the count had a grandson, it was her first time seeing him. Had anyone ever mentioned that he walked with crutches, one pant leg pinned up due to the loss of his right leg below the knee? His face was calm, so if it was the result of an injury, it must have been an old one.

His whole bearing suggested he was comfortable with his grandfather in his bear form, and the sight of it reassured Gwen. Surely this scene wouldn't happen if those under the enchantment risked losing control while in their animal form.

Even so, anger swept through her. Her mother was the mountain queen and responsible for her people. How could she enchant some and terrorize others without qualm?

And what of Gwen's supposed new husband? The revelations of the night had been so shocking that Gwen felt only bewildered amusement at the thought of the unknown prince. How did her mother intend to hide Gwen's nighttime form from a lowlander husband? The entire plan went beyond foolhardy.

Gwen wanted to charge into her mother's wing and demand immediate answers. But enough caution remained to hold her back. As soon as her mother saw Gwen awake in her bear form, she would know her daughter had undertaken the ultimate defiance. It was wiser by far to approach her during the day.

Her best choice, however painful, was to go back to her room and wait until morning transformed her back again. But what about her clothes? In all the shock she hadn't given them a thought.

Remembering the moment of change, however, she was sure they hadn't torn as she grew. They had simply…disappeared.

Dismay swept through her. Presumably they would reappear when she turned human again—she had always woken in the same nightgown she had gone to sleep in—but what about the key concealed in her pocket? That had disappeared along with the clothes. Would it reappear with them? And even if it did, what would she do in the meantime? She was trapped outside her room for the remaining nighttime hours.

She looked down at her huge paws, unsure if she'd even be able to work a key or turn a handle in the form of a bear. With a wince, she remembered she had tried to turn a handle with bear paws once before without much success. On the night she'd discovered her room was locked, the drug had been so strong in her system that she'd barely been able to open her eyes as she dragged herself to the door. She'd been so dazed, she hadn't noticed the strangeness of her body, attributing her heavy, cumbersome limbs to the pull of sleep. But how could she have woken—however partially—and not noticed her change of shape?

She had plenty more hours to berate herself as she waited for the first sliver of dawn. When it came, she welcomed the crawling, itchy sensation and the tearing which she had found so unnerving the first time. When she was driven to her hands and knees, she felt only relief thanks to the sight of her usual shapely hands.

As she jumped to her feet, her hand flew to her pocket. Relief flooded her as her fingers closed around the key. Running through the corridors, she favored speed over concealment in the race for her door.

She dropped the key in her haste to fit it into her lock, but finally she got the door open and herself inside. She even remembered to re-lock the door, although climbing back into bed was more than she could manage.

Thankfully when she heard someone outside unlocking the door, the unseen jailer made no effort to look inside and check on her. She had time to compose herself before the appointed hour for breakfast and her upcoming confrontation with the queen. Time she greatly needed.

She dressed slowly, choosing her clothing with care as she slipped back into the role of the stately, elegant Princess Gwendolyn—the royal heir who always knew how to look the part of a princess, even when she was screaming inside. She had never been so neat and well-dressed for breakfast before, and she entered the room with her head high. It was empty.

Taking her place behind her chair, unable to bring herself to sit, Gwen waited.

GWEN

When Queen Celandine appeared, she paused in the doorway, regarding Gwen with raised brows. "You're here early, my dear." Her tone didn't indicate whether she thought it a good or bad thing.

"I'm here," Gwen said through gritted teeth, trying to hold onto her courage now she was actually facing her mother, "for real answers. You cannot possibly mean for me to marry a lowlander prince."

The queen's brows rose even further. "Really, my dear, must you use that language?" She walked unhurriedly to the table and sat. "I'm not sure why you find the idea so impossible. Who else should you marry if not a prince?"

Something in the look she gave Gwen—as if she knew who Gwen would rather marry and was mocking her for it—sent anger searing through Gwen's veins. The emotion overpowered the instinctive fear she felt in her mother's presence.

"Oh really?" she spat out. "So you're intending to tell the lowlanders the truth about us? Or do you think you can excuse why a husband and wife need separate chambers at night?"

The queen's hand stilled, her knuckles growing white around her fork.

"What do you mean?" she asked, the words coming out a fraction too quickly.

Satisfaction surged through Gwen. For the first time she had succeeded in rattling her mother.

"Oh, I don't know, Mother. I suppose I'm thinking that my husband might be a little surprised to discover his bride turns into a bear each nightfall! And when he finds out I'm not the only one, he may suspect a conspiracy against him."

"Silence!" The queen leaped to her feet, sending her chair clattering to the floor behind her. "How dare you!"

She reached Gwen in two strides, slapping her hard across the cheek. The blow sent Gwen staggering back, her hands flying to her face. Her mother had never hit her before, and the shocking pain brought her fear rushing back.

It was too late to back down now, though. She had revealed her knowledge to her mother, and she couldn't take it back.

"Never say that aloud," the queen hissed. "Anyone might have heard you!"

"So you *are* keeping me a secret from everyone." Gwen tried to keep her voice from shaking. "But why? If the whole kingdom knows the palace's inhabitants become bears at night, why can't they know their princess does as well?"

Her mother clapped a hand over Gwen's mouth, silencing her. Gwen pulled back.

"But why?" she cried. "What difference does it make?"

"It makes all the difference!" the queen growled. "Are you trying to ruin everything?"

For a moment the two stared at each other, both of their chests heaving and their eyes blazing. Distantly Gwen felt curious. Why had her mother kept the condition of the court a secret from Gwen and Gwen's inclusion in the enchantment a secret from everyone else? The two guards who had found her in the garden must have been genuinely worried for her, thinking she was an ordinary girl about to be confronted with something horrifying.

But sharper than the curiosity was the anger, laced with the inevitable fear that underlined every interaction with her mother. Despite her shaking knees, Gwen wasn't going to back down. Not this time.

The queen's brows drew closer, her eyes narrowing. "So you have discovered the truth at last, pathetic girl. I suppose you had to know eventually. But I will not allow you to ruin plans that have been years in the making."

She grabbed Gwen's wrist, holding it tightly enough that Gwen cried out in pain. The queen didn't loosen her grip.

Dragging Gwen behind her, she strode out into the corridor. Gwen struggled to free her arm, but despite her efforts, she was pulled along in her mother's wake.

When they began climbing the winding stairs of the west tower, Gwen considered throwing herself down them, pulling her mother with her. Surely the queen would have to release her hold then.

But Gwen was as likely to be injured in the attempt as her mother. She would have little chance to escape with two broken legs.

She kept struggling, though. It might be futile, but now that she had unstoppered the dam, she couldn't suppress the years of bottled anger and resentment that were flowing out.

It made no difference. Her mother maintained an iron grip, proving herself stronger than she appeared. Only when she had opened a door at the top of the tower did she finally let go, and only then so she could throw Gwen into the room beyond.

Gwen flew forward, losing her balance and landing hard enough on the stone floor to bruise. She scrambled to her feet, wincing, but her mother stood in the middle of the doorway, barring the exit.

Tears sprang to Gwen's eyes. "Why, Mother? Can you really not tell me why?"

"What a fool I was to think you had finally matured into the tool you need to become." The queen regarded her with disgust. "How the court and kingdom can put their hope in you, I'll never understand."

"H...hope? What do you mean?" The queen's unexpected words drove back Gwen's impending tears, a strange echo of those spoken by the girl from the city.

"It's all your fault, you know," the queen snapped. "If it hadn't been for that fool boy, I would never have felt the need to—"

"Fool boy?" Gwen surged forward, grasping at her mother's shoulder. "You mean Easton? What did you do to him?"

"Far less than he deserved!" The queen thrust Gwen backward again, sending her to the floor in a second heavy fall.

But Gwen barely felt the pain. She stared up at her mother. "So he's alive then?"

"As I said, better than he deserved! But I couldn't risk killing the son of a courtier. Not after everything went wrong."

Her eyes snapped and burned, pouring the load of her own anger and frustration onto Gwen. "But how was I supposed to know the object worked in such a way? It was supposed to bind my people to me—ensure their loyalty. How could it turn us into bears and bind us to the mountains instead?"

Gwen slowly stood, giving a shaky laugh. "So it was a mistake, then? The high and mighty Queen Celandine made a mistake, and now you must spend your nights as a bear?" She laughed again, a stronger, colder sound. But her mother was finally talking, giving her answers, and she had to goad her into continuing.

"Silence!" her mother cried. "It may have been a miscalculation at the time, but I can turn any situation to my advantage. Haven't I used it to keep the population quiet? I even found us a way through the mountains—I bought us a future!"

"But it was still a mistake," Gwen said softly. "And every night you're reminded of it. But why did you have to involve me?"

The queen gave her a satisfied look. "That was a master stroke, and I came up with it on the spot. Obviously I couldn't confess I'd made a mistake. I needed to assure my people the enchantment wasn't permanent, but since I had no idea how to reverse it, I needed to give myself time. And thankfully you were safely out of sight."

Gwen sucked in a breath at this description of her torturous imprisonment.

The queen smiled in response. "A humorous fantasy, is it not? But hope is as powerful a tool as fear. A careful wielder of both can hold more power than you can imagine."

"You've been using me to control the court all this time?" Gwen stared at her mother. It was far beyond what she had imagined.

"I'm only surprised they swallowed the notion of a virtuous princess so easily," the queen said with a mocking smile. "A girl so pure, the enchantment couldn't touch her. One who must be protected at all costs because only she could save her people." She chuckled. "But it does sound like something the godmothers would contrive, does it not?"

"But you haven't found out how to reverse it," Gwen said slowly. "It's been ten years, and we're all still trapped. How can the people still look to me with hope?"

The queen's smile turned hard. "Who said I didn't know how to reverse it? A prince is the answer, of course."

Gwen gaped at her. "That's why you're bringing a lowlander prince here? Marrying him is supposed to reverse the enchantment?" She frowned. "But love is usually the key when it comes to godmother objects. You can't possibly think I love this stranger or he me?"

"Love?" The queen's brows rose. "No, who could ever love you?"

Gwen froze, icy tendrils creeping over her. She didn't know why the words shocked her after everything her mother had said over the years. But they hit her in a part of her heart she didn't know was still unguarded.

"A prince was just the excuse at first," the queen continued, "since I hadn't found a way to reverse it by the time you came of marriageable age. I told them it could only be a prince and that stalled them for a while. And then somehow they found..." She broke off, clearly seething too much to finish the sentence.

Gwen frowned at her mother, trying to understand what she wasn't saying. Had it not been the queen herself who had chosen the prince and insisted on Gwen's marriage? Had someone actually called her mother's bluff? Had it been one of her trading teams? Gwen almost wanted to laugh at the idea of her mother's horror when her people returned in triumph with a prince in tow, expecting to be rewarded.

But if they had found a prince and brought him into the mountains, where was he now?

The queen looked up at Gwen, her eyes narrowing. "As always, I turned the situation to my advantage. You would do well to remember that no matter what happens, I will always find a way to control the situation. The time had nearly come in any case, and the princeling has proven useful and will have further uses still. Including him in the enchantment produced unexpected results, but the boy has his own godmother, and her words were far more interesting than the boy himself." She scoffed. "He will soon fail, of course, that much is inevitable. But he will still free us in the process, and then I will have one final use for him."

"Marrying me," Gwen said, the words dull. She couldn't follow half of what her mother was saying, but anything that brought the queen so much satisfaction had to be bad for Gwen.

"You may think you're defying me right now," the queen said. "But it is as pointless as everything else you've attempted. The prince will return to us soon—the painting has shown that clearly enough. So I merely need to keep you sequestered here until then." She tapped her chin. "I will say you're sick and resting so as to be recovered for the prince's arrival." She nodded. "Yes, that will work well enough."

Gwen's heart leaped as she realized her mother meant to lock her in the tower room and leave her there. But it wasn't fear that stirred her. Not when she had the master key still resting in her pocket.

The queen stopped halfway through the doorway, however, turning back with a mocking smile. "I am not such a fool as you apparently think me, daughter. The key to this room is one that only I hold. Your master key will not open it. And so I recommend you reconcile yourself to your stay here and use the time to prepare for your future. Soon our curse will be broken, and you will be married straight after. You will soon be the princess of two kingdoms, and we will begin a new and glorious future for the mountain throne."

"What do you mean?" Gwen asked, her mouth dry.

The queen's lips curved upward. "I've always promised you would one day rule, haven't I? But how could I leave you such a small kingdom, trapped behind walls? The throne I will pass to you will stretch all the way to the ocean. There is no mountain I won't level for your future. Don't worry, my dear. You will be Queen Gwendolyn sooner than you think—but I will always be by your side."

With those haunting words, she disappeared, the key turning in the lock. Gwen threw herself at the door anyway, pounding on it and screaming as she tried to open it.

It remained sturdy, however, and she knew she was too high in an unused tower to be heard by anyone. Even her servant friends wouldn't know to look for her in such an unlikely place.

She had thought her mother might lock her in her room—had even thought she might try a closet again—but she had been overconfident in her possession of a master key. Failing that, she had thought Alma and the others would find some way to reach her. Now that both possibilities were stripped away, she felt raw, exposed, and desperate.

Her moment of defiance had been so long in coming and had failed so spectacularly. She had known her mother had some scheme underway, but she hadn't realized the scope of it. Did she really think she could put her daughter on the throne as a puppet queen, hailed by the court as their savior but powerless in everything but name?

Looking around the barren room, it seemed all too possible. And what had her mother said about leveling mountains? A week ago, Gwen would have dismissed it as grandiose talk. But now she had seen the godmother objects her mother had amassed. Was it possible they had the power to change the geography of the region itself, laying forth a path for her mother to conquer the surrounding kingdoms in Gwen's name?

She looked down at her empty hands, remembering how they had looked as the paws of a bear. Nothing seemed too far-fetched any longer. And her mother would already have a foothold in the lowlands if Gwen's marriage made her a legitimate princess in one of their kingdoms.

Her mother wanted to fool the mountain people into following Gwen as the one who had saved them from the curse. And she wanted to fool a lowland kingdom into accepting her by marriage, opening the door to her planned conquest. But all her plans revolved around her daughter. Her mother had made Gwen the key to all of them.

A different level of desperation sank into her. She couldn't stay in the tower to meekly accept her mother's planned future. Escape wasn't only necessary for her own sake anymore. Her mother said the curse had trapped her and her people in the mountains—explaining why they had never traded beyond those who lived in the valleys of the foothills—and as far as Gwen was concerned, her mother could stay in the mountains for the rest of her days.

Gwen looked wildly around the empty space. The unused room wasn't even furnished, so there was nothing she could use to try to batter down the door.

Her eyes fell on the windows. Rushing toward the closest one, she tried the latch. When it swung open, she had a brief moment of triumph before she remembered where she was.

One glance downward sent her staggering away from the open pane of glass. She wasn't in her room any longer. There was no friendly ground waiting for her, only a fall of several stories.

But desperation still had its fingers deep in her heart. Not even her fear of the drop could compare to her fear of her mother. And if she did fall, at least her death would foil her mother's plans.

Knowing she couldn't wait until her false courage faded, Gwen swung one leg over the windowsill. There were no sheets to make into ropes or anything equally fanciful. She would either scale the rough stone of the castle wall or she would fall.

Her bravado wavered when she reached the point of releasing her death grip on the windowsill. But she had already gone too far to turn back. She was dangling down the side of the wall, and she didn't possess the strength to pull herself back up. There was nowhere to go but down.

The wind whistled past her, making her shiver, although she didn't feel cold. If anything, she felt unnaturally warm. One small slip, and it would all be over.

She wished for a calm day without so much as a breeze that might disrupt her climb, but the wind mocked her, blowing more strongly in response. It curled around her, catching at her hair and dress.

She licked her lips, testing the position of both feet. She had wedged her toes into cracks provided by the uneven stones of the tower wall, but there wasn't much grip. She would have preferred a better foothold, but it was the best she'd been able to find.

She let go with one hand, holding even more tightly with the other as she searched for a lower hold. When she found one, it felt painfully insufficient. Her fingers could barely grasp the slight lip of stone.

You can do this, she told herself, forcing her mind to override her terrified body. She released her final hold on the windowsill above.

Somehow she remained in place as her second hand sought another uncertain hold. Once she'd found it, she froze, her whole length pressed against the stone, her breath coming in desperate gasps.

But the longer she took, the weaker she'd grow. She had to keep moving. She removed one foot and cautiously lowered herself, blindly feeling for another toehold.

The change in position upset her balance, and her fingers slid. There was no time to recover herself. One second, she was still held in place by three points of contact, the next, she had lost them all, and her body was falling backward, drawn irresistibly toward the ground.

She only had time for an awareness of her impending death and the thought of a single face. And in the utter helplessness of that moment, she felt peace.

Except she wasn't falling as fast as she should have been. The wind curling around her had grown more solid, winding its way around her legs and supporting her fall.

Could she even use the word fall? Impossibly, she seemed to be not so much falling as flying. Except it didn't feel like flying. It felt like...riding. An uncontrolled, tempestuous ride, but she could have sworn she felt an invisible mount beneath her.

She glanced over her shoulder and saw the palace retreating behind her. She was actually being carried along by the wind, moving parallel to the ground.

Her invisible mount lurched upward and then dropped abruptly, making her stomach sink to her feet although the wind caught her before she hit the ground and lifted her again.

The warmth she had felt earlier grew, reaching an unpleasant level of heat which seemed to be emanating from one of her pockets. She thrust her hand into it, distracted and confused as she sought the source. It was the opposite pocket to the one holding the key, but her fingers closed around a small metal object.

Gasping, she pulled out the golden halter she had accidentally stolen from her mother a lifetime ago. Given all the revelations since, she had forgotten about the object whose purpose she hadn't been able to guess.

As soon as it was free, the miniature halter cooled. It also began to grow. Within seconds, it was as large as a real halter, and it had leaped from her hands to position itself as if she really were riding an invisible horse made of wind. A golden thread grew from the halter, connecting it with her hand like golden reins that glowed.

She tried pulling on one side, and the wind horse responded, moving in the direction she indicated. Somehow, impossibly, she was controlling the wind.

Whooping in elation, she looked up to see a mountain face bearing down on her. Given her impossible speed, she was already nearing the western edge of the valley. Gulping, she tugged on the reins, and the wind horse surged upward, carrying her higher and higher until she sailed over the mountain's peak.

A brief surge of elation gave way to concentration as the wind raced her down the other side, another peak appearing in front of her. It took all her energy to control the wind horse as she rode it up and down the various peaks and summits that lay before her. Somewhere in the back of her mind, the steady beat of elation kept trying to break free, but she wasn't safe yet. She wasn't free yet.

Finally she rode down the final mountain face, reaching the first of the legendary valleys. They sat on the very fringe of the mountains, but they belonged to a different world—the border of the Four Kingdoms. Far below her she could see roofs and gardens scattered among the trees.

The wind raced her quickly past the first valley, but she angled it downward, and when the next valley appeared, she brought it all the way to the ground. She hit harder than she had expected, sending herself tumbling sideways.

As soon as her hands flew from the reins, they disappeared, and the halter shrank again, dropping to the ground beside her. She scrambled forward, crawling across the littered leaves of the clearing to grab it.

Thrusting it into her pocket with shaking hands, she lay flat, staring up at branches and blue sky. It took a long time for her trembling limbs to still and her heart rate to steady.

As soon as they had, tears took their place. She had done it. After all these years, she had succeeded. She was free.

CHARLOTTE

*C*harlotte stood in her room in front of her full-length mirror, regarding herself in her plainest gown. She had made her rapid decision without even considering what it would be like to meet her family again. What would they think of Charlotte now? Would they think her changed? She felt changed. The Charli who had left them had been a young, naïve girl.

She knew she looked beautiful—her beauty had caused her too much pain in her life to bother denying it—but she felt only listlessness. Her image held no appeal as it had done on the morning after her first night beside Henry. She could no longer see her own golden loveliness without seeing beside it the darker beauty of the princess in the portrait. The unknown woman—who Charlotte felt certain had to be royalty from her bearing alone—made Charlotte feel colorless and washed out.

She shook herself, turning from the mirror. It didn't matter what she looked like for the coming reunion.

Henry awaited her just outside the castle, and it took all her willpower to make herself climb into position on his back, his soft fur gripped in her hands. It had been a long time since their first journey through the trees together, and everything had changed since then.

She stayed awake this time, marveling at the speed of his run. Even knowing how fast they moved, she was taken off guard when she began to recognize their surroundings and knew she was within minutes of her old home.

"We were so close all this time?" she whispered. Their months in the castle had felt so entirely removed from regular life that it seemed incredible the physical distance hadn't been greater.

But she was even more astonished when Henry took her straight to the location of her old home. Had her family not moved after all?

One look at the building told her it wasn't her old home, however. The house that stood in its place was at least four times bigger and more luxurious than any house she had seen in the valley. And the attached stable had been replaced with a free-standing building of significant size, and it clearly housed far more than their original three horses.

"I'll leave you here," Henry said. "I think it's best they don't see me."

Charlotte wanted to protest, but she remained silent. While her heart wanted every extra minute with him, the whole point of this visit was to give herself distance.

"There is one thing I must ask of you, though," he said in a voice turned suddenly serious. "Of course you will wish to talk to your parents of your new life. You may speak freely to them of our home, of our days in the library, even of the bell, if you wish. But our nights together—those belong to just you and me. Please swear to me you will not tell your parents what happens at night."

Charlotte's throat clogged at the way he spoke of their hours in the darkness. She felt in perfect agreement. Even though they maintained physical distance from one another through the night, that time was private between the two of them.

She nodded, managing to squeeze out enough words to reassure him. Her sudden emotion brought a resurgence of his earlier concern, and he hesitated. But voices from inside made him glance toward the house.

"I must be going," he said. "I'll come back for you in three days." He turned to go, only to stop and look back at her, his voice turned urgent. "You will return to me?"

She nodded. "I will be ready in three days. Thank you, Henry."

He examined her face for a moment before nodding and disappearing into the trees.

Charlotte watched him go, barely holding in her longing to call him back, to say she would return with him immediately. But she couldn't speak. She was doing this for both of their sakes, and she had to stay strong.

The door of the house opened, and an unfamiliar older woman came out. She regarded Charlotte with curious bemusement, her eyes growing wider as she took in Charlotte's gown.

Charlotte looked down at herself, recognizing that even the plainest of her new gowns was out of place in the valley. Even with her family's obvious new wealth, she clearly didn't belong.

"Surely you're not the daughter who married the bear!" the woman exclaimed. "Your parents claimed you were living in luxury like a princess, but I thought..." She trailed off, clearly not willing to voice her previous opinion.

"I am she." Charlotte cleared her throat. "Are my family here?" Seeing the unfamiliar face filled her with urgent fear. Had Henry left her on the doorstep of strangers?

"Oh, aye." The woman was still regarding Charlotte with amazement. "They're inside."

"Who's there?" the familiar voice of her mother called. "Do we have visitors?" She appeared in the doorway and let out a piercing shriek.

"Charlotte! Oh Charlotte! Quick, girls, come quick! Your sister is here!"

Falling forward, she wrapped her arms around Charlotte in a bone-crushing hug. Dazed, Charlotte embraced her back, embarrassed to feel moisture on her cheeks.

She had left in a storm of righteous fury, and all this time she had been happy to be far from her family. She had thought Henry's company was all she needed. But now that she felt her mother's arms around her, the walls she had built inside crumbled. She might have been an adult and a married woman, but she still needed support. And her family, for all their flaws, were the only ones she had.

Elizabeth and Odelia piled out the door, their own cries of surprise filling the air. To Charlotte's surprise, they also fell on her, enlarging the hug so it became an awkward mass of entwined arms.

Apparently her sisters had grown more fond of her in her absence. Or maybe it was merely that they now associated her with wealth and ease. Charlotte was grateful to maintain the peace of the moment, but she couldn't forget the way they had treated her for so long. She had thought their relationship changed once before, but it had all too easily reverted again after her cousin's wedding.

Having heard the stories about Henry's supportive and affectionate relationship with his sister, she wasn't going to be fooled again. Now that their lives were so separate, she felt hopeful she and her sisters could spend time together in peace. But they would never have the sort of close, loving relationship Charlotte had always wanted. Hoping for it would only lead to further hurt down the road. The acceptance and safety Charlotte had found in her marriage allowed her to accept her relationship with her sisters for what it was, instead of always seeing it through the lens of what she wanted it to be.

"Charli!" Her father appeared, and her mother and sisters melted away, leaving Charlotte free to greet him.

"Father." She had intended to speak in a steady, cool tone, but instead her voice broke.

His face crumpled in response.

Stepping forward, he also swept her into a hug, and just as with her mother, she responded instinctively, wrapping her arms around him. The hurt still lingered, but unlike with her sisters, there were years of warmth and affection behind it that she couldn't forget.

The shining, perfect father of her childhood had turned out to be flawed, and it had been hard to accept. But she had overreacted to his words that day in the forest. While he might have misunderstood her heart, he had still been trying to act out of love toward her.

"How have you been, Daughter?" he murmured. "Has the bear kept his promises to you?"

She clung on tighter as she nodded. She could hear the worry in his voice, and all the resentment that had built up inside her washed away like a sandcastle before a wave.

"He gives me everything I ask for, Father," she said. "I live in greater luxury than even you." She pulled back and offered him a weak smile. "Though it looks as if you live in plenty of luxury yourself these days!"

He stepped back and smiled proudly, but she could see the truth behind his attempted good cheer. He had never wanted wealth for its own sake, and the family's good fortune was tied up with her departure and the end of his frontier dreams.

"Actually, it's not just from your bride price," her mother interjected, sounding proud. "Although we were all shocked when the house suddenly grew around us."

"Did it really?" Charlotte laughed at the image. "So my wish reached you after all." She had seen the bell work often enough to guess how shocking it must have been for her family, coming without warning or context.

"But it was only a short time later that your father's efforts to win his place with the valley elders finally bore fruit," her mother continued. "Even if you hadn't left us, our fortunes would have been looking up."

Sorrow tinged the pride as she finished her words, and Charlotte could easily read the message behind it. They could have kept their daughter and had eventual wealth as well, even if not as much.

"Oh, Mother," she whispered.

Her mother stepped forward. "I'm sorry, Charli," she murmured back. "I failed you as a mother. I was tired and weak, and I thought our poverty was the root of all our problems. But once you were gone, I realized I could never enjoy luxury and ease that came at the expense of one of my daughters. I shouldn't have let you go."

Tears filled Charlotte's eyes at the apology, but before she could reply, her mother continued.

"But that's not all I have to be sorry for. I've spent so many weeks thinking of you and remembering the past, and I realized I failed you long before I sent you away. I'm sorry I let our home become such a painful place that you would marry a bear to escape it."

Charlotte tried to smile, but her lips were trembling too much to manage it.

Her father slipped an arm around her mother's shoulders, although his eyes stayed on Charlotte.

"I realize much of the blame is mine," he said. "I moved us out here because it was what I wished. I convinced myself it could help you all, too, but that was only an excuse to justify what I wanted. When it took so much longer to establish ourselves than I expected, I should have moved us back to civilization."

Charlotte shook her head, sniffing as she held back the tears. She hadn't come home to hear their apologies, but their words healed something broken deep inside her.

"Be at peace, Mother and Father," she murmured. "I accept

your apologies, and I'm even glad we moved here, as difficult as it was. I am truly well, and I don't regret my choice. If we hadn't moved here, I never would have found Henry."

Despite all the newfound pain, and the prospect that she might have to give Henry up in the future, she couldn't wish away her love or her months with him. When she had left home, she had believed herself fully grown up. And in some ways, she had been. But now, after only a short time away, she understood better how much growth still lay before her. She had already experienced so many new emotions, and with them had come an understanding of her parents she had never expected to have.

She knew what it was to hurt someone despite your love for them—even because of it. It was clear that her unhappiness and her abrupt departure pained Henry. And yet, she had left anyway. She had done it not because she didn't care about him but because of her emotional weakness. She needed space before she could discuss their future without heaping guilt and hurt on his head. And so she had chosen to leave not to cause him pain, but because it had seemed, in a collection of bad options, like the one that would hurt him the least.

She could see now that her father had only been doing the same thing. Faced with his daughter's unhappiness, he had looked at the selection of bad options before them and nudged her toward the one he thought would cause the least pain. He hadn't understood the true cause of her suffering—part of which came from him and his choices—and so he had worded himself badly. But as it turned out, he had been right about her potential for future happiness. So she couldn't blame him now for doing his best.

The weight that lifted off her shoulders as she let go of the last of her resentment toward her parents lightened the pain she still felt over Henry, and her tears started flowing again.

"Charli?" Her father gazed at her with worry.

"They're happy tears," she managed to say, smiling from him

to her mother. "I'm so glad to see you again. I didn't realize how glad."

"Come inside, come inside," Elizabeth gushed, oblivious to the emotional exchange that had just taken place. "Let us show you all around our new house. It's the nicest one in all the valleys, and everyone has come to admire it."

"I was surprised to find you still here," Charlotte entering the house in Elizabeth's wake. "Weren't you going to move to Arcadia?"

Odelia, who had followed them inside, pouted. "According to Father, the bear said we have to wait for that. But we're going to move still!"

Charlotte frowned, wanting to ask her to explain further but knowing Odelia wasn't the one with answers. Why had Henry told her family to wait?

Elizabeth began to show off elements of the house, but from the way she was preening and positioning herself, she clearly wanted a comment on the fine gown she was wearing. Charlotte bit back a smile and supplied it. She extended the compliment to Odelia who lit up in response. Her absence had forced her parents into self-reflection, but clearly the same wasn't true of her sisters.

"Your gown is very nice, too, Charlotte," Odelia said before leaning closer. "Wait, are those real gems?"

Charlotte glanced down. "Perhaps? You may have this one, if you like. I would prefer to borrow something plainer for my stay, if you have it."

Elizabeth and Odelia locked eyes over Charlotte's head, and she realized she might have spoken too carelessly. If her sisters understood the wealth she now enjoyed, would all their old resentment return?

"I would rather have my sisters than any gown," she added brightly, and the tension passed.

Both her sisters smiled again, sweeping her inside to find her a change of clothes. She was paraded through every room in the house where she forced herself to dutifully admire everything. Her family really was living in comfort, and with her new forgiveness of them, the knowledge brought her joy instead of a surge of resentment.

But by the time she had seen every nook, been fed until she was bursting, met the three helpers who lived in the rooms attached to the stable, reassured her parents again of her husband's kindness, and regaled her sisters with descriptions of her days spent reading, she felt as wrung out as the rag her mother was using to wipe the table.

"Do you really do nothing but read all day?" Elizabeth exchanged a look with Odelia. "What's the point of a fancy gown like yours if your only audience is books?"

Charlotte smiled, pleased that her story of the library—incomplete though it had been—had erased any lingering effect of her earlier careless words. Neither of her sisters would feel any jealousy toward her now.

"I do read all day most days," she said. "And so I must confess I'm longing for one of my old walks in the forest."

"Of course you would be missing your old haunts," her mother said. "Give your sisters a moment to change into something more practical and—"

Charlotte threw a beseeching look at her father, and he came to her rescue as he always had before on the worst days.

"Peace, my dears," he said. "Elizabeth and Odelia need not bestir themselves. Charli won't have forgotten her way in such a short time. She'll be safe enough on her own."

"Yes, indeed!" Charlotte said quickly. "I don't want anyone put out for me."

She leaped up and was out the door before her mother could protest. She hoped none of them took offense, but she desperately needed some solitude.

As soon as she lost sight of the house, she felt her chest

expand. Breathing deeply, she turned her face toward the sun and smiled. Shut in the castle, she had registered the change of season, but she hadn't had a chance to experience it properly. Out in the forest, the ground was a riot of color, spring filling her senses.

The pain of her love for Henry and the uncertainty of their future still sat in her heart as a constant ache. But for the moment she was content to be alone with the flowers and the forest's new life.

Charlotte walked for what must have been hours, losing herself in the forest without ever actually being lost. She knew the ground too well for that.

She had seen no one the whole time—the one advantage of such distant neighbors—so she was shocked when she stepped around a bush and into a small clearing only to find an elegant woman sitting on the small patch of grass at its center.

The woman rose as soon as she caught sight of Charlotte, and Charlotte's astonishment grew far greater, hitting her with the force of a speeding arrow. For the face smiling a hesitant greeting was one she recognized, although she had never met the woman before.

Here, in the middle of her familiar forest, she had found the woman from the portrait. Henry's lost love.

INTERLUDE

QUEEN CELANDINE

Queen Celandine stared at the empty room and then down at the key in her hand. What she was seeing was utterly impossible.

Gwendolyn couldn't have escaped. Only the queen herself had the key for this room. And, if Gwendolyn had somehow tampered with the door, she would have at least left some evidence behind. But the door had been whole and locked when the queen arrived moments before.

She had prepared the remote room years ago, thinking it would be needed. But Gwendolyn had proven more biddable than she could have dreamed. Until now, when the girl had suddenly developed a new defiant streak, only to then vanish in a way that shouldn't have been possible.

A slight creak caught the queen's ear, and her eyes narrowed. Striding across the room, she pushed against one of the windows. It swung open.

Celandine sucked in a breath. The girl had gone out the window. The wind must have pushed it closed again afterward, but it had failed to completely latch.

She leaned out, peering downward with an unfamiliar spike of fear. If the pathetic girl had managed to get herself killed, all of Celandine's plans would be for nothing.

But no crumpled body lay on the ground beneath the tower. The queen's gaze moved across the western palace grounds, but no sign of movement caught her eye. She drew back inside and clicked the window shut, scowling.

Soon she would need to return and resume a mask of calm indifference. She had already told the court the princess was recovering from an illness, so nothing needed to change immediately. But she had to get her back, and quietly.

If only that fool of a count hadn't rushed matters. She ground her teeth as she slowly descended the flights of stairs that wound down from the tower.

When she had been pushed into declaring that only a royal prince was a suitable groom to marry the princess and lift the curse, she hadn't expected her courtiers to actually produce one. The enchantment wouldn't allow them to travel further than the valleys. What had the fool boy been doing there?

But it was the defiance of the action that made her seethe more than anything. After all these years, they thought they could push her?

She drew in a calming breath. Anger would get her nowhere. She had felt enough anger to drown a ship or level a village in the years she had spent in her father's home. And after she had found refuge—thinking herself safe with one more powerful than her father—she had felt its fire again. That second betrayal had been even worse than the one by her blood parent.

But all that impotent fury had won her nothing. It had been worse than useless, in fact, since it had blinded her to the valuable lessons to be learned. She could not trust to the power of others to save her. That power only enabled them to treat her as they wished.

When she set aside emotion for clear thinking and cold

revenge, the answer was obvious. She had to seize her own power. She had to rise so high that no one could ever stomp on her again.

It had taken planning and effort, but she had succeeded. And those who had once made free use of their fists had been forced to kneel at her feet and pay homage.

Remembering that moment usually calmed and stabilized her, but now it only brought back the hated wave of anger. She returned to her breathing exercises, trying to drive back the emotions. She couldn't afford to crack now.

She pressed a hand to her head. Was it never to be enough? She had become queen—had ruled with a tight rein for twenty years. There should be no one with the power to assail her.

And yet...

She clenched her teeth. The breathing was no longer working. The court thought they could manipulate her, control her. They thought they could free themselves of the bindings she'd used to ensure their loyalty after that boy had questioned her rule.

She glanced back up the stairs, feeling the cracks in her wall widen. How dare that child flee from her! It was impossible. Unthinkable.

Had someone told her? Celandine stilled mid-step. But after a moment she shook her head and resumed her descent. After what had happened to the boy, no one in the court would be so foolhardy. It had been ten years, and no one had dared.

Princess Gwendolyn still believed Celandine to be her real mother. She must. Given the girl's earlier tantrum, she would have thrown that in the queen's face as well if she had known.

Some of her secrets were still safe.

But her hold on power was slipping. She had kept it secure all these years with the promise that everything would change once Gwendolyn was on the throne in her place. If they discovered the princess was gone, what would they do?

No. She couldn't be gone. Even if she had managed to climb

down the wall, she couldn't have gone far. Celandine would find her.

She stalked through the corridors, and her expression was enough to send anyone she encountered hurrying in another direction.

The guard at the entrance to her wing bowed deeply, avoiding eye contact. He was frightened too.

Yes. She drank it in, reveling in the reminder that her power hadn't cracked yet.

Inside her chamber, she flung open the curtains, pausing to check the portrait behind. It had changed yet again. The girl in gold was now turned toward the bear, her arms wrapped around his neck.

Hours before, Celandine would have been pleased. Soon she would have the prince caught in her snare. Her courtiers had thought to force her hand, but they didn't understand who they were dealing with. The queen had already turned their empty scheming to her own advantage. They thought the wedding would be their moment of freedom, but it was only the beginning.

She had thought the power she had amassed sufficient, but from the moment the count made his move, she knew it wasn't so.

She pulled on the lever and let the portrait swing open, stepping through. As always, the hidden room calmed any lingering unease.

Her people had no idea of the power she had stored here—power she could use to gain even more. When they had seen her level the mountains, when she was seated as empress on a throne that spanned kingdoms, she would finally have climbed too high for anyone to touch her ever again.

She would be safe.

But for now, she needed to find the princess—the girl was still a tool she would need in her stepping stones of conquest. One of these objects would surely help her locate the runaway.

Her eyes flicked between the plinths until they came to rest on one holding a tiny golden whip. She sucked in a breath, her cheeks growing pale.

Instantly she could recall the earlier scene and the place where the princess had been standing. Gwendolyn had taken the golden halter. She had brazenly picked it up and walked out under the queen's nose.

The earlier storm of fury was nothing to the tidal wave bearing down on her now. How dared that girl enter Celandine's innermost sanctuary and steal from her! The queen had offered her grace when she had found her here, and the girl had laughed in her face.

But the wave bearing down on her could sweep away everything she had built. Celandine strode over to another object and placed her hand on it. Instantly the overwhelming and unwanted emotions disappeared, leaving stillness in their wake. The empty bliss of nothingness.

The queen drew a steady breath and assumed a serene smile. This had been her first object, the one that was the foundation of everything. Without her emotions, she was truly free. Without them, she could manage the cold calculation needed to ensure no one ever threatened her again.

The situation wasn't lost yet. The selfish girl had taken the halter and would no doubt be gone from the mountains already. She was probably in the middle of savoring her victory. But she had been more foolish than she realized.

She had left the whip.

INTERLUDE

EASTON

Easton stood on the seawall and gazed out at the endless stretch of ocean. He had always liked this spot. Standing here, he felt surrounded by the sea in a way that could only be rivaled by standing on the deck of a ship.

The wildness of it reminded him of his childhood home in the mountains. And thinking of his home reminded him of her.

There was little point in thinking of Gwen. When he had been cast out, it had been made very clear to him that he would never see her or his family again.

He had even accepted it, in his own way. Or at least he had made the necessary peace that allowed him to forge a new life and to continue on each day. But he hadn't been able to purge Gwen from his mind. He wasn't even sure he wanted to.

Was she all right? It seemed a foolish thought. Of course she wasn't. Nanny was already gone, and now Easton was gone too. She was alone in that castle of stone with only her stepmother.

He regretted that he hadn't told her the truth about her real mother. If only he had run to Gwen when he found out instead of rushing to confront the queen like a hotheaded child.

But there was no use in such regrets. He couldn't change his actions now. He could only hope someone else would muster the courage to tell her the truth.

He didn't regret being free from under the queen's oppressive watch. He only wished Gwen could join him in his freedom. If she and his parents were by his side, he could happily make Ranost his home forever. The coastal town wasn't large, but it had work enough. And it had the sea.

He breathed deeply, tasting the salt on the wind.

He dreamed of the princess sometimes. And the Gwen of his dreams always wore the same face—a grown up version of the one he used to know. Sometimes, she was alone, looking sad and wistful. Occasionally she laughed with a friend, although the other girl always seemed to be cleaning on those occasions, as if the presence of soap and water lightened the princess's mood.

And other times she wandered beneath the moon, her hand resting on the shoulder of a large white bear. He liked those dreams the best. It comforted him to think of Gwen with a silent protector at her side. He had filled that role once—doing more to shield her than she had realized—but he was gone now, and he hated to think of his childhood playmate alone.

The wind gusted against him, caressing his cheek and rifling through his hair. If only it could bring him news of his old home.

Were his parents still alive and well? Had they suffered for his defiance? If they had been banished from court, he didn't think they would regret it. Life in the city was at least a little freer than life in the palace, if only because it wasn't so close to the queen. Neither of his parents had ever desired power. They had only escaped the purge of the king's old inner circle because they had never been close to him.

Familiar anger rose at thoughts of Queen Celandine. He let it come, let it wash over him. For a moment his hands balled into fists.

But then he gazed out across the ocean and breathed in the salty air. He let the steady pull and crash of the waves pull the emotions back out again.

"You are right and just, Anger," he murmured. "But you cannot serve me in this moment. I still have life and breath and work to sustain myself. That is what I must focus on in this moment."

He felt the calm of the ocean seep into him—the calm that came when he remembered that his was just one life among countless in the kingdoms and that even Queen Celandine's power was nothing compared to the vastness of the ocean.

The last time he had faced the mountain queen, he had still been on the threshold of childhood. But now he was a man grown. If he ever faced the queen again, he knew the anger would be there, ready.

It would take courage to face her, he knew that. And his anger at all the wrongs she had committed would spur that courage. If he had another chance to stand up for Gwen, he wouldn't fail again.

CHARLOTTE

*T*he woman in the clearing smiled hesitantly at Charlotte. But as she took in Charlotte's obvious shock, her smile faltered. She stepped closer, staring more intently at Charlotte's face, and then let out a cry.

"You're the girl from the portrait!" she exclaimed, stealing the words from Charlotte's own mouth.

From the woman, they made no sense.

"I don't know what you mean," she managed to say through numb lips.

"Your dress is different, of course," the woman said, smiling at Charlotte in a friendly way. "And you're missing the bear." She laughed as if she'd made a joke, but tension shot through Charlotte at the mention of Henry.

"Excuse me?" she asked before remembering that the whole valley must know she'd married a bear. This woman couldn't know his real identity. "Are you saying someone here has painted a picture of me with…a white bear?"

The woman's eyes widened. "It *was* white! How did you know? Don't tell me you actually have a bear companion?"

Charlotte shook her head, trying to shake loose her brain. The whole interaction felt like a dream. Perhaps she'd stopped to rest somewhere and had fallen asleep. She'd spent enough hours thinking of this woman that it was plausible she would appear in her dreams.

Examining the woman again, Charlotte had to admit the scene felt too real to be a dream. And if it was one, shouldn't she understand—in the magical way of dreams—why something in the conversation had brought a shadow to the other woman's face? There was tension there that hadn't been there earlier.

"It wasn't in this valley that I saw the portrait," the woman said after an awkward moment. "Perhaps I shouldn't have mentioned it."

"Great." Charlotte sank down onto the grass. "So the story has spread to the neighboring valleys too."

What she really wanted was to run away, but her legs wouldn't let her. They wouldn't even hold her upright anymore, so there she was, sitting at the feet of the woman from the painting. Charlotte couldn't lie to herself and pretend it didn't sting.

But the woman immediately sat as well, resuming her original position so she faced Charlotte. Her expression was a mix of curiosity and sympathy, so she must have sensed something of her new companion's inner turmoil.

Of course, if she knew who Charlotte actually was, she would no doubt hate her. Unless Henry's love had been one-sided. Charlotte couldn't believe that, though. What woman could resist loving Henry?

"Are there a lot of...white bears in this area?" the woman asked after a long moment of silence.

The way she asked the question made Charlotte's head snap up. She sounded hesitant and wistful and almost afraid. Before Charlotte could formulate an answer, the woman continued.

"I've been in the area for a few weeks now. I'm only passing through, but everyone has been more than friendly. The local official and his family have taken me under their wing and include me in their meals, although I prefer to sleep outside now the weather is warm enough." She looked uncomfortable, and Charlotte wondered if she was unused to sleeping in the company of strangers.

"I try to repay them by gathering what I can," the woman continued, gesturing at a half-full basket Charlotte hadn't noticed before. Her lips twisted in a self-deprecating way. "I'm not very good at it, though."

"You've been staying with Master Harold and his wife?" Charlotte asked.

The woman's brows lifted. "You know them? Are you a local, then?" Her brow furrowed. "I thought I met everyone from this valley when they celebrated the birth of the new baby from three houses over. I would have noticed you, though."

Charlotte wondered fleetingly why none of her family had mentioned Harold having an extended guest—an odd one who refused to sleep in his house. But she could hardly blame them for the omission given Charlotte had fled into the woods at the first opportunity.

"You probably met my sisters," she said dully. "Elizabeth and Odelia?"

"Oh yes!" the woman said, but she sounded cautious.

Despite herself, Charlotte's lips twisted upward. "Let me guess, they weren't delighted at the arrival of a new and beautiful young woman in their midst?"

The woman bit her lip and looked to the side, clearly uncomfortable. Charlotte winced. She shouldn't have said that, but she still felt so off balance. The woman was being friendly, but the last thing Charlotte wanted was to become friends with her. And yet, at the same time, she couldn't suppress an insatiable desire to know more about her.

"I'm sorry," she said softly. "Forget I said that. I'm Charlotte, by the way. I used to live here before my marriage."

Mentioning Henry, even in passing, sent a jolt of pain through her. The woman seemed to notice and frowned in response as if concerned, but she didn't comment on it.

"My name is Gwen. It's a pleasure to meet you, Charlotte."

Gwen. Charlotte regarded the woman in the painting who finally had a name. Gwen. She moved with the same elegance Charlotte had picked up from the portrait, and her gown looked like Charlotte's—too fancy for a walk in the woods.

Just seeing her image had been enough to plant the idea that she was a princess. Meeting her in person did nothing to erase that impression. But despite herself, Charlotte felt the same curiosity and sympathy growing toward Gwen that Gwen seemed to feel toward her.

They had met by chance in this forest, but neither of them belonged here—not anymore. On the outside, this place might be home for Charlotte—or an old home, at least—but inside she was lost, alone, and in pain. If she felt the pull of a kindred soul toward Gwen, did that mean Gwen felt as she did inside? What had brought her to this place? Why was a young woman traveling the kingdom alone?

"So you've returned from your new home to visit your family?" Gwen asked, clearly trying to inject some cheerful normalcy into the conversation. "You must be so happy to see them."

"Yes," Charlotte said, the answer surprising her with its honesty. "I am." She hesitated, but again she felt the unexpected pull toward Gwen and the desire to be honest with her. "We didn't leave on the best terms, so it's been a relief to reconcile with them."

A wistful look came into Gwen's eyes, and on impulse Charlotte reached out and clasped one of her hands.

"What about you?" she asked. "Have you left someone behind in need of reconciliation? I left my home once in anger and bitterness, so you'll receive no judgment from me."

Gwen shrank in on herself, but it didn't seem to be from

offense at Charlotte's words. Instead, after a moment, she shook her head.

"The one I'm fleeing is beyond reconciliation." The stark look in her eyes shook Charlotte, and she knew instantly that if she could help Gwen, she had to do so.

Her jealousy didn't matter beside whatever horror this woman was fleeing. If Charlotte truly loved Henry, she would do anything she could to aid Gwen in finding escape and healing. It was what he would want.

Charlotte squeezed her hand, putting every bit of sympathy and compassion into her expression that she could.

"I hope you know that you're safe here," she said. "No one in this valley will hurt you. And though Rangmere isn't the warmest of kingdoms, it has changed greatly since Queen Ava and King Hans took the throne. If you head for the capital, I believe you will find assistance there as well."

She paused to consider. The one thing—the only thing—she couldn't do for Gwen was offer her a home. Not when Charlotte and Henry lived alone in an empty castle. The situation would be intolerable for all of them.

"Arcadia is well regarded as being a place of prosperity whose people are warm and welcoming," she said in a rush. "My family has plans to move there. I could talk to them. I'm sure they would be willing to take you with them."

A guilty part of her wondered if she was trying to send Gwen as far away as possible, but she pushed it aside. Gwen was clearly fleeing something, so distance was likely what she wanted.

Gwen hesitated, however, pulling her hand free just so she could wring both hands together. When she looked up at Charlotte, she looked tormented, and Charlotte's heart seized.

"I don't know what to do!" Gwen burst out. "There's someone I have to find, but I don't know where he's gone. I don't even know if he's alive." Her voice dropped to a whisper that was almost a sob. "I have to believe he's alive."

Cold washed over Charlotte, robbing her of proper thought. She put her hands in her lap, hoping Gwen wouldn't notice them trembling.

"You've lost...*him?*" she asked carefully.

Gwen nodded, silent tears running down her face. "It's been so many years since I've seen him. Maybe he doesn't even remember me. But he's the only one I trust. Now that I'm free, the only thing I want to do is find Easton. But I have no idea where to even start looking." She wrung her hands together again.

Charlotte's thoughts, which had seemed mired in molasses, sputtered and flared back to life.

"Easton?" she asked. "Did you say his name is Easton?"

Gwen leaned forward, excitement sparking in her face. "Do you know him? Have you met someone by that name? Someone else without a home?"

Charlotte quickly shook her head. "No, I'm sorry. I don't know any Eastons."

"Oh." Gwen sat back, all the animation leaving her.

But Charlotte felt alive in a way she hadn't since discovering the portrait. It was all she could do to keep sitting still and talking to Gwen as if nothing had happened.

"Do you love this Easton?" she asked, holding her breath as she waited for the answer.

Gwen flushed, the color making her even more beautiful. "I haven't seen him for ten years. He may be married with children by now for all I know. But I certainly loved him fiercely as a child. He was my only playmate and companion."

"Did his family move away?" Charlotte asked.

Gwen's brows contracted, her face growing dark. "No, he just disappeared one day."

Charlotte gasped. Did Gwen think he had run away? Surely she had considered the likelihood of a more awful possibility.

"You…you don't think he met with an…accident?" she asked hesitantly. "Was he the type to run away?"

"No!" Gwen said fiercely. "He wouldn't have run away and left me without a word. He didn't leave by choice."

Charlotte bit her lip, and Gwen winced.

"I know how it must sound," she said. "Sometimes in my most despairing moments, I think he must have fallen down a ravine or met a wild animal and be dead. But he was strong and clever and resilient. When he was cast out, he would have found a way to live. I'm sure of it."

"Someone sent him away? As a child?" Charlotte asked horrified. "Surely not!"

Gwen shivered. "You don't know my—" She cut herself off. "You don't know the woman who rules my home. I used to fear she killed him, but she claimed not to have done so. Just removed him." Her voice dwindled. "I sometimes think she would have gotten rid of Nanny too if she hadn't died."

Charlotte's face paled. What sort of horrible situation had Gwen escaped from?

She had wanted to help before, but the rush of warm feeling had grown in the wake of Gwen's revelation. Gwen wasn't searching for Henry, but for Easton. He was the sole focus of her memories and hopes.

That knowledge gave Charlotte the hope she had been lacking. If Henry's love had been one-sided, it changed everything. She had thought his enchantment and Charlotte herself stood between Henry and his lost love. She had thought it might be her duty to remove herself so he could be happy.

But if a future with Gwen had never been possible, then perhaps she didn't have to leave. Perhaps, Henry was in the process of forgetting the past and growing happy in the new life he had created.

"Where are you from?" she asked Gwen, filled with determination to repay the gift Gwen didn't even know she had given

Charlotte. "If you're right, and he was banished from your home, we can use it as a starting point and work out a search plan. There may be somewhere obvious he would have gone."

She gazed expectantly at Gwen. The other woman grew first pale and then red again, her hands tightening convulsively on each other.

Charlotte frowned, instinct telling her what Gwen feared. "Have you been keeping your home a secret? Because you're scared of the people you left behind? I promise I won't tell anyone anything about you unless you want me to." Indignation filled her voice. "And if the monsters you've left behind ever come searching for you, I certainly wouldn't reveal anything about your whereabouts."

Gwen smiled, a shaky gesture. "Do you think if I had been born here, we would have been friends? I've never had an ordinary friend before. But I always wished for one."

Charlotte reclaimed one of Gwen's hands. "Of course we would have been friends! I only wish you had been born here." She paused, examining the other woman's face. "Would you like to stay here? I'm sure I could find a household in the valley that would be willing to take you in permanently if that's what you'd like. Are you sure you want to search for Easton? You might never find him."

Gwen was already shaking her head before Charlotte finished.

"Logically I know the search is almost hopeless. But I can't just give up on him. Not without at least trying."

"Then you have to try," Charlotte said stoutly. "Which leads us back to making a search route." She gave Gwen a coaxing look. "Can't you tell me where you've come from?"

In the back of her mind was the thought that whatever community Gwen had left, it wasn't a healthy one. If she'd come from one of the valleys, Charlotte would have to convince her to report them to Master Harold. And if she came from somewhere further away...Perhaps Harold could still report them to Rang-meros. The capital had responsibility over the whole kingdom, and she doubted they would be happy to hear of a community that had gone as rogue as Gwen's clearly had.

"I come from the mountains," Gwen whispered, silencing Charlotte's thoughts.

"The mountains?" Charlotte looked instinctively toward the ranges that towered over them. "You mean one of the valleys that's deeper in? I've heard there are a couple..." She trailed off since Gwen was already shaking her head.

"I come from the mountain kingdom." She still spoke in a whisper.

Charlotte stared at her, struck silent by the claim. The mountain kingdom was just a legend!

But was it? Henry had asked her to look for information about them, and she had heard the occasional hushed whisper in the valley. But none of those instances had convinced her the mountain people were anything other than stories created by those who gazed up at the impassable mountains in awe.

Gwen's claim was another matter, however.

"You're saying you grew up in the mountains?" she clarified. "Not in one of the valleys but actually deep in the mountains? And there's a whole kingdom there?"

Gwen nodded, her face pale. She seemed to understand the import of what she was revealing.

Charlotte leaned back, trying to absorb it. Gazing at her new friend, she noticed her straight posture and thought of every-thing she had said—and not said. After seeing her portrait in Henry's castle, Charlotte had been certain she was a princess. But sitting in the forest with Gwen, it had seemed nothing more than fancy. Not only was she alone in the depths of Rangmere, but Charlotte had learned the royal families of all the kingdoms as a child and none of them had contained a Princess Gwen.

She had never learned about the royal family of the mountain kingdom, however. Her earlier certainty returned. She wasn't just talking to a girl from the fabled lost people. She was talking to the mountain princess. And something was terribly wrong in their kingdom if she had been forced to flee.

Charlotte swallowed down the enormity of the revelation and nodded slowly. "Very well, then. Is it possible Easton is somewhere in the mountains? I have no idea how you would search the peaks for a lone person." She gazed again at the glimpse of distant stone visible through the canopy.

"It would be an impossible task." Gwen slumped before rallying with a determined look. "But the mountains are a death sentence, and the queen said Easton was banished. There are ways out of the mountains—we have a few traders who make the trek in secret—and I think she might have abandoned him on this side of the mountains."

Charlotte raised her eyebrows at this information, but it made sense. If the mountain kingdom existed, then the stories hadn't been mere fancy after all, and they must have originated somewhere.

"Do you have any idea where the paths exit the mountains?" Charlotte asked. "If we could work out where he came out…"

Gwen grimaced. "I wish I knew. But I came out by…another means." Her hand strayed to her pocket.

Charlotte waited, full of curiosity, but Gwen said nothing more. Charlotte would have liked to press her for more information, but it seemed rude, so she let it go. She had secrets enough of her own, so she couldn't fault others for keeping their own counsel.

"I think Harold might know something about the routes," Gwen blurted out. "It's why I've stayed with his family so long. I've been trying to convince him to tell me, but he won't talk about it. From what I can gather, only a chosen few valley folk are permitted to meet and trade with the mountain delegations. I think the queen's people might have threatened those valley folk that if word gets out more broadly, they'll lose their trade."

Charlotte's mouth fell open as several things clicked into place. Her aunt and uncle were clearly among the chosen few to be permitted to act as traders—it was the source of their extra wealth. And it must have taken her father all these years to gain enough trust to be included in their number.

But that new knowledge did nothing to help Gwen. "The most obvious place to look is the valleys," she said briskly. "So you've done well coming here. Have you asked Harold if he's met anyone by the name of Easton?"

Gwen nodded. "He says he hasn't."

"Hmmm…" Charlotte hummed to herself as she thought. "That rules out all the closer valleys. We should ask him for help, though. He could provide a map of the remaining valleys and mark off those where he knows all the residents. That will narrow the initial search a little. Unless Easton changed his name when he arrived." She looked to Gwen. "Would he have felt the need to do that if he was on the run from…your kingdom?"

Gwen frowned. "I suppose it's possible. But I did ask Harold if he knew of any boys who had arrived alone ten years ago, and he seemed certain there was no one like that in any of his valleys."

Charlotte nodded. "Good point. Even if his name has changed, it's a unique enough situation that people should remember him." She frowned. "But are you really going to travel through Rangmere alone?"

Gwen shivered. "What other option do I have? It's not that I want to be alone, but I have no one. As it is, I feel terrible for imposing on Harold and his family just because he's the local official."

"Don't worry about that," Charlotte said as cheerfully as she could. "I'm sure they're glad of the company. Society so restricted out here that all newcomers are a matter of interest."

"That's what everyone keeps saying, so I've allowed myself to be talked into staying this long." Gwen didn't sound happy about that weakness on her part.

"They're not making excuses," Charlotte said. "They really mean it."

Gwen gave her a tremulous smile, and Charlotte wanted to give her a hug. How quickly her feelings toward the other woman had undergone a complete shift.

"You also haven't heard of an Easton," Gwen said after a pause. "So that might be another valley I can cross off the search. Which valley are you living in now with your husband?"

It was an innocent question, but it sent a surge of longing through Charlotte. Her thoughts and emotions had been trapped inside her, in such intense turmoil, and she hadn't been able to speak of them to anyone. Even now that she had returned home, she couldn't talk about the truth with her parents and sisters. Her husband had asked her to remain silent, but she would have known it was a bad idea anyway. Her relationship with her family was tangled enough, and they had only just reached a new place of peace.

But here in this secluded clearing, real life seemed distant. She had made a friend, and impossible as it had initially seemed, one who felt like a kindred soul. For the first time, she felt it was possible to talk about the incredible turns her life had taken since her wedding, and she couldn't help wanting to be honest even though she had known Gwen for less than a day.

Somewhere in the recesses of her mind, Charlotte felt a twinge of discomfort. Henry had only told her not to speak of their nights to her parents, but surely he had meant to keep it private in general. He knew her history, and he wouldn't have thought there was anyone else she would be tempted to tell. He couldn't possibly have guessed she would run into Gwen.

Charlotte ignored the small voice of caution. She was so full of emotions, she was going to burst if she couldn't get them out.

Or do you just want to make sure Gwen knows Henry is yours? a less pleasant voice asked.

Charlotte brushed that one aside too. Of course it wasn't jealousy motivating her. Gwen had Easton.

"Actually," she said, her voice trembling with a heady mix of excitement and nerves now that she was finally telling someone the truth of her strange situation, "my husband doesn't come from the valleys. I don't know where he comes from originally, but we have a castle in the nearby mountains."

"A castle? In the mountains?"

Before Gwen could ask any more questions, the story poured out of Charlotte. She told how the white bear had approached her family and about the wealth and escape he'd offered in exchange for marriage. When she mentioned his name, she watched Gwen closely, but there wasn't so much as a flicker of recognition or curiosity.

Charlotte's hope surged afresh. Gwen didn't appear to even know a missing man named Henry. If his love for Gwen was not only one-sided but had developed from afar, then surely such a hollow emotion might have already been supplanted by the wife he spent all his days with? Now she knew Gwen was the mountain princess, it seemed more than possible that Henry—who must also be from the mountain kingdom if he knew Gwen— might have loved her from a distance.

Charlotte had been too hasty in leaving him, and now the hours before his return stretched out far too long.

But in the meantime, she'd found a new and completely unexpected friend. Buoyed up by her relief and the heady excitement it created, she continued on with her tale. She described the castle he had taken her to, and the building provoked more questions from Gwen than the revelation that Charlotte had married a bear.

The more detail she gave on the castle, the deeper Gwen's frown grew. But now that Charlotte had begun, she couldn't stop.

The rest of the story followed, culminating in her discovery that Henry was really a man and the way they spent their nights lying side by side in the pitch darkness.

When she finished, silence fell on the clearing. It lasted until Gwen spoke in a voice that trembled slightly.

"You're married to a man who turns into a white bear every day?"

GWEN

ear nearly immobilized Gwen, but she wasn't sure if it was general dread or fear for Charlotte, who seemed so bright and lovely. Gwen had allowed herself to be swept up in excitement at the unexpected discovery of a friend and in their exchange of confidences. The feeling—however brief —of being part of a team, united in the search for Easton, had been heady. But reality fell far too quickly.

From the bright, almost tender, expression on her face, Charlotte had no idea of the danger she was in. Gwen guessed she even felt affection for her husband, despite his transformations. But Gwen couldn't brush aside the coincidence.

Away from her mother's sleeping drafts, Gwen had been forced to endure her own transformation every night since her escape. She hid in the forest, away from the valley folk until the sun rose each morning, and she had yet to meet another bear of any sort, let alone one who was actually human.

If there was a man in the mountains who turned into a white bear, he must be part of the same enchantment as Gwen herself. And the only people trapped in the enchantment were her mother's people—the mountain court and the queen's guards.

Bile rose in her throat as she put it all together. She had been swept up in their talk of Easton and forgotten where she had first seen Charlotte. It hadn't been in this clearing but in her mother's bedchamber—in a portrait that had also featured Charlotte's husband.

At best, Charlotte's husband was a member of her mother's court, loyal to someone unspeakable. But her friend claimed he was a bear during the day and a man at night—the opposite of the enchantment on the mountain court. The more she considered the strange anomaly, the stronger grew an even more horrifying possibility. What if this man wasn't a member of the court but the original owner of whatever object her mother had used to create the curse?

Was he even a man at all, or was he some creature of nightmare who had managed to assume the trappings of a man by night? It was entirely believable that her mother would be allied with such a creature.

Creeping fingers of cold slid up Gwen's spine. Her friend had said she only ever encountered her husband as a man in the pitch dark. She had never seen him, not once. Did his dread enchantments allow him to assume the voice and size of a man but not a proper appearance? Was that why he hid in darkness?

Charlotte's bright smile was fading in the wake of Gwen's long silence, and she knew she needed to speak.

"Charlotte," she gasped, "are you sure you've never seen his face?"

"No, never." Charlotte leaned forward, looking concerned. "Are you well, Gwen? You look ill."

"I...I'm well enough." Gwen exerted all her will power to push down the horror that was making her sick. "It's you I'm worried about."

Charlotte laughed and waved a hand as if to brush off Gwen's concerns. "I know it's an unusual situation—to say the least!—but Henry is everything considerate."

Gwen caught the soft glow in her friend's eyes when she spoke his name, and her heart sank. She had spent years forced to attend the events of her mother's court, always watching and listening from the sidelines. While she might have engaged in few conversations herself, she had long ago learned that sometimes the most charming of faces concealed a rotten core. This Henry had clearly won Charlotte over, but that fact provided Gwen little reassurance. He would show his true colors eventually, but when he did, Charlotte would be trapped alone in his castle.

What could Gwen do about it, though? Charlotte had known her for less than a day. Why would she listen to her speaking against her beloved husband? In any ordinary situation, Gwen would even have applauded Charlotte for that loyalty.

But her friend was caught up in a dark enchantment, and Gwen couldn't leave her to fight it alone. Especially when Charlotte didn't even know the danger she was in.

"Don't you think you should at least insist on seeing him once?" Gwen suggested tentatively.

Impatience crept over Charlotte's face, as if she was disappointed in her friend's reaction.

"I can't do that. Of course I'd like to see his face—I've imagined it too many times to count—but I trust him. He has a reason for keeping it hidden, and he'll show me his full self when the time is right."

But will you like that full self when you see it? Gwen pleaded in her mind.

Aloud, she said, "But surely it couldn't hurt to see him only once?"

Charlotte shrugged. "Even if I wanted to, it's impossible. The castle is Henry's, and he controls the sources of light. None of them work during the nighttime hours. It's not just a matter of taking a peek."

Gwen bit her lip. She could think of strategies that might circumvent the enchanter's machinations, but it was clear her friend didn't want to hear them. Already Charlotte had deflated at Gwen's questions. She feared that if she pressed any harder, Charlotte would close herself off from Gwen entirely.

Gwen couldn't risk that. Not when she had finally found someone who might become a friend, someone who would help her make a plan for finding Easton. And even for Charlotte's sake she didn't want to destroy the fragile beginnings of their friendship. If her suspicions were even partially correct, Charlotte would need every possible ally in the future.

"I'm sorry," Gwen said softly. "It's just such an...incredible story."

Charlotte relaxed, laughing. "Imagine what it was like living it! I wasn't sure if I was in a dream half the time."

The two chattered on a little until Charlotte noticed the afternoon sun waning. She leaped to her feet.

"We really must be getting back. Otherwise my family will start worrying, and you might miss your evening meal." She smiled at Gwen. "Shall we meet again?"

Gwen agreed eagerly, and the two began the walk back, staying together until they had to part ways to reach their separate destinations. As they walked, Gwen's mind raced, and when they paused for a final farewell, she made a suggestion.

"I could meet you at your house tomorrow, if you'd like. I remember where it is, and I'd be happy to have the chance to greet your parents and sisters again."

Charlotte paused for the briefest moment, and Gwen wondered if she'd rather keep their friendship separate from whatever complicated dynamic Charlotte shared with her family. Gwen could certainly understand that desire. In ordinary circumstances she wouldn't have dreamed of intruding. But the circumstances weren't ordinary, and while they were walking, she'd realized what she should do. She just needed a chance for a quiet word with one of Charlotte's parents.

Charlotte might not have a reason to listen to a friend of a few hours' standing, but surely she would listen to her own parents. Gwen just needed to convince them there was something terribly wrong with Charlotte's husband—something beyond the fact he turned into a bear each day.

CHARLOTTE

Although Charlotte had been hesitant at the idea, Gwen's visit to Charlotte's family home had been a success. With no one else present to provoke her sisters' sense of competition and comparison, they were welcoming to the visitor. And Charlotte's parents seemed delighted to hear she had a local friend, even if only of recent standing.

Gwen herself was everything that was charming and polite. She even graciously accepted a tour of the new stable, conducted while Charlotte was caught inside by her sisters. Elizabeth and Odelia had somehow talked her into helping with the food preparation their mother had assigned them, and Charlotte wasn't able to extricate herself before her proud mother swept Gwen off to complete the tour. Given Gwen's true status, Charlotte could only hope she wouldn't take offense. But she couldn't warn her family that Gwen was a princess when her friend hadn't even fully confided in her.

Thankfully Gwen's royal manners were more than adequate for Charlotte's absence. But she still felt guilty enough to stick closely to her friend for the rest of her stay. So it was only after Gwen left that Charlotte noticed how distracted her parents seemed. With the excitement of the visit over it was impossible to miss.

When her mother dropped her third bowl in a row, Charlotte asked what was wrong.

"Nothing, nothing," her mother said, but the look she cast at Charlotte suggested otherwise.

Charlotte sat straighter, frowning. It hadn't occurred to her that her parents' mood might be related to her, but her mother's expression suggested it was.

"Actually," her father said suddenly, "your mother and I were wondering if you would come for a walk with us, Charlotte?"

If her father was using her full name, then something was definitely wrong.

"Of course I'll come," she said, dreading the possibility that her parents might ask her to extend her stay.

She gathered her cloak with a heavy heart. It would be difficult to say no to them, but there was no question of staying longer. She was already counting the hours until she saw her husband again and was able to finally have the too-long deferred conversation about their future. She wouldn't delay her reunion with Henry for anyone.

Sure enough, as soon as they were away from the house, her mother cast a beseeching look at her father, and her father cleared his throat. Charlotte held herself silent, knowing it was only fair to allow them to have their say, even if she already knew the outcome.

But her father's first words took her completely by surprise.

"You seem happy, Charli," he said, "but your mother and I have some concerns."

"Concerns?" Charlotte looked between them, bewildered. "About what?"

"In retrospect, I can see that I took the matter of your marriage far too lightly," her father said. "I made certain assumptions that I have since realized are false."

Charlotte frowned. Where had these concerns been in their joyous reconciliation the day before? Her obvious well-being had seemed to clear away their lingering worry.

"I don't know what you mean," she faltered. "What sort of assumptions?"

"In truth," her father said, "I took certain hints dropped by the white bear—"

"Henry," Charlotte interrupted.

Her father exchanged a look with her mother. "Ah yes. Henry. I took certain hints dropped by Henry and combined them with information from your uncle to reach erroneous conclusions. It was on the strength of that understanding that we agreed to part with you."

"What can you possibly mean?" Charlotte asked, growing more and more incensed. "Henry promised me a life of ease and comfort, and he promised you riches through a large bride price." She glanced back in the direction of the new house, now hidden by the trees. "Can you deny he's provided exactly that for both of us?"

Her mother looked pained, but her father's stern expression didn't waver. "I admit he has so far stayed true to the explicit promises he made. It's the implications that have proven false that now concern me."

Charlotte felt her anger on Henry's behalf peak and then suddenly abate. She let out the breath she'd been holding. Could she blame her parents for leaping to wrong conclusions about Henry when she had done exactly the same? And just like them, she had been concerned when she first learned she was wrong. But just as she had long ago forgotten her thoughts of the Palace of Light, they would soon realize their daughter had more than she could ever need.

"I'm sure I can ease your minds," she said softly. "What is it you were wrong about?"

Her father looked at her without any abatement of his

obvious anxiety. "When we encountered a talking white bear, naturally we assumed he was one of the mountain people."

"Naturally?" Charlotte asked, astonished. "Whatever can you mean?"

"At the time I hadn't met one myself, of course," her father said, "but since the mountain people who visit these valleys transform into white bears, the connection was obvious. I told you as much."

"Told me?!" Charlotte stared at him in astonishment. "What are you talking about? I've never heard such a thing!"

Her mother looked from Charlotte to her husband, horrified, while he merely looked confused.

"Given I was working so hard to be accepted as one of the approved valley traders, your mother and I were extra careful to maintain discretion about their existence. Even after Henry first appeared, it didn't seem wise to mention anything in front of your sisters."

Charlotte frowned, remembering all the times after Henry's appearance when her father had hinted at something unsaid, or trailed off a thought half finished. Even his response to the arrival of a white bear hadn't seemed entirely normal.

"I can understand you not wanting to say anything to Elizabeth or Odelia," she said, incensed. "But how could you not tell me the full truth when I was about to marry one of them!"

"I couldn't say it in the house with your sisters around," he said. "But I did tell you out in the forest when we talked about his proposal, remember? Or at least, I started to tell you, but you became furious and cut me off, running back to the house."

Charlotte gaped at him. The memory of that day was burned into her mind, thanks to the high emotions that had marked it. And now that she thought back to that conversation, she did remember him whispering something that she hadn't heard, too caught up in her heartbreak to pay attention. How could she have guessed he was imparting secrets of such significance?

"I didn't hear you," she said, groaning. "You were whispering, and I was too..." She sighed. Perhaps it had all been for the best. She might not have gone through with the marriage if it hadn't been for her mistaken assumptions.

"But Harold said you knew everything," her father said, still frowning in confusion. "He gave me a whole lecture about how I should have warned you to be more discreet. He said you nearly blurted it all out in front of his children. I thought you must have already heard about it from one of your cousins and were protecting them by not mentioning as much to me."

Charlotte shook her head, her emotions shifting toward amusement. She remembered the conversation with Master Harold as well. She had been confused to receive a similar lecture to the one her father had been given and even more confused when he had spoken about some in the valley not trusting Henry's people. If she hadn't been so emotionally worked up, maybe she would have hesitated long enough to demand a full explanation.

"None of my cousins ever mentioned a thing," she said.

"You really didn't know?" her mother frowned. "But you can't have married him thinking he was genuinely a bear!"

"I thought he was one of the High King's creatures from the Palace of Light," Charlotte said. "I thought he meant to take me there!"

Her mother gasped, and her father's jaw tensed.

"What?" he asked. "You thought what?" He looked thunderstruck.

Charlotte shrugged. "It doesn't matter now. I'm perfectly happy in Henry's castle and have no desire to go to the Palace of Light instead."

Her parents exchanged worried looks.

"But what is this castle?" her father asked. "Is it not in the mountain kingdom?"

Charlotte shook her head. "Actually, it isn't far from here. It's certainly not up among the proper mountains—which is where I assume their kingdom must be. I've recently found out some information that makes me think Henry must have come from the mountain kingdom originally, but he doesn't live there now."

"You really do live all alone?" her mother asked. "I thought your stories sounded a little strange, but I didn't realize you were so totally isolated." Her expression was growing more and more alarmed, and Charlotte tried to think how to reassure her.

"Did Henry ever say he had come down from the mountain kingdom or that he meant to take me there?" she asked slowly.

Her father sighed. "No, he didn't. We assumed as much because he was a white bear. How could we think anything else? But he was obviously wealthy, and he dropped certain hints that gave me the impression he was a prince among them—or a senior member of their court, at least. I know some in these parts mistrust the mountain people—it's why the traders wish their existence to remain secret so as to avoid any prejudice or hostility. But the mountain kingdom has brought new prosperity to the valleys. Its people aren't evil—they're just unknown. And if you were their princess, what danger could there be? Henry assured me you would have a life of luxury, privilege, and power, and that you would be free to come and go as you wished." He audibly ground his teeth together. "It sounds foolish now to say that his manner convinced me he could be trusted. I shouldn't have been so credulous."

Charlotte put a gentle hand on his arm. "I know what you mean. I sensed it from him myself. It's a large part of the reason I agreed to the marriage. And you needn't be so alarmed, Father. He may not be who either of us thought, but he has done nothing to betray our trust."

"I know now he's not a prince," her mother said, sounding eager, "but you said he is one of the mountain people?"

Charlotte bit her lip. Since meeting Gwen, she had concluded he had to be, but they had all been wrong in their previous assumptions.

"He has never said so," she admitted reluctantly.

"He hasn't taken you to visit the mountain kingdom?" her father asked.

Again Charlotte was reluctant to answer, but a lack of communication was what had caused the problem in the first place. "No. We've never been anywhere but his castle, which, as I said, isn't far from here."

"And you live there completely alone," her mother said slowly, looking at her father with eyes of concern.

"We may be alone, but it's still a life of luxury," Charlotte said quickly. "Henry's godmother object provides for all our needs."

She had thought mention of a godmother object would reassure them, but they merely exchanged another significant look.

"So this Henry is neither a resident of the Palace of Light nor one of the mountain people," her father said slowly. "And he keeps you isolated and alone, far from any communities. It seems impossible that he could be a white bear and not be one of the mountain people, but they have never mentioned one of their own living isolated within the valleys. If he isn't one of them, then we must know—who and what is he?"

Both her parents fixed her with such intense looks—compelling, anxious, and charged all at the same time, as if they were ready to wrench her away from Henry and never allow her near him again.

Fear made Charlotte's heart lurch and race, words falling out of her.

"Henry is a man! You're talking as if he's something horrible, but he's just an ordinary man under an enchantment."

Her father's stance didn't relax, but her mother slumped a little, the first hint of relief appearing on her face.

"You're sure?" she asked. "You've seen him as a man?"

Charlotte bit her lip. "I haven't seen him, but…" She fell silent, remembering her promise to Henry. Would he still want her to keep it in the face of this terrible misunderstanding?

Her mother let out a soft cry. "You haven't seen him! How can you know he's a man, then? Oh, my daughter!" She flung her arms around Charlotte. "We should never have let you go. This is all our fault!"

"Mother!" Charlotte struggled to free herself from the suffocating grip. "You really don't need to be so concerned. I'm happy in my life with Henry." She drew a breath as she finally extricated herself. "I love Henry."

Her admission, which felt so weighty and significant to her, seemed only to fuel her parents' unease. They exchanged yet another look, and this time she could read it. They found the idea discomforting—as if it were further evidence that she was under the thrall of someone malevolent.

"He isn't like that!" she cried. "He's kind and considerate, and he knows me—the real me. I belong with him." Tears ran down her face as she realized the truth of her own words and how foolish they made her doubt and uncertainty seem. Why had she been so overset that she couldn't even manage a conversation?

"Hush, my dear, hush." Her mother rubbed her back. "We'll find a way out of this marriage for you."

Charlotte pulled back. "Aren't you listening? I don't want to leave my marriage!"

"We should all calm down," her father said. "Charli, we're only worried about you. If everything is as you say, we will be delighted. But how do you know he's really an ordinary man? Do you have anything to rely on other than his own words?"

He looked at her so intently that she squirmed. She had to defend Henry. Surely she could do so without telling them the full truth of their nights together.

"It's not just his words," she said slowly. "I've talked to him as a man."

"I thought you said you hadn't seen him in any form but that of a bear." Her father was watching her carefully and must have caught her grimace.

"I didn't say I've seen him, I said I've talked to him."

"That sounds like nonsense," her mother said. "If you've talked to him, why don't you look at him as well?"

Charlotte hesitated, worrying at her lip. "Because it's always dark," she finally blurted out. "He is only a man at night and the palace is shrouded in complete darkness then."

She didn't mention the specifics of their nights spent side by side in bed, but it was clear that even without those details, her words had confirmed her parents' fears rather than allayed them. She should have just remained silent as Henry had asked her.

Fresh tears threatened. She had only wanted to defend him, but instead she had terrified her parents.

Her mother's voice softened. "You say you love him. Don't you want to see his face? Just once, so you can be sure—so we can be sure—that he's really what he claims to be."

Charlotte scoffed. "What else could he be?" Even as she said the words, she could feel the warmth of his arms around her on the night he had comforted her, his heart beating so close to her own. Of course Henry was a man.

But she couldn't deny the insidious appeal of her mother's suggestion. She did want to see his face. She wanted it desperately.

"We don't really know anything about him," her father said. "But it would be reassuring to know he truly is an ordinary man. There are clearly strong enchantments at work, and you yourself have pointed out that not all creatures in this world are entirely... natural."

Charlotte frowned. The creatures that lived in the Palace of Light with the High King weren't something to be afraid of. But then, neither were any of the godmother objects when they were first given to humans. And yet, some had been corrupted and misused.

Charlotte didn't believe Henry was someone who deserved her fear. But she wanted a future with him—one in which they could be fully husband and wife—and she longed to see her husband's face. Even if she only saw it once, for a moment, it would be enough for now. Once she had seen it, she would be able to picture him as he lay beside her in the darkness. Nothing else would need to change, but she would truly know him the way he knew her. And maybe if she truly knew him, their marriage could become real, the way she longed for it to be.

"But I can't," she said, sounding more regretful than she should have. "His object controls all the sources of light in our castle."

"I have an idea about that." Her mother gave her father a look that made Charlotte wonder about the source of her mother's idea. "I'll give you a candle from home and a way to light it. Keep it hidden on you, and when night comes, you can light it and see him for yourself. If that upsets him, then he's not being honest with you, and at least you'll know…" She hesitated. "Whatever there is to know."

Charlotte bit her lip. Her parents didn't know that Henry slept beside her at night. If she looked at him while he was asleep, he wouldn't even need to know about it. She could light the candle for a brief minute and then hide it again. She would even destroy it the next morning so she wouldn't be tempted again. Nothing would need to change.

"Fine," she said in a rush. "If it would relieve your mind, I'll do it."

Both her parents smiled at that, although it didn't quite relax the tension in her father's frame. She could only imagine what he was thinking. If she did discover something terrible about her husband, what would she do about it alone in their castle? But she wasn't worried about that aspect because, unlike her father, she knew there was nothing terrifying to find. All she was going to see was the face of the man she loved. The face of her husband.

CHARLOTTE

*B*y the time Henry arrived to collect her the next day, Charlotte was a wreck. The candle had been received and stowed carefully inside her gown, but she might as well have stored a nest of ants there. She could barely stay still, one minute seized by the certainty she should throw it away and the next by a burning impatience for night to fall so she could finally see Henry's true face.

She waited outside for him, but since her entire family waited with her, he couldn't avoid them this time. They greeted him politely enough—even with curious excitement on the part of her sisters now that he had provided the promised wealth. Charlotte just hoped he didn't notice the tension in her father's shoulders or the way her mother clung to her and avoided looking straight at the bear in front of her.

Henry himself said as little as possible until they had departed and were traveling through the trees.

"How did it go?" A world of tension lay beneath the words. Had he been worrying about her for the last three days?

Charlotte leaned forward, resting her cheek against the fur of his neck. Had he been taking proper care of himself? What had he done alone at night in his human form? Without her to sleep beside had he roamed the empty corridors?

The only thought she couldn't stomach was the idea that he might have spent those nights alone in the dining room. But memories of the portrait—once so painful—led her now to thoughts of Gwen and her search for Easton. Even if Henry's feelings still lingered, she would find a way to drive them out. Now that she knew there was no bereft love waiting for him, nothing could make her give him up. Henry was hers, just like she was his, and she would hold onto him with every bit of her strength.

"Lottie?" he asked at her silence, and warmth rushed through her at the nickname. She had missed hearing it. She had missed him.

"Thank you," she said. "For suggesting I go home and for taking me there. I didn't realize how much I needed to reconcile with my parents. Even my sisters were kind to me like they used to be when we were small. Now that I'm gone and they're rich, everything is forgiven."

She couldn't keep a hint of sourness from appearing in the last sentence, but it was tempered with amusement. Her sisters were who they were, and there was nothing for Charlotte to do apart from accept that fact. She couldn't force them to change, and she would only make herself miserable hoping for it. They wouldn't be bothered in the least.

"It was a good time." Henry repeated, both relieved and pleased. "I was worried I'd done the wrong thing sending you to them. They have never treated you as you deserved, and I spent the whole time you were gone worried I'd only delivered you into further heartbreak. Perhaps you'd be better without them in your life at all."

"No," Charlotte said quickly. "My parents apologized for the past, and everyone treated me well. I know my life is with you now—I welcome that—but my past is still important to me. They're still important to me."

Henry grunted as if not entirely convinced.

"I'm sorry you worried, though," Charlotte said softly.

"I just hope it won't make you feel more lonely in the castle," Henry said, still sounding concerned.

"No," Charlotte said fervently. "As much as I liked seeing my family again, I missed home. Our home." Her voice dipped shyly on the last two words, and he rumbled in response.

"Our home," he repeated, in his deep, gravely voice, and the sound filled her with happiness. She was with Henry again, and they were going home.

And soon it would be night.

The trees flew past, and when the castle finally appeared, Charlotte felt actual tears at the sight of the sober gray stone. She never would have guessed how comfortable a home the castle would become.

They parted ways as usual, but Charlotte could barely make it through her usual evening routine. Food might as well have been paper in her mouth for its lack of taste, and the candle still burned beneath her dress, although it had never been lit.

When it came time to undress, she hid it carefully beneath her pillow. Almost as soon as she'd extinguished the normal candelabra—triggering the accustomed descent of pure darkness—the door opened. Henry had never arrived so promptly before, and she dared to hope he had missed her some fraction of the amount she had missed him.

He sighed as he slid between the sheets, keeping to their usual distance.

"It's nice to have you back," he said simply. "I managed alone here without you before our wedding, but now…"

Charlotte glowed at his words. He really had missed her. He wanted her here. Maybe she was right in hoping he had already started to forget his youthful interest in the princess and was turning toward his wife instead.

"I'm glad to be back," she murmured, wondering if the extent of her emotion sounded in her voice. "I won't leave you again."

"It was a fortunate day when I first saw you and your sisters in the woods." The sound of his voice told her he'd rolled over and was lying on his side facing toward her.

"You mentioned you'd seen us before," Charlotte said. "But how did you decide to propose to me? And why me?"

She asked the questions shamelessly, the fear she had felt before over his answers gone.

"From the moment I saw you, I couldn't take my eyes off you, Lottie."

She laughed, unable to help the glow of satisfaction.

"Do you not believe me?" he asked. "How could I look away? You're like sunshine itself. I knew I needed to find a wife, and as soon as I saw you, I knew I wanted it to be you. Seeing you made me feel like I'd spent the last months beneath solid gray cloud and the sun had finally appeared."

She considered his words. "You needed a wife. Because of your enchantment." She was skirting dangerously close to topics he had declared off limits, but she couldn't help herself. "And you picked me because you thought I was beautiful." She wasn't sure whether to be amused or offended.

Henry groaned. "That sounds terribly shallow, doesn't it? But it wasn't like that. Of course I noticed your beauty—it would be impossible not to. But I've seen plenty of beautiful women before. What drew me to you was something else. The brightness in you was in your expression and your words, not just your features. Even the way you carried yourself…"

He groaned again. "I'm not explaining it well. I'm just saying that your beauty isn't only physical. It shines out of you. I could see it in the way you approached simple tasks like gathering food and in the way you interacted with your sisters. I suppose, objectively speaking, they are attractive enough, but they seemed like gray clouds beside your sun. I know it sounds foolish, but I felt as if I knew you. And then after we talked..."

The rustle of sheets gave away his restless movement. "After we talked, I was really sure. If I hadn't managed to convince you, I don't know what I would have done. Thanks to the enchantment, I would still have needed a wife, but how could I have married someone else?"

Fresh warmth suffused Charlotte. Henry had seen her from the very beginning, just as he had seen her all these weeks in the castle. She had come home ready to fight for their future, but was it possible he was already won?

Her heart soared at the thought even as she cautioned herself. If he loved her as she loved him, why did he keep such a careful distance, never treating her as anything more than a friend and companion?

Unless he's just keeping his promise, a new voice whispered.

As soon as she thought it, Charlotte realized how likely it was. Her husband—her good and true husband—had made promises to her that he would consider absolutely binding. Promises he wouldn't break, no matter his feelings.

She let out a sound that was half sob, half laugh. Whatever Gwen had once been to him, his attention now seemed solely for his wife. Everything she longed for was in front of her. She just had to reach out her hand and grasp it.

"What is it?" he asked sharply, worry in his tone. "Are you all right?"

Charlotte was tempted to say no, just to see if he would cross the divide to comfort her again. But she couldn't bring herself to say something so untrue.

"I'm just happy," she whispered. "I'm happy to be back."

"Oh." He settled back, rustling the sheets at his movement. "Then we can be happy together."

"Yes," she murmured. "Together." She knew her voice sounded a bit watery, but she didn't care.

Soon she would tell him all her heart and admit her foolish fears. But she didn't want to mar this perfect moment with her confession. They had the rest of their lives to be together as husband and wife. There was no rush.

"I think I might actually be able to sleep tonight," Henry murmured in a voice that was already half slurred with sleep.

Her heart contracted. Had he lain awake without her beside him? Or perhaps he had prowled the corridors as she had feared. As much as her heart ached for him, it also rejoiced to know she had so much sway over his emotions.

"Sleep, dear husband," she whispered. "And in the morning, we will begin afresh."

And she would know his face by then. She would be able to picture him as his true self, and there would be no more barriers between them.

Swept up in her emotions, even the enchantment seemed like nothing. With their combined effort, how could they not find an answer to it?

His breathing evened, slowing into the familiar rhythm of his sleep. She lay for a long time, listening contentedly to the sound of his presence. But finally eagerness overtook her, and she stole out of bed.

With trembling fingers, she retrieved her mother's candle and flint. It took her several tries to light it, and part of her thought it wasn't going to work. But then flame blossomed in the darkness.

She squeezed her eyes shut, waiting a moment for them to adjust before cracking them open. She had never realized how bright a single candle could be until she had seen the depth of full darkness.

Shielding the single flame with her hand, she crept around the end of the enormous bed, approaching the far side where her husband lay. Her heart pattered far faster than her feet, sounding so loud she feared he would hear it and awaken.

But he slumbered peacefully, clearly deeply tired. When she had approached close enough, she leaned in, holding the candle so it would illuminate his face.

Her breath caught at sight of him. How was it possible that he was even more handsome than she had dreamed? He looked so peaceful in repose, giving her a full chance to admire his straight nose, strong jaw, and the riot of dark brown hair. The candlelight caught on his head, suggesting a hint that was almost auburn amid the brown. She couldn't see his eyes, but she didn't need to see them to fall even more in love with him.

Her body swayed toward him, pulled by something beyond conscious thought. But as she shifted position, a drip of candle wax fell. She only had time to gasp and jerk backward as it landed on the hand he had thrown over the blanket.

His eyes sprang open, and she forgot everything else at their piercing blue. With his eyes closed, he had been almost painfully beautiful, but the animation and intensity of his eyes only amplified the effect. The startling blue stood out against his dark hair, creating a whole that robbed her of breath. Could this man truly be her husband?

His expression, which had started out with the confusion expected from someone who had been woken from deep sleep by burning wax, softened at the sight of her. Their eyes locked together. Looking at his true face—at his unguarded response to her—she knew he already loved her as completely as she longed to be loved.

But the joy had barely registered when his expression changed. His thoughts had caught up with his instincts, and his gaze dropped to the candle in her hand. Instantly his face changed to a look of such profound horror that she fell back before it.

"What have you done?" he cried. "What have you done?"

"I...I just..." She moved to blow out the candle, panicked by his response, but he leaped forward and gripped her wrist in a steel hold.

"No," he said sharply. "There's no point now. The damage is already done. At least let me see you for these last moments."

"What do you mean?" she gasped as he removed the candle from her now trembling hold and placed it on the small table beside the bed. "What last moments?"

"Three months," he said. "That's all we needed. Three months' worth of nights. We were nearly there."

"I don't understand." Charlotte's trembling had spread from her hands to her whole body.

"When I left home to go adventuring on my own—a foolish notion I know now—I was captured in these valleys. The people who captured me wanted me to break their enchantment through my marriage. But something went wrong. I don't know why—I don't think they do either. I was supposed to be a bear at night, not during the day. It ruined their plans." He gave a harsh laugh. "Many marriage ceremonies are too elaborate to be completed between a human and a bear."

Charlotte swallowed painfully, putting together the pieces he hadn't said. "The mountain kingdom. They stole a husband for their princess. They wanted to marry you to Gwen!"

"Who?" he asked blankly.

"The mountain princess," she cried. "The one in the portrait."

"The portrait?" He frowned for a moment before his brow cleared. "Oh, you mean the one in the dining room? I never go in there."

"You...never go in there?" Charlotte whispered, trying to understand the seismic shocks that kept hitting her.

He laughed again, another bitter sound. "An empty castle except for one furnished room? This place didn't come from the bell—it's part of my enchantment, and it was a little obvious in its efforts to sway me with that one."

"They...they weren't your portraits?" Charlotte stammered.

"There were others?" He sounded genuinely surprised.

"In the side tables. And those came from the bell, after I arrived."

"When the bell interacts with the castle, it's affected by the castle's enchantment." He shrugged. "I never even met the princess. If they ever told me her name, I don't remember it. I certainly had no desire to eat my meals with her looming over me. She's the reason for my capture, my imprisonment in the body of a bear, all of it. Even if she didn't order it herself, she's still at the root of my involvement."

Gwen wasn't his lost love, she was his enemy—although she didn't know it. From her reaction to Charlotte's story, she clearly had no idea who Henry was or what had been done to him in her name.

"So you didn't create this castle yourself?" Charlotte gasped out.

"I came here from the mountain kingdom, and the castle already existed when I arrived. Even with the bell, I could hardly change anything until you arrived."

He spoke in a dead, hopeless tone, and Charlotte feared she might be sick.

"How did you escape them?" she asked.

"I didn't. When it all went wrong, she released me."

"Who is *she*?" Charlotte whispered.

"The mountain queen. The ones who captured me were her people, and she's the one who enchanted me. As I said, I was intended to marry their princess, but when the enchantment went wrong, she gave me the bell and told me that if I wanted to live, I had to find my own way to break the enchantment. She tied me to her with a second enchantment so that if I did break it, I would be forcibly returned to them. So I had two choices: live as a bear forever, or reclaim my true form and be forced to marry the princess as they planned."

"But why free you in the first place?" Charlotte asked, trying to make sense of the nightmare she had suddenly found herself in.

"The mountain court has been enchanted for as many years as we've been alive," he said. "If they had the answer to breaking the enchantment, they would have done so long ago."

"And they expected *you* to find a way free?" Charlotte asked.

Henry shrugged. "I'm a prince and uninvolved in their schemes. There are always ways for one such as me to free themself. All the stories say it."

"A…a prince," Charlotte gasped. "What do you mean? I thought—"

"That's another thing I loved about you," he said sadly. "That you didn't know I was a prince. You knew me only as Henry, not Prince Henry, soon to be crown prince of Arcadia."

Charlotte gasped again, remembering his promise that he would move her family and establish them in Arcadia. She had even known Crown Prince Maximilian and Princess Alyssa's only son was called Henry. But it had never occurred to her to put those things together. Had he been planning to move her family after he broke his enchantment?

"But if you're a prince, you must have a godmother," she said, clutching desperately at possibilities. "We need to call her!"

"I already did." He sounded grim. "She told me the mountain people were partially right about the way to break the enchantment. It was through a royal marriage. But it would take love as well as a wedding. The moment I looked into my wife's eyes with my own human eyes and felt nothing but love, the enchantment would be broken. But she told me something else as well. There was a way for me to break the second enchantment, the one tying me back to the mountain kingdom."

"What…what did you have to do?" Charlotte whispered although she could already guess at the answer.

"I had to find a girl to love who would marry me despite my

being a bear—someone who didn't know my true identity or the details of my enchantments. A girl who would sleep beside me for three months' worth of nights and trust me without ever seeing my face. The queen's enchantment creates a false bond and forced loyalty, but it could be broken by trust that was freely given and a bond created by choice. If I could find someone who would believe in me and trust in me enough to sleep beside me in darkness without knowing why, her faith would win my freedom from both enchantments."

He smiled, but it didn't reach his eyes. "You married me, Lottie, and I can assure you I felt nothing but love when I looked into your eyes just now. You've freed me from my life as a bear. I will never be one again. But now I cannot escape the mountain queen. My godmother has already done as much as she can for me."

Charlotte stepped forward, fisting his nightshirt in both hands. "Surely there's a way! There has to be something I can do!"

"Can you find the mountain kingdom?" he asked in a voice that would have been mocking if it wasn't so gentle and full of love. "Can you find a place whose only direction is that it lies east of the sun and west of the moon? Can you tear me from the grasp of a queen who has spent two decades consolidating her power? A queen who spends half her time as an enormous bear?"

"Yes," Charlotte sobbed. "I can do anything! I will do anything to free you. I promise!"

He stared deep into her eyes, his breath coming ragged and fast.

"Lottie," he finally groaned and yanked her toward him.

For one breath, his blue eyes devoured her face. And then his lips descended on hers.

There was nothing soft about his kiss. It was demanding and possessive and burned with the longing of all their weeks together.

She melted against him, glad for his strong arms pressing her close. She didn't want the kiss to ever end. She couldn't accept that he was about to be ripped from her.

But too soon he pulled back, gazing hungrily down at her face again. "Do you know how much I've wanted to hold you like this? To gaze human face to human face?"

"I'm sorry!" she wailed. "All I wanted was to see your face once."

"If only you'd waited!" he cried in tones of fresh anguish. "Do you know how much self-control it took to lie beside you each night—my wife!—and keep my distance? But I endured it in the hope of a future where I could stay by your side night and day in my true form. If only you could have waited as well, then that future could have been ours. But now everything is destroyed!"

"I'm sorry," she repeated, sobbing in earnest now. "I'm sorry. I love you, Henry."

He stilled, only the muscles in his arms jumping in response to her words. His face softened as he gazed down at her.

"I love you, too, Lottie," he murmured, and then he was gone.

CHARLOTTE

"*H*enry!" Charlotte sobbed, her empty arms reaching for a man who was no longer there.

"Henry!" she screamed more loudly, but it wasn't only her husband who had disappeared.

Her bedchamber was gone, along with the candle and the entire castle. Soft moonlight illuminated a clearing at the base of a mountain face, and nothing blocked the stars that twinkled uncaring overhead.

She fell to her knees, the sobs shaking her so strongly it hurt. But she couldn't master them. She had won Henry's love, had been held in his arms, only to have him ripped from her.

She couldn't accept it. She wouldn't.

She screamed again, wordlessly this time, shouting her defiance at the cold sky and the unmoving mountain.

Her anger burned against the mountain queen who had stolen her husband, but it also turned inward. Why had she been so impatient? Why hadn't she trusted in the man she loved so much?

From there, the spark of it leaped to her parents. It had all been their fault. They were the ones who had pressed her and given her the idea. They were the ones who had given her the candle. Why couldn't they have trusted her when she assured them of Henry's character and her own happiness? They had married her off, and yet they still thought of her as a child whose judgment couldn't be trusted.

Distantly, some part of her knew she wasn't being fair. They had acted out of fear for their daughter, whereas she had acted from selfish desire. She was the one who knew Henry, and yet she had been the one to accept the candle, the one to light it. But in that moment she didn't care. If it hadn't been for them, she wouldn't have lost Henry. The idea of the candle would never have occurred to her on her own.

Anger, grief, pity, fear, and fury bit as deeply as the night's cold, and she collapsed on the patch of grass where the castle had once stood. Consumed entirely by her tears, she cried until her exhausted body collapsed into unconsciousness.

When she woke, the emotions were waiting for her, prowling and circling while she slept, ready to pounce when she opened her eyes. But she fisted her hands, letting her nails dig into her palms, and wrestled them under control.

If it had only been for herself, maybe she would have succumbed to them. But she had made her husband a promise, and this time she wasn't going to let him down. It didn't matter how high the mountain or how impossible the task. She would find him and rescue him before he fell to the mountain queen's schemes.

He had trusted her with his hand, his heart, and his enchantment. She would not allow that trust to be entirely in vain.

Her first instinct was to stand up and start walking uphill, heading into the mountains. But her determination hadn't robbed her of all sense. She would find nothing but a quick death if she braved the mountains alone and without provisions.

East of the sun and west of the moon.

The words taunted her. She needed proper directions if she was to find the mountain kingdom.

She sprang to her feet. The mountain kingdom! She knew someone from the mountain kingdom. She knew its princess!

She hadn't pressed Gwen for answers about her home before. But somehow Gwen had traveled from the mountain kingdom to the Rangmeran valleys. She must know the way. And Charlotte would beg and plead without a trace of pride if it was necessary to pry an answer from Gwen. Surely her friend would help once she knew Charlotte's husband had been stolen by Gwen's own mother.

With an actual, achievable goal, Charlotte couldn't start quickly enough. But the trees passed much more slowly than they had when she rode a white bear. Her will was strong, but she was still bound by her short legs. It would take her more than a day to reach her home valley. She just hoped Gwen was still there when she arrived and hadn't already left on her search for Easton.

Eventually, as the hours passed, Charlotte had to give in to her hunger and spend some time foraging. As little as she wanted to waste any daylight hours, she would be slower in the long run if she lost her strength due to lack of sustenance.

If the moon had been full, she would have tried to keep going even when night fell, but it was too dark to make any progress realistic. As with the food, Charlotte knew a twisted ankle would only slow her down.

She slept fitfully, however, her arms always reaching for Henry, only for her to start awake when they found empty air. And each time she woke, her cheeks were wet with tears.

As soon as the sun rose, she continued her journey. The forests around her had finally grown familiar—the very furthest reaches of what she had explored while she lived with her parents.

Back on familiar ground, she could take a more purposeful route—aiming not for her old home, but for that of Master Harold. Gwen was the one she sought, and Charlotte had no desire to see her parents—not while she was still lost in the height of her anger and grief. They had become inextricably entwined with her betrayal of Henry—the greatest mistake of her life—and the searing loss that had followed.

But long before she could reach Harold's home, she heard movement in the forest nearby. Her first instinct was to hide. But she was still too far out for it to be any of her family—they never came so far.

What if it was Gwen herself? Charlotte could think of no reason for her to be moving eastward toward the mountains, but she still raced forward, hope lending her speed.

And, sure enough, when she sprinted into view of the sound's source, it was the mountain princess herself.

"Gwen!" Charlotte gasped. "Oh, Gwen! You have to help me!"

"Charlotte!" Gwen paled, racing forward to take her friend's hands. "What is it? What is it? Is he after you?" She looked wildly behind Charlotte as if searching for a white bear in full chase.

Charlotte ripped her hands free, anger surging easily to the surface.

"Of course he's not after me! Henry would never hurt me." Her anger collapsed and her body collapsed with it, leaving her sitting on the grass. "He's gone, Gwen. He's gone, and I have to get him back."

Gwen knelt beside Charlotte, her face somehow growing even paler. "I don't understand. What do you mean?"

In halting words, devoid of all emotion, Charlotte told her the whole story. At some point, Gwen fell back, as if Charlotte had struck her. But she remained silent until she had finished.

"Henry—your Henry—is the lowlander prince my mother and the court wanted me to marry? That was the reason he was a white bear?" The thought had clearly never occurred to her.

All of Charlotte's animation returned, making her surge forward and grasp Gwen with both hands.

"You'll help me, won't you? You know how to get east of the sun and west of the moon?"

"I...East of the..." Gwen clearly had no idea what Charlotte was talking about.

"The mountain kingdom!" she exclaimed impatiently. "Your mother. That's where the stories claim it's located. You can help me get there, right?"

"Oh." Once again Gwen's hand went to her pocket. "I didn't know the stories described us that way. I don't know what it means. But I think...I think I might be able to get back there."

Charlotte fell back, relieved, her good sense finally starting to reassert itself.

"But what are you doing out here?" she asked. "Surely you can't be foraging so far, and so early in the morning?"

Gwen looked away. "As to that. Well..." She drew a breath. "I was worried about you. I wanted to come and check on you."

"You were coming to our castle?" The possibility hadn't occurred to Charlotte. How happy she would have been to receive her friend's visit if only she had never lit that candle.

How different everything would have been if Charlotte hadn't acted like a fool from start to finish.

GWEN

*H*er friend fell into silence, lost in her own reflections. They were unhappy ones from the look of her, and the familiar sensation of guilt wrapped itself around Gwen.

She had been worried for her friend—worried enough to attempt to find the castle on her own. But she had never dreamed of the damage she herself had done. Charlotte must blame her parents, but that was only because she didn't know it was Gwen who had spurred them on to it. She had purposely maneuvered them outside without Charlotte or her sisters so she could tell them her concerns about Henry.

They had still believed him a mountain prince until she had told them there was no such person. She had even been the one to suggest the candle. She had let her fears consume her, had spread those fears to others, and now this was the result. How many lives had she ruined?

The thought of her mother's plans of conquest seized Gwen's throat, threatening to close it over. There were still so many more people who could be hurt as a result of her misjudgment.

Should she confess everything to Charlotte? Even as the

thought occurred to her, she was already rejecting it. She wanted to help her friend, but would Charlotte let her do so once she knew the truth?

And under that, the uglier reality. She didn't want to see the hurt and disgust that would surely fill Charlotte's eyes once she heard what Gwen had done behind her back. Gwen had finally found a friend, and she couldn't lose her already. She couldn't be alone again.

"We'll go together," she said instead, the words surprising her. "Together we'll find both Easton and Henry." The thought of going back home, in reach of her mother, terrified Gwen. But she couldn't abandon Charlotte after causing her suffering. And if she was honest, the mountain kingdom was the most obvious place to look for clues as to where Easton had gone. She would have started there already if her fear hadn't gotten in the way.

"Yes!" Charlotte leaped up, her earlier despair evaporated, her face alight with purpose. "We'll go together and find them both." She paused, her brow creasing. "So where exactly are we going? You'll have to lead the way."

She flashed her friend a smile, and Gwen took strength from it, even managing a smile of her own.

"Actually," she said, "about that…" She drew the golden halter from her pocket. "I didn't walk here when I escaped, I rode the wind. And I think that's our best hope of getting back."

"You…rode…the wind…" Charlotte startled her by letting out a loud whoop. "That is far more amazing than I was expecting. You are amazing, Gwen." She shook her head. "You escaped your mother on the back of a wind horse. I think I picked the right ally."

She eyed the halter in Gwen's hand. "Although the horse that would fit that might be a little small to carry both of us."

Gwen chuckled in spite of herself. She didn't deserve Charlotte's admiration, but she couldn't help being swept up in the other girl's enthusiasm.

"It gets bigger," she said.

Charlotte laughed. "Of course it does. So how do we use it?"

She looked at Gwen expectantly, and Gwen's heart sank. "Um...that might be the hard part. I've only used it once, and then it sort of...well, it caught me while I was falling from a tower."

"You fell from a tower?" Charlotte eyes widened. "Someday you really need to tell me your whole story. But for now..." She looked around them. "Do you think that would be tall enough?"

Gwen followed the direction of her finger to a tree. "Tall enough for what?" she asked, her heart sinking.

Charlotte flashed her a challenging smile. "To fall from, of course."

"Of course," Gwen repeated weakly. She wasn't sure if she had the courage to throw herself purposefully from the top of a tree, but she also didn't know another way to activate the halter. "What if it doesn't work this time?"

Charlotte was already walking toward the base of the tree. "It'll work."

Gwen wished she had half her friend's certainty, but she could sense Charlotte was in no mood to be dissuaded. She would take any risk to rescue Henry, and Gwen owed it to her to offer what assistance she could.

When they stood on the highest branch, however, she was no longer so sure she could do it—even for Charlotte.

"Are you sure about this?" she asked, her voice coming out a squeak.

Charlotte threw her a mischievous glance. "No." She already had one arm wrapped firmly around the bark, but she wrapped her other arm around Gwen. "I think we'd better be connected, though. Do you have the harness ready?"

Gwen held it up. Her hands were sweating, but she had her fingers wrapped so tightly around the golden object they were white with the effort. Even the wind that tugged at them given their height couldn't pry it from her grip.

"Well, then," Charlotte said. "Here we go."

Before Gwen realized what she intended, her friend pushed herself off the branch, pulling Gwen with her. She had angled them away from the other branches, attempting to jump into clear air rather than lower boughs.

She had succeeded partially, but there was still one large branch beneath them—one they had both made use of to haul themselves so high. For a dizzying second, Gwen was sure they were going to collide with it. But then the harness in her hand began to grow.

A blink of the eye later, she had the golden reins in her hand, and the wind beneath her, as steady as any mount. A whoop in her ear and hands clutching at the back of her dress told her Charlotte was safely behind.

"Did that mad plan really work?" she murmured, but the wind snatched the words away before they could reach Charlotte's ears.

She didn't know the exact direction of her home, but on the way out, she had been able to steer the wind at will. If they circled high enough over the mountains, eventually they would catch sight of the mountain kingdom. It was too large to miss, especially from the air.

She tried to direct her wind mount upward and east, toward the nearest mountain peak, but it pulled north instead. She pulled harder on the reins, and the wind bucked in response.

Charlotte gasped, grabbing tighter to Gwen. "What's going on?" She had to shout to be heard over the rushing noise around them.

"I don't know!" Gwen cried back. "This didn't happen last time."

She tried again to direct their wind mount right toward the

mountains, but it wouldn't respond. When she pulled harder, it suddenly disappeared beneath them.

They both dropped, screaming and flailing before it suddenly caught them again. Gwen only had a second to catch her breath before it surged upward, carrying them terrifyingly high.

"This is too high!" Charlotte shouted in Gwen's ear.

Gwen gritted her teeth and didn't reply. All her attention was focused on wrestling with the uncooperative reins. She couldn't understand why they were behaving so differently to the previous occasion.

The wind lurched, almost exactly like a bucking horse, and the reins nearly slipped from Gwen's grasp. Charlotte threw herself forward and grabbed them as well, the two girls holding on with everything they had.

And all the time they fought the wind, it carried them northward at breathtaking speed, the mountains rushing past on their right. She didn't know how many valleys had passed beneath them, but they had long since left their starting place far behind.

"I...don't...understand..." Gwen forced out, her teeth still clenched.

"It's like someone's driving it with a whip and spurs," Charlotte gasped from where she was awkwardly squeezed against Gwen as they both fought the golden reins.

Charlotte's words sparked memory in Gwen and suddenly everything made horrible sense. There had been two objects on the one plinth—a pair. She had been repulsed by the whip and without thinking had grabbed the halter. It had never occurred to her that overlooking the whip might cause her a problem.

But if the halter controlled the wind, wouldn't the whip be a matching pair with it? The halter could tame the wind, and the whip could control and drive it. And her mother still had the whip.

"Is the wind getting stronger?" Charlotte cried as their pace picked up even further. "How do we get back to the ground? At this speed we're going to create a storm and destroy something!"

Gwen pulled on the reins as she had done last time, and the wind thankfully dipped in response. But almost immediately Charlotte cried a warning. Gwen craned to see what her friend was indicating and caught sight of a village approaching below at a terrifying pace.

She pulled their mount sharply back up again. If they went any lower, a wind as strong as the one they rode would rip the town to pieces. As it was, she could see the trees swaying and loose objects blowing wildly about.

She twisted in her invisible seat to see the town disappearing behind them. At least all the buildings looked intact.

Trying again, she pulled the reins up, and the wind lowered them toward the ground. It appeared her mother couldn't prevent them landing, at least.

But just as she was wondering what to do about the speed of the approaching ground, another cluster of houses appeared. She flinched, starting to direct them upward again, but Charlotte prevented her.

"No, it's too late!" she shouted. "We won't get high enough fast enough to miss them. We have to land!"

Gwen realized she was right. As they lowered, the wind was losing strength, so the lower they got, the less force would hit the hamlet.

She pulled with all her strength, no longer worrying about the speed of their own impact. She would have to trust in the object to keep them safe. All that mattered was to slow the wind as much as possible before it hit the defenseless houses.

She couldn't lower them fast enough, however. Their wind mount swept them between two houses, tearing the roofs off both as it went and filling the air with wreckage.

Gwen screamed, the sound seeming to echo around her as Charlotte also cried out. And then her shoulder, hip, and back hit the ground, and all she could do was breathe, the effort a frantic struggle.

When she finally managed to draw a proper breath, she realized the wind had disappeared completely. She looked down at the tiny halter still gripped in her fingers and quickly thrust it into her pocket.

Charlotte recovered a second behind her, leaping up and offering her hand to pull Gwen the rest of the way to her feet.

"We have to find the people," she said breathlessly, ignoring the disarray of her hair and the dirt smeared down her night-gown. "They might be trapped or hurt."

Gwen nodded, scrambling upright. She had brought the wind to this hamlet. Whatever had happened here was her responsibility, and she would do what she could to help, little as that might be.

CHARLOTTE

*C*harlotte followed at her friend's heels as Gwen raced back toward the destroyed houses. She could see from Gwen's expression that she was feeling tormented, considering herself responsible. But neither of them had foreseen the possibility of the wind turning against them and becoming an unchecked weapon.

"What made the wind fight you?" Charlotte asked Gwen as they ran.

"My mother," Gwen panted back. "There was another matching object that I left behind. A whip. I didn't know what it did, but it's obvious now. She must be able to tell when I've activated the halter, and she started using her object to interfere."

The hard ball that burned inside Charlotte flared up. Another crime to lay at the feet of the mountain queen. It seemed there was no end to them, and Charlotte meant to hold her accountable for every last one.

"Help!" A desperate voice called, directing their steps.

They raced around a wall—one that stood starkly upright, no longer attached to the building it had once supported—and

Charlotte crashed into her friend's back. Peering around her, she saw a woman attempting to lift a large beam off a young man.

Charlotte and Gwen hurried forward in unison, one on each side of the woman.

"I'm all right, Ma," the man said, although he looked pale to Charlotte's eye and his breathing was strained. "It's just a pity our roles aren't reversed—I'd have this off you in a moment."

"Hush now," the woman said sternly, "and save your breath." She sent a desperate look at Charlotte. "It's on his chest, and it's getting harder and harder for him to breathe."

"We'll help," Gwen said from the woman's other side. "If we all pull together..."

The three women reached down, all three of them straining with the effort to pull up the beam. But they couldn't shift the heavy bar of wood.

The mother kept trying even after Charlotte stepped back, so she pulled her away. The woman fought, trying to get back to the beam, so Charlotte snapped at her, trying to pierce the mother's mounting fear.

"We're not giving up! We just need to try something different. Is there anything we can use as a lever?"

"Over here," Gwen called, and Charlotte turned to find her already dragging a wooden post toward the other two women. It looked as if it might have been a fence post before the wind ripped it from the ground.

She ran forward to help her friend carry the post.

"Where do you think...?" She didn't need to finish the question before Gwen was placing the shorn-off tip underneath the beam, just above the man's head.

The mother realized what they were doing and ran forward to help. The fence post was only just long enough for the three women to all get a secure hold at once, but as soon as they had, they all pushed downward.

For a second, Charlotte thought it wasn't working, and then the beam lifted slightly, raising one inch and then another.

As soon as they had it high enough, the trapped man rolled sideways, freeing himself. The moment he was clear, the mother let go, and the beam clattered to the ground.

She ran to her son, pulling him up.

"Wait!" Charlotte called, rushing after him. "He might be injured. We should check him first."

"No, I'm fine." The man managed a pained smile. "Thanks to your assistance."

Charlotte exchanged a guilty look with Gwen. He would never have needed help if they hadn't accidentally brought a gale to his home.

Fortunately for Charlotte and Gwen, the mother and son were too relieved at his rescue to ask where the two young women had come from.

"There might be others in need," Gwen murmured, and Charlotte followed her to the next house.

Once they had rounded a particularly large pile of rubble, they got a proper look at the rest of the hamlet. None of the houses were untouched, although they weren't all as shredded as the one of the mother and son.

Several people were still being retrieved from two of the houses, and Gwen rushed to help. Charlotte was about to follow her when she noticed an old lady standing on her own at the edge of the chaos.

She crossed over to her, concerned.

"Are you all right, Grandmother?" she asked. "Are you injured or missing someone?"

"I'm not your grandmother," the gray-haired woman snapped, but there was an amused twinkle in her eye that softened her tone.

"No, indeed," Charlotte said politely. "But I would offer you aid anyway if you're in need of it."

"Aid, is it?" The woman raised her eyebrows. "And here was I, thinking you were the one who brought this on them."

Charlotte paled. So someone had noticed them riding in on the wind after all.

She bowed her head. "It wasn't our intention. We ride in rescue of others, but the person who has wronged us is a powerful foe." The fire in her belly flared up again. "She is the one truly to blame for this catastrophe."

The woman chuckled. "I'm glad to hear you see things clearly. So what do you intend to do about it?"

Charlotte glanced back at Gwen, who was ferrying a bucket of water toward a small fire that had sprung up in the wake of the various collapses. Others rushed to help her, and they soon appeared to have the fire under control.

"We'll do everything we can, although I fear we're ill equipped for this sort of work."

"Not about the hamlet," the grandmother said, exasperated. "About this powerful foe."

Charlotte winced. "I'm not sure what we'll do about her either." Her eyes narrowed. "But we'll find a way."

The woman patted her on the arm. "That's the spirit." She leaned close as if about to impart a secret, and Charlotte responded instinctively, also leaning in. "You have to be in the fight if you want a chance of winning it."

Charlotte pulled back, fighting a smile. From the old woman's air of great significance, she hadn't expected such a familiar saying.

"Very true, Grandmother," she said. "I'll keep it in mind."

The woman gave her a tart look, as if she could read Charlotte's thoughts. "See that you do."

Charlotte turned to leave. "If you're truly uninjured, I should see if there's someone who needs my help."

"Wait a moment, wait a moment," the woman cried testily. "You young things are always in such a rush. Give me a moment."

Charlotte waited obediently, trying to hide her impatience to join Gwen and do something to help.

"It's here somewhere," the woman muttered before giving a cry of triumph and producing a golden ball.

Charlotte stared at it, bewildered. When the woman held it toward her with an imperious gesture, she reached out her own arm, and the woman dropped it into her hand. She stared down at the ball, which fit comfortably into her palm.

It looked and felt as if it were made of real gold, but it was far too light to be solid.

"I don't understand," she said. "What is this?"

"It's a gift," the woman said with satisfaction. "Rumor says it will help you find your true love."

Charlotte looked up sharply, and the woman smiled. "You are looking for your true love, aren't you?"

"Yes, but—"

"Don't bother me with silly questions," the woman said with a return of her earlier tartness. "Don't they teach young people manners in this part of the world? If you receive a gift, you should thank the giver, not pester them."

"Thank you," Charlotte said obediently, still shocked.

A moment later the woman's words registered, and she frowned. She spoke as if she wasn't a resident of this hamlet after all. And neither did she look as if she'd just been caught in a gale.

"No more nonsense from you, youngster," the woman said with a knowing look. "I'll look after these people, so you can focus on what you must do."

"And what is that?" Charlotte asked, watching the woman closely.

But despite her attention, she couldn't help blinking, and in the half-second her eyes were closed, the woman disappeared.

Charlotte gasped. In the second before she had gone, she could have sworn she saw something shimmering behind the woman's shoulders.

"Were those wings?" she whispered, although there was no one near enough to hear the question.

The woman couldn't possibly have been a godmother. It wasn't as if Charlotte was a princess.

Except...she was. The thought hit her for the first time. If Henry was a prince—one in the direct line to a throne—and also her husband, that made her a princess. The thought was enormous. Too enormous to be grappled with in the moment. But it was enough to make her believe in the identity of the woman who had disappeared before her eyes.

Her fingers closed around the ball. It had been a strange enough gift already, but it had just become infinitely precious. Even after her marriage and residence at Henry's castle, she had never imagined she would someday receive a godmother object directly from the hands of an actual godmother.

Reverently, she placed it in her deepest pocket. Turning toward Gwen, she was about to call out to her friend in excitement, but something snatched at her dress before she could speak.

The sharp wind pulled at her again, making her stomach tighten. The wind that had died when they landed was returning.

She ran toward Gwen and the others, shouting for everyone to take shelter. She didn't know how she knew it was necessary, but the certainty filled her.

Gwen looked up, frowning, and Charlotte called only two words. "The wind!"

Gwen's eyes snapped upward, although there was nothing to see in the sky. Her hair whipped around her face, though, and her skirts flapped. It wasn't just Charlotte's imagination. The wind had returned and was growing stronger by the second.

"It's back," she panted as she finally reached Gwen. "And it's going to destroy what's left of these houses if we don't do something."

"But what can we do?" Gwen wailed.

The grandmother's earlier words—increased in significance in Charlotte's memory now she knew they were the words of a godmother—came back to her.

"You have to be in the fight if you want a chance of winning it!" She grabbed Gwen's arm. "Your mother has sent the wind against us again, but we can't fight it from down here. We have to be riding it if we want a chance at controlling it."

Gwen wanted to argue. Most of all, she didn't want to return to the sky to be buffeted and thrown about at her mother's whim. But she couldn't deny the logic of Charlotte's words.

A particularly strong gust made a child cry out in fright, and Gwen's fingers plunged into her pocket.

"Hold onto me," she said grimly as she pulled out the halter. She didn't think they were going to need to fall from a height to be caught in the wind this time.

Sure enough, Charlotte barely had a hold on Gwen when the halter grew and the reins appeared. The next second, both girls had been swept into the sky.

"Go higher!" Charlotte shouted in her ear, ignoring the cries of shock and fear from below them.

Gwen pulled on the reins, relieved when the wind responded and leaped skyward, taking them high enough not to touch the houses or even the trees.

"What now?" she cried, but Charlotte didn't know how to answer. When she had directed them to resume their journey, she'd been thinking of the villagers below and following the directions of the godmother. She didn't know how to control the antagonistic wind.

"Forget about the mountains," she cried as loudly as she could. "Just try to keep it away from people and anything it could damage."

Gwen nodded, her attention focused on the reins as the wind lurched first one way and then another, trying to throw them off.

Charlotte held onto Gwen, but she kept herself poised ready

to grab the reins as she had done before. If the wind grew strong enough, it would take both of them just to keep hold of it.

The land raced beneath them, so distant Charlotte hardly noticed it. But eventually a bright light ahead of them caught her eye. It took her a long moment to realize what she was seeing, and when she finally caught on, she gasped.

Spread from one side of the sky to the other was the ocean, reflecting the sunlight so that it winked and glowed.

"We're going to have to land," she shouted, and Gwen nodded. "I see it."

Charlotte had always wanted to see the ocean, but she didn't want to be swept out over it, carried far beyond the reach of land. Gwen obviously felt the same because she directed them downward immediately. But just as she did, a large town appeared, nestled on the coast and protected by a vast sea wall.

Both girls cried out at once, and Gwen pulled them up again. Charlotte could see her trying to wrestle them either left or right, but the wind wouldn't cooperate. It was determined to sweep them out to sea.

As they left the land behind, unreasoning terror gripped Charlotte at the vastness that was now apparent in three directions. She knew the sea was big—endless, some said. But she hadn't been able to comprehend the reality.

She wrestled the fear down, however. There was no time to give way to it. Even if it killed them, they couldn't let the wind lay waste to a whole town. And neither was she ready to give up on the two of them. They had to force the wind to bring them back in.

Gwen tried to direct them left just as the wind lurched in that direction. They swerved so violently in response that both girls were nearly unbalanced. But it gave Charlotte an idea.

If she could find a way to communicate it to Gwen, they would possibly have a chance of getting back to land safely without destroying the town. She leaned in, about to shout in

Gwen's ear, when a spot of brown caught her eye, followed by a white sail. The wind was sweeping them straight for a fishing fleet—one that was out on the open ocean, far from the protection of the sea wall. On their current course, they would reach them in less than a minute and every one of those ships would be sunk.

There was no time for explanations. Charlotte lunged around Gwen and grabbed the reins. As soon as she had control of them, she held herself in readiness, the reins slack in her hands.

Gwen started to protest, but Charlotte ignored her, all her senses on edge. The second she felt the wind lurch in one direction, she threw the reins the same way, using every bit of her strength.

They swerved so violently that the wind carried them in a half circle, sweeping them back toward the land. Gwen cried out in surprise, but Charlotte couldn't break her concentration to explain.

The wind pulled them sideways again, and she did the same thing, bringing them all the way around in a full circle this time until they faced land again. It happened again in the other direction and then again. And each time they circled, they were closer to the land than they had been the time before.

At last they grew close enough that Charlotte began to consider how to direct them around the town. But before they reached the harbor, the wind cut out as it sometimes did, sending them falling toward the waves. Both girls screamed, but the wind caught them just as their feet broke the choppy surface of the water.

It swept them back up again, only to cut out again. Charlotte's stomach lurched, but she couldn't miss the opportunity. She pulled on the reins in anticipation so that when the wind caught them again—more quickly this time—she was already directing it downward.

They weren't going to make the actual land, but they had a

chance at the sea wall. She angled toward it, screaming for Gwen to brace herself.

Charlotte let go of the reins as they skimmed just above the wide wall of stone, throwing herself sideways and landing on the stone with a painful series of bumps. She lay for a minute, listening for the whistle of the wind and hearing nothing.

Sighing in relief, she rolled over to find a young man offering her a helping hand. She took it, glad for the extra assistance since every one of her muscles ached.

"Did you just ride that wind in?" he asked, his eyes wide and his curly hair looking as if it had just been through a hurricane.

Charlotte winced. "Yes, I'm sorry. I hope it didn't hurt you."

"I'm fine," the young man said quickly and offered her a grin. "Just astonished."

Charlotte smiled back weakly, glad the stranger was taking it so well.

"I have a friend," she said as she turned to look for Gwen. "We should—" Her eyes caught on Gwen, sitting frozen a few feet behind them, her eyes on the young man behind Charlotte.

Charlotte turned to follow her gaze and found the young man equally frozen, his eyes fixed on the young woman still sitting on the stones.

"Gwen?" he asked in a breathless voice. "Is that you?"

GWEN

*G*wen hit the ground hard and rolled. For a second, she thought she might roll all the way off the wall and drop into the terrifying depth of water on both sides of it. But she stopped in time, her hand somehow still clenched around the now-miniature halter.

She pushed herself slowly into a sitting position, feeling bruised all over in body, mind, and emotions. If it wasn't for Charlotte's intervention, untold numbers would have just died. She had wanted to escape her mother's reach, but she hadn't gone far enough, and now she was bringing calamity to others.

The sound of voices broke through her haze, and she looked toward Charlotte. Someone had approached her and appeared to be offering assistance. Gwen hoped that meant they weren't going to be driven out of the town for bringing the wind in the first place.

The man straightened, Charlotte beside him, and her friend turned toward her, revealing the face of the man at her side.

Gwen's breath caught, everything around her stilling into silence. The face wasn't exactly the one she had been picturing for years, but it was close enough. And the hair was exactly the same, even the messiness of it, as she remembered.

"Easton," she breathed, just as he called her name in tones of equal shock.

Her heart swelled. He was alive. And he hadn't forgotten her.

He ran forward, sweeping her onto her feet and into his arms.

"You did it," he murmured against her hair. "You escaped her!" He pulled back to grin down at her with the same broad smile she remembered. "You escaped by riding the wind? I can't say that option ever occurred to me."

She was too overwhelmed to respond with anything but a smile.

A clearing throat caught her attention, and she turned her head to see Charlotte watching them with amusement.

"How about an introduction?" Her expression suggested she already guessed who the man must be.

Easton let his arms drop and stepped away, and Gwen felt instantly bereft.

"Yes," he said cheerfully, smiling at Charlotte. "I'm curious as well. I don't remember you from the mountain court."

Instant jealousy sunk its claws into Gwen. She had told herself that if only Easton was alive and still remembered her, it was all she needed to be happy. But she had now seen his true adult face and felt his arms around her, and she was already greedy for more.

He might remember her affectionately, but what if he saw her as a friend or younger sister? He might already have a sweetheart or wife. He might like Charlotte more than he liked—

She cut herself off. Charlotte was already married, and Gwen was being ridiculous. If only she could have a few minutes to gather herself after the wild ride and shock of emotion.

"I'm Easton," he said, holding out a hand to Charlotte when it became obvious Gwen was still too overwhelmed to speak.

"I'm Charlotte." She shook his hand. "And I've never been to the mountain kingdom. Gwen took a...detour on her way here."

"I didn't know where you were," Gwen murmured. "I didn't even know you were alive."

Easton's face—the one that still looked as if it had been made only to smile and laugh—darkened.

"This sounds like a conversation for somewhere other than a sea wall," Charlotte said, looking hopefully at Easton.

He quickly agreed, directing them both toward a small home on the harbor. It was tucked just to one side of the sea wall, away from the action of the loading and unloading of boats, but with a breathtaking view of the ocean.

Easton saw Gwen looking at the endless stretch of water and smiled. "I like to be near the sea. It makes me feel free." His face darkened again. "I don't like feeling constrained."

Her insides squeezed as she imagined what sort of restraints her mother might have placed on him and for how long.

"What happened to you?" she whispered, wondering how he could face her after what her mother had done to him.

Somehow they had made it inside the small house, although she couldn't clearly remember stepping inside, and somewhere along the way Charlotte had disappeared.

"I got angry and confronted her," he said matter-of-factly, not having to specify who he meant. "I should have come to you instead, but I went storming off to her and got myself banished. She made me drink some sort of potion, and when I woke up it was days later, and I was here. My parents were always warning me about what would happen if I ever lost my temper at the palace. I should have listened to them. I just hope she didn't punish them as well."

"As far as I know their only punishment was expulsion from the court. I believe they're living quietly in the city." She paused, unable to stop herself stepping closer to him. "I'm so sorry. It was all my fault."

"What are you talking about?" he sounded genuinely surprised. "I'm well aware where the blame lies, and it's not with you. It's not with me either, not really. But since I was drugged and hauled over the mountains unconscious, I've had no idea how to get back."

"You've been here in—" She stopped, realizing she had no idea where they were.

"It's called Ranost," he said with an amused twitch of his lips. "Rangmere's northernmost coastal town. We fish the north-eastern oceans, among other things."

"And you've been here the whole time?"

He nodded. "I've been fortunate enough to build a life here."

"A life?" she asked hesitantly, looking around again. There was no indication in the room that anyone lived in the house other than Easton.

"The years have been kinder to me than they might have been," he said. "I have much to be grateful to the locals for. But it never stopped feeling like I was waiting for my real life to begin." His smile grew warm, his eyes capturing hers. "I never stopped believing you would find a way to stand up to her."

Gwen flushed, soaking in his attention and presence. The reality of him was so much better than her imaginings and being in his presence triggered a flood of memories from their shared childhood. He was just like the companion of those days, and yet at the same time not. She couldn't help noticing how tall he had grown, and how broad his shoulders had become. He filled the space in the house in a way he never had before.

But at the same time, she felt his admiration as a pressure. He believed in her beyond what she deserved. She sat heavily on a nearby sofa.

"I didn't really stand up to her," she said miserably. "I tried to investigate, but as soon as I discovered about becoming a bear and confronted her with it, she locked me up. Honestly, it was luck as much as anything that kept me from dying in my poor escape attempt. If I hadn't accidentally stolen a godmother object from her that turned out to allow me to ride the wind…"

"I'm sorry, becoming a bear?" Easton stared at her, and Gwen flushed darkly. She'd forgotten that the enchantment had begun after she confronted her mother over Easton's disappearance and was locked up. He must have still been in the mountain kingdom somewhere at that point, drugged unconscious, but apparently he hadn't been one of those the queen included in the binding enchantment.

She swallowed. "My mother cast an enchantment, after you… After we…" She sighed. "The queen and I and all her courtiers and guards turn into bears from sundown to sunrise."

Easton rocked back, his eyes growing wide. "That is another surprise."

Gwen watched him closely, but she could see no sign of disgust in his eyes. Catching her scrutiny, he sat beside her. Taking her hands, he smiled at her. "Clearly a lot happened in the years I missed. But what matters is that you found out the truth about her in the end, and you can even ride the wind now! That must be a helpful tool in confounding her. Have you come here for more allies?"

"A…Allies?" Gwen blinked. "I came here to find you. Or at least, that's what I was trying to do. I wasn't coming here specifically because I didn't know you were here."

He smiled, but it didn't quite reach his eyes, overtaken by a quizzical expression instead. "I'm flattered, and I'll help you, of course. I've been waiting for ten years to do so. But I'm not sure how much value I can bring. You'll need more allies than just me to bring her down. Or have you already disrupted her that significantly?"

"I…" She swallowed. "I think you've misunderstood. As soon as I discovered I could direct the wind, I came over the mountains. I came looking for you."

He dropped her hands, his brows drawing together. "But I've

heard rumors about traders from the mountains and further tales about people disappearing. The locals might not have put those two things together, but it must be obvious to anyone who knows Queen Celandine. What has happened to her captives? Did you just leave them there? And what about the people in the city? Your people."

Gwen went hot and then cold. After meeting the girl from the city, Gwen had been ashamed of herself for never thinking of the city's inhabitants. But then she had turned around and forgotten about them all over again. Whereas Easton—who hadn't set foot in the mountain kingdom for ten years—still thought of them immediately.

He surged to his feet, striding away from Gwen only to immediately come striding back. He ran a hand through his hair, further disrupting the messy waves.

"You just abandoned them?" he demanded. "But you're the true heir of the mountain kingdom, Gwen! You're the only one who can stand up to her, the only one who can bring her down. How could you just run away?"

All the joy that had filled her on finding him drained out. She leaped up, her hands covering her face. After everything he'd said, after seeing the disbelief in his eyes, she couldn't bear for him to see her tears.

Blindly she ran from the house, fleeing down the harbor, away from the noise and movement toward the quieter section. Distantly she heard him calling after her, but she didn't slow.

Only when the sounds of the town completely fell away did she finally stop. She had reached a bluff that gave a sweeping view across the ocean. A flat rock provided a place for her to perch, and she pulled her feet up onto it, hugging her knees as she looked out over the waves.

The tears had stopped, but the emptiness they had brought remained. At home, she had always felt lonely, the walls of the palace closing in around her. But for a brief window, she had thought herself free. And yet, here she sat in a whole new town, with friends at her side, but just as trapped by loneliness as ever.

Physically, the expanse of the sea stretched out before her while a breeze ruffled her hair. But she felt the enclosing walls just the same, this time made of guilt.

Charlotte's presence only reminded her of the guilt of her secret. She had betrayed her friend, and her friend had paid the price. And now Easton's presence carried the weight of another betrayal. Everything he had said was true. She was the only other royal in the mountain kingdom, the only heir. She had known others suffered under her mother's hand. And yet, when given the chance, she had fled without a second thought, intent only on saving herself.

She could come up with a list of excuses. She could say she was powerless before her mother. But she had been telling herself that for years, and it was wearing thin. Faced with the one person who had always believed in her and supported her, she was forced to confront the truth.

She had used her powerlessness as an excuse to wallow in weakness. As long as she told herself there was nothing she could do, as long as she passively accepted her mother's control, she didn't have to risk her own safety.

Never once had she truly attempted to best her mother or stand up for anyone else. Even when she finally snapped, she had fought only for her own escape and freedom.

She had done everything Easton had claimed, and now he would never see her the same way again. She had ruined everything.

GWEN

"*Y*ou look like you could use an apple." The kind tones of an older woman interrupted Gwen's despair.

She blinked, wiping away the lingering traces of tears, and scrambled to her feet. The old woman gestured for her to sit again and then sat beside her.

She held out a yellow apple, indicating for Gwen to take it.

Gwen wasn't hungry. Her stomach couldn't possibly take any food given her emotional turmoil, but she didn't want to be rude, so she accepted the fruit anyway.

Only once it was in her hand did she actually look at it properly and realize it wasn't yellow but gold. Actual gold. The metal. It wasn't a fruit at all but a valuable, and amazingly light, treasure.

She looked up. "I can't possibly take this!"

"Whyever not? You need it more than I do. And you never know when it might come in handy. Put it away now, there's a dear."

Gwen blinked, reminded strongly of the affectionate but iron-willed nature of her old nanny. One glance in the woman's eyes told her there was no point arguing.

Bemused, she tucked the golden apple away in a pocket as

instructed. The woman gave an approving nod and gazed out over the ocean.

"The castle east of the sun and west of the moon isn't an easy target," she said. "But I think you know that better than most."

Gwen stared at her. She had read that princesses always had godmothers, and she had often wondered if she had one too. She suspected she had just found her.

The apple in her pocket grew heavier as she considered it in a new light.

"That place has already taken more from you than you should have had to give," the godmother continued. "Do you want to be finished with it now? Do you want to walk away?"

She said the words with a look of such sympathy that Gwen nearly started crying again.

"Well?" the godmother asked when Gwen didn't answer. "If I told you that you were free to walk away right now—that I would find someone else to take your place—would you choose to do it?"

"Someone else?" Gwen asked. "Someone better suited for the role?"

The silver-haired woman shrugged. "They might be. Or maybe they would be worse. That isn't something I could say in advance. It would depend on both your decisions and theirs."

Gwen rubbed at her head. She wasn't sure if it was a real option being offered her or just a theoretical exercise, but it was incredibly tempting. She longed to let go of the guilt and walk away from everything.

But could she leave the guilt behind? Who else could fill her role? Who else knew her mother and all the corners of their palace? Who else was known to every member of the mountain kingdom as their heir? Gwen might be a poor heir, but she was the only one they had ever had. Would they accept someone else?

It was all too easy to think of some brave soul facing Queen Celandine, underestimating her, and being struck down. Gwen didn't know if she could ever defeat her mother, but she didn't know anyone else who could either.

How could she hand over something like that and walk away?

"No," she said at last, the word heavy. "I wouldn't."

The godmother smiled as if unsurprised at her choice, although it had surprised Gwen.

"See, you aren't weak," the woman said. "You're just still in the process of finding your strength—and learning who else's strength you can rely on."

"I turned my back and rode away from them all," Gwen whispered.

"So?" the godmother said. "Are you going to ride back?"

"Yes." Again Gwen was surprised by her own answer, this time by its strength and speed.

"In that case," the godmother said, "you didn't truly abandon them."

She sighed, patting Gwen's hand. "In the past you chose weakness because you thought you were weak. But that isn't your fault. You were a child, and the person who should have protected you instead told you every day that you were weak. But now you are a woman, and you have a choice. You can choose to continue believing those words, or you can choose to reject them and believe the words of others instead. If you believe you're capable of standing up to the queen, then you can begin to find the strength to do so."

"Do you truly think that?" Gwen asked.

The godmother raised an eyebrow. "Haven't you been listening? The relevant question is whether you believe it. You let the queen tell you who you are. Are you ready to listen to the people who love you instead?"

Gwen swallowed, thinking of what Easton had just said to her. Did she want to hear what others thought of her? Was there anyone who loved her?

"The High King didn't make you princess of the mountain

kingdom by mistake," the godmother said. "You matter to him, and you matter to others."

"Why did he give them Queen Celandine as their queen?" Gwen asked, struggling to completely let go of her bitterness.

"Who said he did?" the godmother asked sharply.

Gwen looked at her with a frown. What was that supposed to mean? How could the High King have made her their princess and yet have had no hand in her mother being queen?

"I can think of one person who might have something to say about who you are and your value," the godmother said with a sudden chuckle. "I think a certain young man is on his way here, bitterly regretting his hasty words." She nodded in the direction Gwen had come, and Gwen caught a glimpse of a familiar figure. Easton was hurrying toward her, his expression intent.

She turned back to question the godmother on what she had meant about her mother, but the rock beside her was empty. She blinked at it for a moment, but the woman was definitely gone.

Climbing slowly to her feet, she considered what her godmother had said as she waited for Easton. Could she believe she had been chosen? Could she believe she was worthy even after all the mistakes she'd made?

A wave of something that felt more like peace than guilt washed over her, settling deep into her bones. The godmother had said it was up to her to choose whose words she would believe about herself. That meant she could choose this peace. And she could choose to let go of the mountain queen's poison. She could break the walls that closed her in and refuse to ever build them back into place.

"Gwen!" Easton reached her, seizing both her hands and looking into her eyes with frantic worry. "I'm so sorry."

"It's all right." Gwen felt a smile stretch across her face. "Everything you said was true, at least in part. I did run away, but I haven't abandoned them. I realized that while I was sitting out here. I'm going back to free them all. I have to."

She tipped her face up to him, her smile growing. "You're right about the ocean. It's helpful for thinking—and breaking down restraints."

Easton sucked in a breath, his eyes still intent on her face. "You shouldn't forgive me so easily," he whispered. "It only makes me feel worse. I know what you went through in your childhood, but I can only imagine how alone you must have been in the last ten years. I've been living a free life, but you've been under her thumb every moment, trapped in her enchantment, her castle, and her control. And yet, you managed to free yourself! You held onto who you are through it all. You're brave and resilient and incredible, and yet the first thing I did was berate you! You should tell me you never want to see me again. I deserve it."

Gwen's eyes had grown misty as he spoke, but her smile returned at the end of his speech.

"Should I?" she asked playfully.

He looked down at her, his gaze changing as his eyes darkened with an entirely new emotion.

"No," he said thickly. "You shouldn't. You should let me do this."

He pressed his lips down on hers, pulling her into his arms and kissing her as thoroughly as she had always dreamed he one day would.

"I don't think I can steer this time." Charlotte gazed uncertainly at the halter resting in Gwen's palm. "I know I did it last time, but that was a simple matter of getting us back to land. I don't know the way to the mountain kingdom."

Gwen glanced at Easton, a question in her eyes. He just smiled back at her, the warmth in his gaze making her flush while his trust in her ability buoyed her up.

She was the one who had fled the mountain palace. She was their princess. It was her job to lead them back.

"I wish we could take more than three of us," she said mournfully, remembering Easton's talk of allies. "But we could never get an army across the mountains. This will have to be done through stealth, not force of arms. It will be dangerous."

Charlotte propped her hands on her hips. "You should know by now that you're not talking either of us out of it. And while I can't speak for Easton—who looks like he'd follow you wherever you go—I'm not going to the mountain kingdom for you, remember."

Gwen nodded, her flush deepening at her friend's mention of Easton's devotion. He didn't follow her around, but he had waited for her, and that was more than enough.

"It's time to go home," he said softly, capturing her eyes.

She nodded back. It was time.

"But do we really have to jump off this bluff?" he asked, eyeing the fall to the sea below.

Charlotte snorted. "Think of it as an opportunity to impress your lady love with your courage."

Easton grinned at her. "What if I don't have any?"

Gwen rolled her eyes, grasped both of their arms and pulled them all off the cliff.

Easton gasped and Charlotte screamed, but it seemed to be a scream of delight more than fear. The halter in Gwen's hand grew, the reins appearing in her curled fingers.

She looked back over her shoulder to see the other two lined up behind her. She noticed with smug pleasure that the object had placed Easton behind her. His arms immediately wrapped around her waist, securing them both in position.

"Why am I at the back?" Charlotte complained, and Gwen smiled again. She knew the excitement underlying her friend's words. She was finally on her way to the kingdom where her husband could be found.

They soared high over Ranost, heading for the mountains. But as soon as they hit them, the wind began to fight her.

Her first instinct was to pull against it, as she had before, trying to compensate for its lurching, jerking motions. But she forced herself not to respond on instinct.

Charlotte had shown her the way, and she would need every bit of her strength and concentration to lead them through the more difficult path through the mountains.

She had wanted to follow a low-lying valley to their right, but the wind pulled them left. She scanned the landscape in that direction, comparing it to the maps she had often studied in the palace library. They hadn't included the trails through the mountains, but they had shown the locations of the landscape itself. And from the air, the ground below her looked almost like a map, stretched out for her perusal.

She spotted a crevice that opened into a deep valley. Leaning into the wind's leftward motion, she sailed them into the dark gash in the mountain face. As she had expected, it opened into a valley, the high walls forcing the wind to flow down its length and giving her a chance to breathe.

But all too quickly they reached the end of it, and the wind jerked them wildly again, trying to send them spinning uncontrollably toward the ground. She let it take them downward, waiting until they caught the inevitable cross breeze that flowed along mountain canyons. As soon as it nudged their direction, she leaned into it, pulling upward again until they soared over the first peak.

Charlotte called triumphantly from somewhere behind her, but Gwen didn't respond. Every ounce of her concentration was needed in the life and death wrestle she was undertaking.

And it wasn't only her life at stake. She carried Easton and Charlotte with her, and a whole kingdom depended on them. She would not fail this first challenge.

Valley by valley, crevice by crevice, and peak by peak, she led them through the maze of the mountains, fighting the wind every step of the way. Sweat dripped down her hairline, and she might have slipped from her perch on their wind mount if Easton's arms hadn't held her securely in place.

Exhaustion began to creep in, and she was nearly out of strength when she finally spotted a final, familiar mountain.

"It's over that one," she cried, forgetting all her restraint and yanking the reins in the direction she wanted to go.

But she wasn't the only one who had grown weary. The wind tried to buck, but the movement was light. It wasn't fighting her anymore but losing force entirely. For one breathless moment, Gwen thought it wouldn't make it over the peak.

Then they were past, and it was sinking down the other side. But it didn't matter. They wanted to descend anyway.

She guided it in as accurately as she could, acutely aware that her mother had just battled her through the mountain range and must therefore know of her return. Gwen could only hope the queen was unable to pinpoint the exact location of their dismount.

She aimed for the edge of the city, where they could quickly lose themselves in the streets. As soon as their feet hit the ground, she pushed the miniature halter into her pocket and led the others forward. They both seemed to have realized the danger because they followed her without question.

But once they reached the first intersection, Gwen stopped. She might have spent her whole life in the mountain kingdom, but she didn't know the city at all.

"Psst!" The hissed whisper caught the attention of all three, but only Gwen recognized the girl gesturing urgently for them to join her. It was the fourteen-year-old who had snuck into the palace to complain about the taxes.

She led the others to where the girl was lurking behind a building.

"Are you talking to us?" Gwen asked.

She nodded. "Who else would I be hissing at? I came to get you."

Gwen stared at her in astonishment. "How did you know we were here?"

The girl gave her a scornful look. "You do know you *flew* into the city, right? I've been watching for you so I could hardly miss that."

"You've been watching for me?" Gwen asked, her astonishment growing. "But why?"

"Because they told me to, of course," the girl said impatiently. "Now hurry. We need to get off the streets."

The others looked at Gwen, and she shrugged. They had to find a place to hide, and she would as soon trust this girl whose name she didn't know as anyone else in the kingdom, except perhaps Alma or Miriam.

But as they followed her down a series of dark streets and alleys and finally into a dirty basement, she couldn't resist asking.

"But who told you to watch for me?"

The girl shrugged. "He did, of course. And the others. Everyone who opposes the queen and has been waiting for your return."

Gwen stared at her in even greater astonishment. "There are people waiting for my return?"

"Of course," the girl said. "You're our princess. Who else is going to stop *her*?"

"She's been growing more and more unstable since your departure, Your Highness," said a new voice from the depths of the basement. "She's becoming dangerous on a whole new level. And since the prince returned, she's only gotten worse."

Charlotte pushed herself forward, her face alight. "He's here? Henry's here? Is he in the palace? You're sure he's still alive?"

The man stared at Charlotte, clearly unsure what to make of her intensity. Gwen felt almost as off balance as the man appeared to be, but somehow hearing the way they talked about her—the certainty in their voices when they talked of her return —made her feel like she could be the strong person they imagined.

"Allow me to make some introductions," she said. "You'll know Easton already."

Easton nodded respectfully, and the man started. Apparently he hadn't recognized him.

"Your parents will be very glad to hear of your safe return," he said, making Easton smile.

Gwen gestured next toward Charlotte. "And this is Princess Charlotte, Prince Henry's wife."

"His wife?" The man's eyebrows rose toward his hairline. "That is likely to cause some problems, considering our plan to marry the prince to you, Princess Gwendolyn."

Easton growled quietly, the sound so low only Gwen heard it. She placed a gentle hand on his wrist and smiled at him. He had to know she was past the point of allowing anyone to bully her into marrying Prince Henry.

"And this," she said finally, gesturing at the man, "is Count Oswin—who is, apparently, not my mother's most trusted advisor after all. I think, together, we might be the heart of the resistance."

NOTE FROM THE AUTHOR

Find out what happens to Charlotte and Gwen in To Steal the Sun, the final book in the Four Kingdoms duology.

Or if you missed discovering the Four Kingdoms, try the rest of the Four Kingdoms books, starting with the very first book, The Princess Companion: A Retelling of The Princess and the Pea, or if you want to skip ahead and meet Charli as a child, try the final book, The Abandoned Princess: A Retelling of Rapunzel.

To be informed of my new releases, as well as new bonus shorts, please sign up to my mailing list at www.melaniecelli er.com. At my website, you'll also find an array of free extra content in my Four Kingdoms world.

Thank you for taking the time to read my book. I hope you enjoyed it. If you did, please spread the word! You could start by leaving a review on Amazon (or Goodreads or Facebook or any other social media site). Your review would be very much appreciated and would make a big difference!

ACKNOWLEDGMENTS

This is my first fairy tale to be split across two books and to follow two separate heroines as they discover adventure, loss, love, and strength. It's been an enjoyable challenge to try something a little different, and I hope my readers also enjoy the variety in format.

Family—both the one we're born into and the ones we find later in life—is central to so much of who we are and who we grow into. As Charlotte and Gwen's stories wrestle with the meaning of family and loyalty, I find myself incredibly grateful for my own family—my family of origin, the family I married into, the family my husband and I have created, and the friends of my heart who have become as dear as family. You are all a gift and a joy, not least because of your willingness to continuously choose love over hurt or offense. It is my prayer that anyone who wasn't born into such a family will be able to find them later in life.

In my case, my family have also been an integral support in my publishing journey, and I am so grateful to my mum, my dad, my sister, Deborah, my brother James, and my husband, Marc, for beta reads, edits, website design, tech support, last minute calls, flexible schedules, and lots of conversations about the ins and outs of publishing. I appreciate you all more than I can say.

The same goes to my amazing beta reading friends, Rachel, Greg, Ber, Priya, and Katie. And to my editor Mary who is far more supportive and flexible than I deserve.

Another big thank you to the amazing Karri—I love the covers for this duology so much!

And, of course, thank you to God who teaches us the true meaning of love, devotion, and family.

ABOUT THE AUTHOR

 Melanie Cellier grew up on a staple diet of books, books and more books. And although she got older, she never stopped loving children's and young adult novels.

She always wanted to write one herself, but it took three careers and three different continents before she actually managed it.

She now feels incredibly fortunate to spend her time writing from her home in Adelaide, Australia where she keeps an eye out for koalas in her backyard. Her staple diet hasn't changed much, although she's added choc mint Rooibos tea and Chicken Crimpies to the list.

She writes young adult fantasy including books in her *Spoken Mage* world, her *Mage's Influence* world, and her various *Four Kingdoms* series that are made up of linked stand-alone stories that retell classic fairy tales.